The Life and Love (Attempts) of Kitty Cook

Helen Aitchison

Cahill Davis Publishing Limited

Copyright © 2023 Helen Aitchison

The moral right of Helen Aitchison to be identified as the Author of the Work has been asserted by her in accordance with the Copyright, Designs and Patents Act 1988.

First published in Great Britain in 2023 by Cahill Davis Publishing Limited.

First published in paperback in Great Britain in 2023 by Cahill Davis Publishing Limited.

Printed and bound in Great Britain by Clays Ltd, Elcograf S.p.A

Apart from any use permitted under UK copyright law, this publication may only be reproduced, stored, or transmitted, in any form, or by any means, with prior permission in writing of the publishers or, in case of reprographic production, in accordance with the terms of licences issued by the Copyright Licencing Agency.

All characters in this publication are fictitious and any resemblance to real persons, living or dead, is purely coincidental.

ISBN 978-1-7398015-9-5 (eBook)

ISBN 978-1-7398015-8-8 (Paperback)

Cahill Davis Publishing Limited

www.cahilldavispublishing.co.uk

To Paul, my happy ever after.

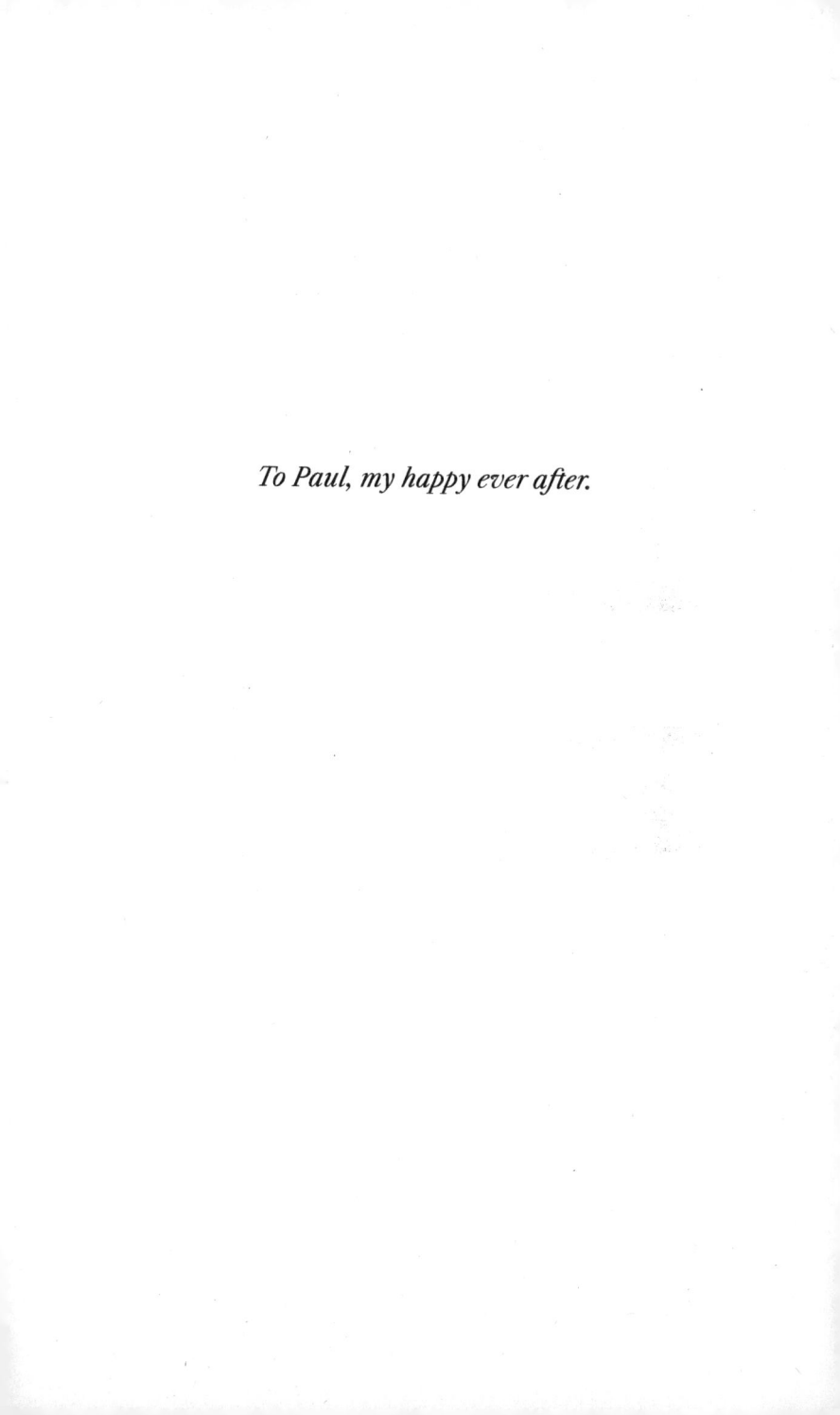

Chapter 1

Breakup day two. My alarm wakes me with that adrenaline startle you get when your body hasn't had enough rest and your energy levels are fraught. Heart racing and sinking at the same time, I almost crawl out of bed, feeling like my heavy head is about to topple off my neck. I sigh, taking a deflated walk to the bathroom. I look into the mirrored cabinet, eyes fixed in a haze of cloudy reality, and sob. My heart feels sore and raw, and my eyes sting, as if wasps were feasting on them all night. Then the flood of tears start again as I wonder how I can possibly get through the day ahead.

I haven't been able to get Liam out of my mind and I'm still yet to get used to going to bed and waking up alone. I know we don't work—I knew it while we were together and I'm still sure of that now—but five full years, sixty full months, 1,826 days is a long time, and it feels even longer when you've turned thirty and are being reminded of your age by society and family almost daily. Almost like I should be settled by now. And I was. Kind of. I just didn't feel 'settled'. The relationship was terminal for months before we had the mutual courage to cull it.

Memories, history, young love, the friendship beforehand when we were at uni—these factors all made it harder to extinguish the final struggling flames keeping our relationship mildly heated. But the warmth had gravitated to toxic nastiness in times of disagreement, with both of us becoming people we didn't like. The ugly combination of modified personalities and conflicting goals left the relationship more relationshit. Even memories and history couldn't keep the stitching together.

I don't have long before I have to be at work, and I've probably only had about three hours of sleep. Makeup is applied like I'm a sales assistant at one of those department store make up counters, certainly not as neat, but the quantity is there. I apply and reapply it in a desperate attempt to camouflage my puffy, bloodhound-esque eyes, my blotchy, bloated cheeks and ragged skin around my nose and mouth from hours of sobbing. Although I'm now borderline clown, my face paint most definitely means people won't just be looking at my eyes.

Taking one last look at my face and deciding clown is definitely okay for today, I leave my house and climb into my car, ready for the drive to work. I'm a sociology teacher at the local secondary school, Richardson High.

Whilst both career-orientated, Liam has the dreamer's disease and thinks he's going to be the next Ryan Gosling. He focuses his time, money and energy on auditions, chasing Hollywood for empty promises. We were living separate lives, separate dreams and visions. It felt as if we were talking completely different languages. So, time was called, there will be no 'take two'. Liam can chase the yellow brick road, or red carpet, or whatever the hell he likes, and I will be the responsible, independent woman that I am.

So, yes, on deep reflection, perhaps the breakup is for the best. But love is love, even when it's a bit crap, isn't it? Even the shit love needs some getting over and can fester for a while until it is eventually flushed away for good.

Feeling sick with emptiness and already praying for the day to end, I pull into the car park, not quite sure how I made it here with my mind this scrambled. But here I am, even though every cell in my body wishes I wasn't. I stay in my car for a minute, trying to regulate my breathing, before putting on my metaphoric mask and sauntering into the staffroom.

Sadie, my colleague and one of my closest friends, turns to the doorway when she hears me come in. Her eyes widen, and she immediately discards her cup on the side before heading over. Her steps are normal and deliberate, trying not to draw attention to the fact she can sense something is up by my clearly rubbish acting. As she approaches, her arms go out, and she gives me a breast-enveloping cuddle, or cwtch as Sadie would say.

Before anyone else can catch sight of the fact I'm close to tears, she grabs my hand and quickly leads me to an office side room. We have fifteen minutes before the Monday morning staff meeting, and her eyes are telling me I need to spill. I don't need much coaxing though, as everything comes out about the events of the weekend.

'Why didn't you bloody ring me, Kit? I would have come straight over,' Sadie says, shaking her head.

'I know, I just wanted to be alone.'

Sadie reaches for my hand, and I can tell there's upset that she wasn't there for me despite the fact I didn't give her the opportunity.

'It's a strange thing when you know something is never going to get better, never going to work and there's always going to be a problem. But, well, I guess sometimes we wish for things that aren't ever going to happen.' I take a deep breath. 'So many times, I knew our relationship was wrong, but I just waited for it to turn right. To be different. I think I ran out of wishes and patience.' I put my hand to my mouth, feeling my bottom lip quivering.

'Things can be dead a long time until we realise we have to let go. And it always hurts. Love can be made in an instant, but love can be hard and not always good for us. You've had some great times with Liam, and even if you had some shit to go through, you still had the good.' She squeezes my hand as I nod, letting a tear fall down my cheek. 'But it's not enough, and you deserve happiness, Kit.'

'You're right. I know it'll just take time and I know it's for the best. I just can't imagine stopping loving him despite the horrible times. He could be so nice, so perfect, when he wasn't being an arse.'

'Emphasis on the arse.'

I run my hand through my hair and let out a sigh. 'He's not right for me and I'm not right for him. But, well, he was the comfortable hoody as well as the irritating thong.'

Sadie throws her hands in the air and her head back as I can't help but giggle. 'Oooh those irritating, fart-trapping thongs. Just the worst.'

'Totally the worst.'

Coming back off the laughter high, she places a hand on each of my upper arms, her face now serious again. 'You'll be okay, Kit, I promise.'

I weakly smile at her.

'Love, you can do better than man-baby Liam, and you know what they say, don't you, Kitty?' She pulls away and looks at me with the eye of Barbara Windsor in the smutty Carry On films. I know something soaked in innuendo is coming.

'What do they say, Sadie?' I ask, rolling my eyes but half laughing. The floodgates have already halted.

'The way to get over a bloke is to get straight under another.' Sadie howls, clapping her hands with delight, then going back to grabbing my hand with her manicured, tiny fingers.

I squeeze her hand, grateful for her humour, then the tears flow with force as I remember Liam and I had a dinner reservation for a restaurant in town tomorrow night.

Chapter 2

Breakup day three. I'm starting to feel increasingly sorry for myself. My body posture has turned decisively saggy and a frequent exhale of melancholy is becoming a bad habit. Even though I have a magnificent family and friendship support around me, there's a massive void in my life. A five-foot-eleven, thirteen-stone void. Whilst Liam and I had our separate hobbies, friends and interests and had only been really living together for a year, it's still loneliness I'm feeling for much of the day, so much so that I've noticed I keep talking to myself at home to cover the deafening silence. Despite our relationship being far from romance-novel perfect, there were some good times.

It's now evening, and I'm watching the news on TV. I say watching, but I'm mostly staring, not absorbing a single story. Whether it's from too much already on my brain or subconsciously not needing any more negativity in my life, my mind is unable to focus.

Not seemingly able to get out of my own head, I decide to ring my friend Jane. She's always known about my arguments with Liam, and as much as she tolerated him and respected our relationship, it's clear she has always wanted more for me, as good friends do.

Having already updated her at the weekend by text, declining her offer to come over, I now feel more able to talk without getting too emotional. After Jane answering the phone and once again offering to come over and me telling her not to be so silly at this time, we chat for a bit about nothing in particular, and as usual, Jane makes me feel better. But the conversation is bound to hit the main point sometime, so it might as well be now.

'I just want to be loved.' I sigh into my phone. 'Love is one of the most sacred of things. It may manifest and present itself in diverse and unique forms, but it's all love.'

'Did you read that in a bloody magazine, Kit?' Jane asks, laughing.

'You aren't helping,' I reply, trying to be firm, 'but yes, actually, I did,' I mumble.

'Kitty, you've fallen in love with a bag before. Remember the five hundred and sixty pounds Mulberry Roxanne that was your true love ten years ago?'

I can't help but giggle, knowing she's right.

'You had it as your phone screensaver for months. People have their pet or their child, and you had a designer bag that flashed up on your mobile.' I can almost imagine her shaking her head at the other end of the phone.

We both laugh.

'It was so pretty; I wanted the world to see it. Well, my small world anyway. But alas, our relationship wasn't meant to be. Roxanne didn't love me back, turning her affections to another who had money.'

'Seriously, you'll be okay, Kit. In a few months, weeks even, you'll be completely over Liam. I love you and you know I only want the best for you. Liam is a dick. He won't ever put you or anyone else first, you know that in your heart of hearts, and I can say it now that he's gone. Good luck to him getting anyone who will put up with his carry on.'

She's right, of course, it just doesn't make it any easier. And I'm not making things any easier either, checking social media twenty plus times an hour for any communication and stalking his accounts. I don't even know what I would do if he got in touch anyway. It's one of the many headaches I'm constantly experiencing.

'Let's go out Saturday night,' she suggests.

I find myself immediately agreeing, a distraction with my also single best friend sounding perfect. One less night alone, talking to myself. We always have a great night out together despite it usually ending in one of us vomiting. Maybe that's exactly what I need, minus the vomit. Perhaps with my newly single status, my freedom could lay the foundations for a spontaneous, excessive social life and create opportunities for debauchery and fun. Then again, I'm a creature of habit in many ways, so maybe the wild me will just be a slightly more outgoing, amplified version. That would be fine too.

The thought of a night out will get me through the last two days of work this week, where I'm just about getting away with wearing a mask of pretence and not managing to either cry or bite anyone's head off for most of the day. Although Sadie knows about the breakup, I'm not ready to share it with the rest of the team. I'm not ready to tolerate the pity looks. I'm not ready for the 'what happened?' queries. Or even worse, the 'I've got a single friend' lines that people love to use, solidifying my already encroaching feelings that I shouldn't be single and my whole life's identity is based on my relationship status.

I come off the phone to Jane and shuffle weakly to the fridge, trying to muster some enthusiasm for a dinner that isn't a tin of spaghetti hoops. Combing my fingers through my hair, I ponder on why life has to be so bloody complex and confusing at times. I think back to my late teens and twenties and sigh. There's a beautiful naivety in the late teenage years, where you have no worries of having to get up in the morning for work and functioning on five hours of sleep. Where you haven't got a backlog of emails you must sort out immediately and winter tyres to get put on before the weekend. Where your priority isn't ensuring you get to Metafit twice a week, you remember to drop your friend's child's birthday present off and make time to pop in to see your aunt, who you've been meaning to visit for three weeks.

Sometimes I wish I was that person again. Carefree, perhaps for selfish reasons. Pulling a potato out of the fridge and some leftover quiche, I wonder if I could be. Maybe I just need to let myself live a little. After all, I don't have a man-baby to put first anymore, to look after and ensure he has a packed lunch and the bills paid. I spent years trying to make Liam someone he isn't to my own detriment. Maybe it's time to be more laid-back, be more spontaneous, put myself first and even perhaps be a little reckless. Well, okay, perhaps not reckless—I don't want to be struck off from teaching. Losing my job is the last thing I need.

Chapter 3

Breakup day four. Just like most humans, my circle is very important to me. My family and friends, my soul food, support and champions. Luckily, I get to see my closest friends frequently. Jane and Sadie in particular. I met Jane at university and I see Sadie at work most days.

Sadie is one of those women whose age you can never guess. You know the type—is she thirty, forty, fifty even? Part of this is the playful zest that is omitted from her like Tigger on his spring, part of it is her glamour and the aura of sparkle that surrounds her. I remember in my first week of working with her, I came into work with my naturally wavy hair slightly crumpled around the crown of my head due to my lack of straightening it properly. I was aghast yet completely amused when someone I had only met a few times said I had 'shag hair' and called me a 'dirty, dirty girl' before letting out the cheekiest giggle. I looked at Sadie, this little Welsh woman, with her bleached blonde, jaw-length hair and bright red lipstick and burst out laughing.

We then heard a cough at the office door. The head teacher, Mr Dryden, had been standing there for longer than I wished, and Sadie just turned around and used her usual magnetic charm. It was 'The Sadie Effect', and I was hooked.

That's Sadie—risqué, a bit eccentric, humour like a bartender. But phenomenal at her job and a heart the size of a frying pan. It was almost love at first sight for me with Sadie, and we soon became soul sisters, inside and outside of work, spending lunchtimes talking rubbish and eating gingerbread. She's a forty-two-year-old, five-foot-nothing, big-boobed parcel of wonder.

Then there's Jane, who came into my life nine years ago at uni. I can't remember a life before Jane. We've got an unbreakable bond and at times our own little world of humour, language and understanding. Jane, like me, was in a long-term until ten months ago, when she eventually called time on her exhausting relationship. Jane's two years younger than me, and she's one of those friends you can scrape your hair back and wear old, torn jogging bottoms with. Someone you can cry in front of until you look like a teething baby, but she'll still tell you you're beautiful and make you laugh. A friend who knows chocolate, belly laughs and planning a night out are always the medicine you really need.

As I reach the staffroom at work, the scent of expensive creams and indulgent perfume hits me, indicating Sadie's already here. You always know when Sadie's around because she carries the aroma of being a travelling sample of all the duty-free testers. I often wonder if it's a genius distraction technique for her lessons, to hypnotise the nasal passages of the year eleven English students she teaches. Alongside her scent of the Chelsea Flower Show, she always seems to have a sprinkling of glitter on her and jewellery that could rival a pirate.

'So, you're out on the pull at the weekend, are you, my little Kitty Kat?' she says, clasping her hands together.

Kitty Kat—one of Sadie's many pet names for me.

'I'm not sure about that, Sade. I think I've forgotten how to flirt. I'll be like the female *Mr Bean*,' I say, letting out an exasperated sigh.

She waves my comment off with a flick of her wrist. 'Shut up, you daft bint, you'll look delectable and be fantastic. You'll need a shitty stick to bat off those blokes.'

Sadie looks over my shoulder and grins. I turn, spotting Will walking awkwardly into the staffroom, blushing and shaking his head. Sadie and I look at each other and giggle.

'You go out and get your flirt on, love, and if no one takes your fancy, get on the internet dating lark. My friend Emma swears by it. She's had more cock ends than weekends.'

'*Sadie*,' I shriek as she bursts out laughing, throwing her head back in utter amusement and elbowing me in the side.

Will turns away, stirring the contents of his mug, pretending to be appalled but clearly desperate to hear more of the conversation as he leans in our direction.

'You're like a bloody old man down the social club, you scruffy bugger,' I say playfully as she continues to almost snort.

'Right, I've got a class. I suggest you do some work as well.' I smile meekly, holding back a yawn, my nights still mostly sleepless right now.

Sadie reaches for my hand affectionately, her eyes turning serious. 'Enjoy, my little Kit. Be kind to yourself,' she replies, handing me a gingerbread star in a paper bag.

I've managed to muddle through classes this week so far. The kids have been well-behaved and too self-involved to pick up on a deviation to my persona. Well, that and the fact I should have probably gone into acting, given how well I've been wearing the mask of 'happy-go-lucky Kitty'. Maybe it should have been me chasing stardom rather than Liam. That's one good thing about absorbing and dealing with any trauma at Richardson High—the kids are always too busy thinking about social media and selfies to worry about anything else around them. I shake my head, smiling a little as I think about when I was the same age as the kids. How lovely it used to be when the only dilemmas I had were whether I was going to wear the red or khaki green top, or whether we would be going to Sophie's garage or Claire's garage for our Friday night hang outs.

As the kids set about their work on the influence of media to social constructs, I sneak a look at my mobile phone for the fifteenth time this morning. A stupid part of me still expects Liam to be texting throughout the day, like we always did. Sometimes it would be more serious, but it was often the *I just had a big poo* or *Look at Dave's dog* photos. Or me texting, asking if his sandwich was nice at lunchtime. Boring as they were, they were part of our routine, and a routine I've been missing this week. I stare out of the classroom window, the longing in me feeling all-consuming.

Liam messaged on Monday night just saying he hopes I'm okay. It was one of those closed statement text messages where the sender doesn't really want a reply. Of course I replied anyway saying I was okay-ish and that I hoped he was also. I deleted the *I miss you and love you* off the end. It was pointless. I knew and know that Liam and I split for a multitude of decent reasons. We're different people since we met at uni over eight years ago and different still to the couple who eventually got together five years ago. People change, we evolve, grow, adapt.

Sometimes having a history just isn't enough.

Sadie's comment about internet dating has been playing on my mind all day. And not because of the cock remark. Perhaps chatting to random men would give me a confidence boost. I don't have to go on any dates, just do a bit of harmless flirting. I'm not ready to date, but I have to get Liam out of my mind, and attention focused elsewhere could help send thoughts of Liam on their merry way. I need to know more about online dating, and I know the perfect person to ask.

After making a cup of tea, I sit on the sofa, a notebook by my side in case I need to jot down anything important. I call Sophie, one of my oldest friends and former housemate. She is the type of friend who you don't need to see every week or even every month, but when you reconnect, it's like you've never been apart.

'Hey, stranger.'

I immediately smile. We shared so much in the six years we lived together that we have an affinity of comfort and support intertwined in our friendship, her voice now wrapping me in warmth like the cosiest blanket. It was hard getting used to her not being around when she first moved out, even harder that she moved fifty miles away to be with her fiancé, but we've kept in touch and meet up when we can. And the fact she met her fiancé online is the exact reason I need her advice.

'Go for it, you could meet the man of your dreams,' Sophie says confidently after I tell her I've been thinking about online dating.

'After filtering through the weirdos, you know how great it was for me. I got to know Chris without the pressures of alcohol, nerves and shovelling makeup on, well, until we eventually met. I've told you before, he could have looked like Sloth from *The Goonies* by the time we met, but I was already smitten with him.'

I laugh, thinking how happy she and Chris are. However, as romantic and deep as their situation sounds, I don't want a Sloth lookalike on my arm. I have a distinct type, and Sloth is not on the list as my ideal man.

'In all honesty, Soph, you're really lucky. Chris is a decent bloke and loves you so much. You're the perfect case study of internet dating. But not everyone is as fortunate. I've heard some nightmare stories, and there are a load of liars and pervs out there,' I say, part of me still trying to put myself off the idea.

'Sure, there'll always be the odd scammer, cheater, catfisher and sexual deviant, just as there are in in-person situations too, but there's also some genuine folk, Kit. You can't let the bad things in life put you off from possible good things. Good things that could lead to brilliant things. What've you got to lose? You're home alone, feeling sorry for yourself. It's entertainment, if nothing else.' Sophie says it so convincingly that she could be on commission from an internet dating site.

She has a point though—internet dating would definitely help distract me. What's the worst that could happen? A bit of rejection? The possible need to block a few weirdos on an app?

'Maybe,' I ponder. 'Maybe.'

Chapter 4

Breakup day five. I'm relieved that it's finally Friday and I'm so close to the respite that the weekend will provide. Work has been so much harder this week, smiling and pretending all is okay when inside I'm running on empty. I want to shut myself off from the world, be alone and eat chocolate all day, not lesson plan and teach. I've been living on spaghetti hoops on toast and cereal most of the week. My skin is turning grey from the lack of fruit and veg I normally consume like a goat. Tomorrow, Jane and I are going on our night out. I told her I'm even going to meet her at the gym in the morning.

I have wardrobes full of clothes, but much of them are designer and classic timeless pieces bought second-hand. New wardrobe items are only received as presents or purchased using money received around Christmases and birthdays. I mooch around shops like TK Maxx for last season's designer bargains over fast fashion. But tonight I just want to be out and doing something that always makes me happy: shopping.

I decide to deviate from my usual Friday night food shop that Liam and I would do, eating like a sparrow all week meaning I have an abundance of food left.

I soon pull up to the shopping centre and find a parking space. This last year, I've been trying to be more economically and environmentally savvy. I have limited my purchases of items made in countries where production and treatment of staff is questionable and passed on my unwanted items once I've finished with them. I've been cutting up T-shirts that are past their best and using them as cloths to save from using disposable wipes constantly. Liam would find them drying around the house, cut in speed rather than neatness, eventually getting used to seeing orange, turquoise and red scraps of material everywhere. There is even one in his car for wiping down the dashboard. I wonder if he'll think of me when he notices it. If he's thought of me at all.

One of my hands instinctively goes to my chest, near to where my seatbelt still lies across me. The tears start falling as I put my hands to my face, my head a whirlwind of could-have-beens. I know it's normal to feel like this, of course it's normal and something people have to deal with every bloody day, but it hurts. It hurts so much that it feels as if my heart could stop at any moment.

My stomach growling takes my mind away from my tears, lunch of a cereal bar and a banana apparently not being enough. Even if my heart feels starved, my stomach doesn't want to play any part in a hunger strike. I wonder if this is the start of my appetite coming back or just a one-off day. I get out of the car, feeling both demotivated and determined. Like a baby taking its first, reluctant steps.

'Bloody get a grip,' I whisper to myself, throwing my handbag over my shoulder and walking towards the shops. I straighten my shoulders, from the week of deflated posture, and smile, not caring if I look silly.

As I start mooching around the shops, I realise I'm enjoying the time to myself without having to search for Liam in the men's department or saying 'I won't be long' with a sorry look as I scurry with multiple items to the changing rooms. It's autumn and a new season for clothes. Luxurious materials and colours surround me; the shades of purple, red and pink lipsticks wink at me from displays; velvet, lace, thick cotton and a touch of glitter here and there. I rush over to where I see a large display of dresses. Looking through, my eyes widen. I eagerly grab some from the rails and head towards the changing rooms.

'Christ,' I say, trying to pull the first of the dresses over my arms. The double layers are cutting right into my upper arms, with no give in the material. I admit defeat and put it back on the hanger, feeling like a shot-putter.

Next is a velvet dress with a sweetheart neckline in a rich maroon. A tight, bodycon style. I'll need to wear my 'fat suit' underneath, my control bodysuit, I decide as I turn my body to the side and look at my stomach. I sigh at what's reflected back to me, more podge than I would like, then mentally scold myself for being so self-critical. Getting the dress on, I slide into one of my work boots, which has a little heel, as I try to envisage what it would look like. Not bad, I think, nodding to myself and flicking my hair. I take a photo to send to Jane for a second opinion, blowing her a kiss as I pose.

Giggling, it feels almost like a moment of healing. Just me, in a changing room, finding myself again. I shake my head, feeling a little foolish with my changing room reflection session. I look at myself in the mirror—tired eyes from a week of holding emotions and tension, a worry line lightly creasing my forehead from a week of doubt, frowning and feeling inadequate. As my image looks back, I will it to smile. To reach out from the floor-to-ceiling mirror and grab me, hold me, tell me I'm enough and I'm going to be okay. I close my eyes for a few seconds and swallow the build-up of setting concrete in my throat. Opening my eyes again, I tilt my head up. 'You can do this. You are enough.' A deep breath, and I'm almost ready to try the next dress on.

It's a cerise number with a little glitter. Although the material is itchy, I love the colour and it makes a change from my usual choice of black. Maybe I want to play it less safe, be a bit bolder. Once it's on, I'm disappointed to see that it's baggy on my chest and stomach but tight around the top of my thighs. I think about how it's what I'd imagine a unicorn shit would look like—a funny shape of bright pink and glitter. I begin laughing at my own joke and take a photo for the craic.

Jane has replied with her view on the first dress: *Sexy Morticia*. I'm not sure if that's a good or bad thing.

The last dress is a safe but sexy black lace mini dress with long sleeves. Comfortable, classy and timeless. I feel a million dollars in it, which is perfect given it's only twenty-four pounds ninety-nine. So what if it's black again? Perhaps I'll add some colour with my makeup and accessories.

I take a photo and send it to Jane. She sends back a heart emoji and the blowing a kiss emoji. After paying for my purchase, and with the slightest bounce in my step, I continue to mooch about the shopping centre, even indulging in a lipstick and eyeliner to go with my new dress.

Chapter 5

I start getting ready for my Saturday night out with Jane a full twenty-four hours before. Being a woman is a serious chore at times, and although I admire the natural beauties and those carefree enough not to focus time, energy and stress into appearance, I'm not one of them. Without much grooming and effort, I resemble a *Macbeth* witch. I spend the rest of my Friday night doing some 'going out prep'. I shave my legs even though I'll be wearing thick tights, do my toenails even though they'll be covered with thick tights and shoes (it's all psychosomatic) and put some tanning drops on my face (which will definitely not be covered with thick tights).

I plan to apply a layer of fake tan in a delicious shade of caramel in the morning before going to the gym to meet Jane. It will sweat off and wash away a little, but I'll add some instant tan before we go out. The overtly orange look isn't my style, but a little bit of a golden glow on my almost translucent skin will make me feel a little sparklier. It's a very regimented process to achieve.

In between cups of tea, I pluck my eyebrows, which grow faster than a baby's nappy needs changing and resemble a Gallagher brother's monobrow. I've never had the faith to get them done professionally, and the processes bamboozle me. HD Brows, tattooing, threading, dyeing, thickening, shaping. It's all a bit too much. So, plucking is enough, plus a little of my own shop-bought dye for the overplucking that's a frequent occurrence.

It's now 10 p.m. and I'm satisfied with my completion so far of self-chores. They've distracted me from checking my phone every ten minutes and listening to trance anthems (I'm still stuck in the decade before, when I first started clubbing at college and thought Tiësto and Avicii were gods). The night, along with my shopping therapy, have been a welcome distraction and a great start to the weekend.

The next twenty hours go by slowly until Jane eventually arrives at my house to get ready for our night out. She makes me laugh as she tells me about her week at work tutoring in the local prison. She talks about her job with such flippancy despite teaching basic literacy skills to serious offenders. After a messy breakup and being surrounded by male offenders each day, it's no surprise Jane wants a break from men. She's happy being single and has very much adopted the mantra of 'what will be, will be', which is refreshing in comparison to the anxiety I'm plagued with and the pressure to get my life back on track.

An hour later, and a few orange gin and lemonades later, Jane and I check our makeup and hair one last time. I put a little more eyeliner on and Jane sprays some hairspray on her shoulder-length, almost black hair, which is glossier than a puma's coat. We take a few selfies before the Uber arrives, pouting, and I bend my legs a little to fit in the lens better with Jane, who is six inches shorter than me.

We spend a minute looking over them and giggling before we strut to the waiting Uber. It's a mild night for the start of October, and even in sub-zero temperatures, us women of Newcastle are known to never wear coats on a night out partying. The Uber driver smiles at our happy greeting as we instruct him on our destination and get straight into some banter with him. The lack of food this week and a few gins for confidence has me feeling merry already.

We soon pull up at the first bar—a trendy, mid-priced joint that attracts eclectic people. Sauntering in, we go straight to the bar and order gins. It's busy and buzzing, and the atmosphere soaks into me, just like the drinks so far. I feel lucky to have Jane and grateful to be out and about in bars. This time last year, we were all in lockdown, when the future of ever socialising again was unknown. The music of tonight is old-school Usher and Lady Gaga mixed in with more recent chart music. Jane and I guzzle our drinks and dance away, knowing but not caring that our moves are rubbish and not exactly sexy, hands darting up as we lean into each other, singing the words. For all we care, it could be just us two in the whole world, Jane and me, in our own little gin-infused, rubbish-dancing bubble.

An hour later, we move on to the next bar, then the next, before deciding on a nightclub. The club will provide the option to dance like we think we should be on stage but also sit and rest our feet, which are starting to nip from heels that haven't been worn in a while.

We laugh and link arms as we walk to the club, remembering when we used to be out almost every night at uni, then at least once a fortnight when we graduated. Good times that we will always cherish and look back on with fondness despite some of the worst hangovers of our lives. Even the bad parts of being sick in toilets and looking like *The Walking Dead* cast, with smudged eye makeup and tatty hair. And we'd always finish the night at a takeaway before going home, getting cheesy chips decorated with mayonnaise, tomato sauce and lashings of salt. Maybe we will again tonight. I feel truly blessed for the first time in a while, and I thank my treasured friend. Reminiscing at silly memories as we walk, I tell myself I will remember and be grateful for what I do have and not focus on what I don't.

Chapter 6

I immediately feel the impact from drinking too much alcohol the second I open my eyes. Letting out a pathetic sigh, I drop my hand to the floor, moving it around slowly with all the energy I have to locate my mobile, which is always on charge overnight. Not being able to find it with my blind hand, I groan and lean over, my head spinning. It's not there. Putting my palm to my throbbing head and lying back on the pillows again, the panic of 'where's my phone?' brushes past me. Once the room comes into focus again, my hand is back searching, and I eventually locate it wedged in between the pillows.

I look at the screen through half-shut eyes: 7:05 a.m. on Sunday morning. Urgh. I didn't get in and to sleep until after 2 a.m. My mouth feels full of sawdust as I try to move my stiff, dehydrated tongue. Reaching over to the bottle of juice on my bedside cabinet, I let out a moan of the hangover that's enveloping me. I wonder if I'll ever learn the concept of moderation. After swigging the juice, I place my head back down on the pillow. The room is spinning, and I know if I don't get back to sleep, there's a high chance I will vomit.

I wake up again, the battle of the bands in my head slightly less vocal than they were earlier. It's going to be a long day. I greedily drink the rest of my bottle of juice. As if in a kettlebell class, with monumental effort, I slowly pick up my what feels like seven-kilogram phone from the bedside cabinet. Squinting to focus on the screen, I see some texts from Jane, Sadie and my mam.

I'm desperate for the toilet but it's as if my bed is snuggling me in the folds of it, and I'm struggling to oppose its embrace whilst feeling exceptionally vulnerable with this hangover from hell. I try to ignore my pulsating bladder for a few minutes as I groan back to my protesting stomach churns, head thumping and now bladder pleading.

I touch my stomach, as if to soothe my bladder and feeling of sickness, and notice it's bare, exposed from the lack of usual vest or T-shirt I wear for bed. I lift the quilt slightly, and I'm greeted by the sight of last night's underwear. I put my hand to my head. This is weird, as even when drunk, I always manage to get my pjs on, albeit sometimes inside out. I must have really overdone it, or it's just that I'm not used to drinking so much anymore. Nine times out of ten, I also manage to scrape at least some of my makeup off with a trusty reusable face pad, but there are no soiled ones to be seen. My bladder isn't going to stop throbbing, so I practically crawl to the bathroom, as if on the last leg of an Ironman contest.

While having a wee that goes on forever, I have a sudden flashback and cringe.

'Oh shit,' I say, grasping my mouth as a memory comes rushing back. 'Oh bloody hell, nooooo.'

I put my head in my hands and try to shake away the video playing in my mind. It does nothing but make the brass band in my head start clattering about again. Closing my eyes, I remember Jane and me getting the taxi home, Jane getting dropped off first at her house. I can recall the feeling of needing to vomit and almost hanging my head out of the window as the taxi driver chuntered on in the background. I can't remember getting out of the taxi, but I recall my neighbour, Tracey from across the cul-de-sac, opening my front door and pushing me up the stairs. Crap, she must have put me to bed. I put my hand to my mouth, stifling the shame and perhaps a little bit of nausea rising. What a sight I must have been.

I grab my dressing gown off the bathroom door and stumble back into my bedroom, this time noticing the pile of my clothes on the floor, with splashes of vomit down my stunning new dress.

'You total dick.' I crawl back into bed, letting out a defeated sob.

Unable to get back to sleep, I ring Jane to update her on my discovery that the neighbour put me to bed.

'Eeeh, that's hilarious. You were really mortal, like,' Jane exclaims after laughing through the entire story.

'How bloody embarrassing that a neighbour had to take my clothes off me and put me to bed. God, I need to move house.' I bite my lip as Jane giggles down the phone. I would find it funny if it hadn't happened to me.

'Shame it wasn't that fit one from over the back.'

'I'm gonna have to do a completely different type of walk of shame today,' I reply, letting out a sigh.

Two hours later, I'm washed, dressed in joggers and have managed to get down some scrambled eggs on toast—a guaranteed hangover helper. I'm going to see my parents today but know I have to knock at Tracey's house beforehand. There's no point in putting the embarrassment off and delaying the inevitable.

I sheepishly walk over the road, looking around and desperately hoping no curtain twitchers are watching. Taking a deep breath and straightening my hungover and ashamed posture, I knock on her door as one of her cats, Silky, comes rubbing against my calf.

Tracey immediately opens the door, a grin on her face. 'Rough today, are ya, love?' she says playfully but loudly enough that had it been summer with windows open, the whole cul-de-sac would have heard. 'Come in,' she adds, gesturing into the house.

I scurry inside, desperate to get out of view. 'Tracey, I'm, erm, I'm so sorry,' I stammer as I feel my cheeks flush.

'Don't worry, hun, we've all been there. Christ, I'm fifty-two and still don't know when to stop.' She snorts, tipping her head back.

I wonder how often a neighbour has had to put her to bed. It was definitely a first for me, and I never want to have to put anyone else in this quiet street to bed, although I'd probably have to make an exception for Tracey after last night. I nod as she continues.

'It's the voddie for me, love. Lethal, it is, and I'm a greedy cow once I start,' she states boldly, seemingly very proud of her alcohol gluttony.

I laugh nervously. 'Yeah, me too, evidently, although it's gin for me.' I want to get out of here. I can't help but feel like a teenager, and I also get the sense that Tracey's weirdly in awe of my almost blackout and me having to be stripped off by her.

'Erm, thanks anyway, you know, for looking after me.' I glance at the carpeted floor, a cup and half-filled ashtray drawing my eyes to them, wondering whether to explain. 'You see, I split up with Liam, so it was a bit of a blowout, I guess, but fellow greedy cow here also,' I say, raising my hand and trying to make light of what's making me feel like crying.

'Ah, hun, I didn't realise you'd split. You're a bonnie lass though; you'll have your choice of blokes and be loved up again in no time,' she says, the wrinkles around her eyes turning up.

I smile despite sadness creeping up my back and threatening to strangle me.

Tracey touches my forearm gently. 'But have a bit of fun before someone snaps ya up, eh? You're only young once. And don't take any shit. You deserve the best.'

I look at Tracey, my neighbour, technically a stranger, and I can't move. Consumed by my sadness, a tear falls down my cheek. Standing here in baggy loungewear, with wet, tied-back hair and stale-alcohol breath, I feel like a child lost in a department store, not knowing what to do.

'C'mon, hun, you're better than that shit. You're a strong lassie; you'll get through this. Some of the most painful times in my life have been times I'm bloody grateful to have experienced. In the future, you'll be grateful, pet. Just remember that.' Tracey lightly hugs me. The random, drunk, heartbroken neighbour that she had to put to bed and now has to comfort.

I wipe my stinging eyes, still coated in last night's mascara, and muster a pathetic smile. Absorbing Tracey's parting advice, I thank her and apologise again as I slope out of her house and back to the sanctuary of mine.

After an hour of staring into space and generally feeling sorry for myself, it's now mid-afternoon and time to head to my parents' for Sunday lunch in the hope of some of my mam's magnificent homemade apple crumble for dessert.

Mam opens the front door shortly after I knock. 'Hi, pet.' She gives me a cuddle and kiss before I walk into their hallway. 'Hungover, are you?' She lets go of me and gives a concerned eyebrow raise.

'Yeah, something like that, Mam,' I reply, taking my trainers off.

She tuts. 'You need to be careful, pet. Learn moderation.'

I decide it's probably best not to mention the escapades of the night before.

I nod a greeting to Dad and Henry, who are watching sport on TV in the lounge, as I walk past them and follow Mam into the kitchen.

'How are you, pet?' Mam asks, studying me intently. 'You look a little pale.'

'That'll be the hangover, Mam,' I reply, trying to laugh it off.

'I know my Kitty. How are you really? Have you heard from Liam?'

Mam watches me as I lean against the kitchen bench. She does know me, even when I try to put on an act. She's my mam, the first person to learn my body language, but there's also the maternal instinct and the maternal knowing.

'No, I've not heard from him really. I don't want to, Mam, yet part of me really does.' I can feel myself getting emotional and grit my teeth. 'He's not been in touch for a few days,' I admit quietly. 'I've deleted him on Facebook. All the checking on him and my messages was driving me mad.' I can't keep letting the breakup dominate my feelings. People care and I'm grateful, but people asking also means he has another performance in my head.

Mam's still watching me, as if she's waiting for me to admit more, maybe regret the breakup, but I stay silent. I hate these questions. I get asked how I'm coping by so many people but it's like *Groundhog Day* of heartbreak and lying constantly. Pretending you're okay, when more times than not you aren't, feels more exhausting than running a marathon.

'I know, it's not easy... it never is. But this time next week, it'll be a little easier, then easier again in a month, and it'll just keep getting easier. Better now than down the line, eh?'

I nod, pressing my lips together and trying to not think about it. Alcohol always makes me a little bit more sensitive the next day, which isn't the best medicine for fragile emotions. My mam touches my hand reassuringly before going to the pans of cooked vegetables.

I help serve Sunday lunch and then call the men of the family over to the table. Henry's girlfriend, Sarah, often joins us, but she's on shift at the local hospital today, where she's a nurse. Henry sits opposite me, and I immediately look to my plate, waiting for the inevitable subject I know is going to come up.

'I hear you and soft lad split up.'

And there it is already. I roll my eyes at the predictable. 'Yeah, Liam and I broke up last week.'

'Well, he was always a bit of a dreamer in my opinion. Deluded even. You're better off out of that shite.' Henry has never been overly keen on Liam. They have little in common and Liam never made a great effort with my brother.

'*Henry*,' scolds Mam before looking at me tenderly.

Dad stays silent and continues stuffing a Yorkshire pudding into his mouth, as if the conversation is on the TV in the background.

'He was, Mam. A right knob. Remember when he messed our Kit around that New Year's Eve and had her upset?'

I give Henry a weak smile. He's the protective, older brother, even if he spends most of his time poking fun at me. That New Year's Eve was one of the many times Liam upset me when together. Most of the time, I didn't mention it to my family; after all, 'I told you so' is one of the worst lines to ever hear. After that New Year's Eve,

Liam received and never recovered from the black mark against his name after telling me he was going to meet me at a bar, me waiting there for four hours and him going to another of his auditions instead and forgetting the promise he'd made me. I was force-fed a lecture that Liam perhaps wasn't the one for me. But you keep going, don't you? Love makes us unable to see a lot. Clearly, Henry never forgot.

'I am here, you know.' I glare at Henry. He can be bloody insensitive at times.

'Aye, well, forget him. Get a proper bloke next time and let us vet him first. No more men who go on like teenagers, eh.'

I shake my head and stab at a roast potato with my fork, wondering what a 'proper bloke' is.

Chapter 7

Since getting closer to thirty-one years old, my hangovers now last two days. Or perhaps it's just that I'm a gin pig. I just know that even after an early night last night, I have that steamrolled, bloated face feeling and want to eat slice after slice of toast. Luckily for me, Monday is the day of the week where I teach the least number of lessons and use the rest of the day for marking and lesson prep. Also luckily for me, I'm ahead in my lesson prep after sleepless nights last week, so I can afford to be a little more relaxed in the staffroom and indulge in self-pity. My plan is to stuff my face with my emergency pack of custard creams and drink numerous cups of tea.

Walking into the staffroom, I see a paper bag from the bakery in my pigeonhole and know Sadie has delivered some gingerbread. I smile, grateful for such little things that mean so much. The staffroom is quiet, only me and another teacher, Gordon, who's milling around and talking to himself. I nod a hello in his direction as he continues to chunter away. Spreading my files across a table, I have a look at some of the recent assignments by year eleven. The assignments I need to mark are about the concept of food poverty in modern Britain. Ironically, before getting started, I take my gingerbread out of the paper bag and munch on it happily.

An hour later, Sadie comes waltzing into the staffroom. 'Alright, my little love?' she booms, her lip-gloss-soaked smile lighting up the room.

'Hi, lovely. Not bad. How are you? And thanks for the gingerbread,' I reply, pointing to the empty bag.

'All good, Kit. How was your night out? Do any dry humping?' she asks, clapping her hands and giggling like a naughty schoolgirl as she takes a seat next to me.

'*Sadie, man,*' I shriek, tapping her hand playfully.

'Come for tea this week. I'll make my leek and cheese mash and put in extra love for you. I'll send Stu packing for the night.' She squeezes my knee and looks at me through pleading eyes, like a child asking for a pony.

'Well, I guess I can't say no to that.'

'Gotta go and use my Welsh charm on Dryden; I've buggered up the parents' evening schedule.' She giggles as she gets up and saunters out of the staffroom, as if she doesn't have a care in the world.

As I return to my marking, I decide I want to be Sadie Flitcroft when I grow up.

The working day eventually ends, and even though I feel like a fried turd, I decide to go to the gym. I need to get back into some of the normality that I embraced pre-breakup, and I know exercise, as always, will make me feel better about myself. Jane attends the same gym but works late some Monday nights. This evening, I attend solo, with my headphones and dance music to sweat out the toxins of the weekend.

I wait until I get home to shower after my workout. Maybe the tide is turning and things will get easier, like Mam said. I haven't heard from Liam for five days, and now I can't check his social media, it's maybe the healing I need. There's still the heavy heart of loneliness that clings to my body and mind, especially when I'm home alone. Making my dinner, getting a single plate out and leaving the TV on in the background just so the silence isn't deafening. The last week has been 100 lessons a day on how to live single, as one solitary person. Filling the kettle for just one cup of tea, putting the toothpaste on just one toothbrush, the empty side of the bed feeling the size of a football field and being perpetually cold. The daily things we all take for granted that leave voids.

I sit on the sofa with my dinner of jacket potato and beans on my knee. I can't face sitting at the kitchen table alone. I know sitting there solo would make me feel like a dingy in the ocean. Zoning out from the depressing world news on TV, I remember the advice and suggestions people have given me about dating apps. Surely there would be no harm in looking? Suss out the maniac/perv/liar ratio to decent folk actually looking for love? I'm not naive; I know the sites have as many maniacs as genuine folk. I remember when Sophie was on there, although a long time ago, we were looking at the men and saw a guy we went to school with, who was married. These sites can make beautiful connections but can also destroy people's lives.

Nevertheless, curiosity, boredom and loneliness get the better of me, and I search on Google for dating sites. There are some that seem aimed at hook-ups only, friends with benefits and weird, kinky fetishes. It's overwhelming how many results there are. Bloody hell, does anyone meet anyone in the real world anymore? The art of dating has most definitely changed in the last five years, most likely even more online from the Covid-19 pandemic. I click on 'Dating Doctor' and look at the homepage. Wow, it's filled with beautiful people, no doubt some cut and pasted from Google Images. Quotes flash on the page, including one stating 'Only £19.99 a month.' Bugger that. Going back to the Google search page, I click on 'Soul Mates', which looks less Google Images than the last site. To look any further, I have to register for a free, seven-day trial.

My finger hovers over the laptop as I nervously bite my lip. This is all so new, so strange and unknown. I'm not sure what to do or what I want. Straightening my shoulders and taking a deep breath, I wonder what I have to lose. The answer is 'nothing'. I could just register and look around, then probably never bother again. So, why do I feel so nervous? I click on the register button, to see what registering actually entails. I have seen these things before, when you have to register to get a 'free' healthy brownie recipe or a 'free' skincare product, only to have to give your life history, DNA and a nine ninety-nine a month subscription.

Name, date of birth, gender identity and email are all that's required. No cost or optional details if you want to complete your dating profile. I look at the laptop screen as I wriggle nervously in my seat. It's certainly a more popular way to meet people these days, I know that, and I even know of friends and friends of friends who had Zoom dates during the pandemic. There was perhaps a stigma attached to internet dating fifteen years or so ago, when it first really became a thing in the UK, but now, hell, there are more couples than not who met online. So, why do I feel so reluctant? Is it the tiny pang of hoping I'll get back with Liam? Is it that I don't feel attractive enough, slim enough, confident enough? That fear of rejection, or even worse, hurt? Somewhere inside of me is a frightened girl, who never feels quite good enough, trying to disappear in the corner.

I put my laptop to one side. Maybe making a cuppa will give me the courage to register on the site. Not exactly the usual 'Dutch courage', but a good cup of Yorkshire tea always soothes my being and a few ginger nut biscuits dipped in will be a welcome addition. Five minutes later, I curl back up on the sofa, with a fleece throw over my legs, and put the laptop back on my knee.

'Sod it.' I begin filling in the registration details. I complete the minimum requirements and don't add a photo. One of those grey-blue outlines of a person's head on a white background comes up with my profile name 'K-30'. I've decided against anything cliché that will only encourage people to misuse my name. It's happened before, mainly by drunk men, referring to me as Pussy, with a stupid grin or laugh, after hearing my name is Kitty. Or calling me Catwoman, Kitten or similar rubbish to that. It's tedious and irritating, and Kit-Kat is about as much as I tolerate from friends.

I click on the email link to finish registration that has landed in my inbox and then there I am, 'K-30', on the dating site. My seven-day trial has begun.

Going back to the home page of Soul Mates, I have a quick browse over the site's pages, navigating in the layers of dating exploration before stopping on the 'Find a Partner' page. Here, you filter down the requirements of your search and then people are displayed who match your criteria. I've already given a rough guide, and pictures of profiles keep whizzing by the bottom right of the screen. I need more biscuits for this, so I scurry into the kitchen and grab the biscuit tin before returning to my place on the sofa. As I shove a ginger nut into my mouth, my laptop pings. My first message. The immediate excitement soon bursts when I realise it's a message from the admin, welcoming me to the site. I go back to filtering my search when another ping sounds. There it is, my first non-admin message, from 'Gym Dog 25'.

Hi Sexy!

'Eh? Sexy?' I don't even have a profile pic. So, this 'Gym Dog 25' finds shadow outlines in a grey-blue colour sexy? Christ, I mean, I'm all for inclusion, but this is pushing it.

Back to my search, and the filters go on and on. It's a love labyrinth. I guess you can fill in or skip as many of the sections as you wish, but if I'm having a free trial, I want to be thorough. I start completing the sections.

Gender: Male.

Sexual Orientation: Heterosexual.

Age: 30–45. (There are some hot creeping-into-middle-aged men.)

There are multiple options for 'Build'. I'm not a massive fan of the gym gods, who I can't eat chocolate in front of without feeling like Augustus Gloop. Or super fit cycle/running bods who won't let me lie like a bag of cack on the sofa on a Sunday afternoon. At the same time, I don't want to grow old and obese with someone. There has to be some gluttony but motivation in my ideal man. Treats and exercise, both in moderation and happy unison. I'm also aware that men will say they are five-foot-eleven and athletic and they actually look like the Penguin off *Batman*. Or say they're toned and yet look like a lamppost. I eventually click on what I think is the safest option.

Build: Average.

'Height' is another tricky one. Whilst I'm five-foot-eight myself, I'm attracted to men taller than me when I'm wearing heels. I feel like a cow even discounting the shorter guys, but I guess I'm not going to be everyone's cup of tea either, and I'm fine with that. I want to find my Yorkshire tea, not my Just Essentials cuppa with UHT milk.

What am I thinking? I'm looking too much into this.

I put my laptop to one side and pick up my mobile. There's a text from Jane, asking if I'm still hungover and how the gym was, and a meme from Sadie. I answer and click on Facebook for a mooch. Jane has shared a photo of us from Saturday night. It's filled with smiles and fun, and for having had a rubbish week, I don't look too bad. Jane looks really pretty, as always, and we're both holding drinks, which makes me slightly nauseous to look at now. There are the usual statuses and photos shared of events, kids and food. Someone I went to school with got married at the weekend and her photos are up. She looks beautiful, and happiness covers her face. I smile. True love does exist. I've never been one of those who's envious of other's successes. Why piss on someone's rainbow just because you aren't happy or haven't got something? It's never made sense to me, and I truly believe that good things happen to good people. Being bitter, jealous and miserable for others is something I find repellent. Looking at the stunning wedding photos and depictions of love, I don't feel the void of Liam or the need to get married, although of course it would be lovely in the future. Instead, it makes me realise that we're born to love and be loved and that giving up on love is surely giving up on life.

I shut my laptop down for an early night, but I know I'll finish my search requirements tomorrow and even add some more into my own profile. Love will come to me in time.

Chapter 8

I wake up twenty minutes before my alarm, having dreamt about Liam. Maybe it was more of a nightmare. In it, I kept seeing a man who I was searching for disappearing around corners. Each time I got closer, Liam would pop out and shout, 'Gotcha', but he had an old man's face. I feel disturbed and my heart is racing. I shake my head at my weird dream. Maybe Liam knows I'm on the dating website. Perhaps he is 'Gym Dog 25'. I sit up in bed and rub my face.

'You're an absolute idiot, Kitty.' I've always been one of those people whose mind is like a crazy, trippy cartoon akin to The Beatles' "Yellow Submarine" when I've just woken up. My dreams are always vivid, and my imagination can quickly turn to overdrive. Great in some ways, for work and planning events in my own time. However, as an overthinker and a bit of an eccentric one, it's unnecessary mental torture at times.

The working day is just as odd with classes, like pulling teeth from the year elevens, nosebleeds, fights, confiscated mobiles and a general pre-half-term lethargy.

'There's something in the water today,' I say to Sadie at lunch, shaking my head.

'Yeah, I know what you mean. I'm going to give mine extra homework over half-term if they don't behave. Fancy coming for dinner tomorrow night, love?'

'Please,' I reply, grateful to be looked after.

'Great. Right, chicken, I'm off. Love you.' She blows me a kiss.

It's soon home time, and I'm looking forward to a veggie pizza in the fridge that I got courtesy of shopping at The Cooks' on Sunday.

'It's a thin-crust one, pet, so less calories,' my mam had said lovingly, knowing I'm always trying to watch my weight.

Once home, I jump in the shower and then put my fleece pjs straight on. With the autumn nights, it feels acceptable to get straight into pjs when getting in from work, even at 4:30 p.m.; after all, it's getting dark. I light my bioethanol fire and put the oven on. Usually I'd have dinner later, but I'm hungry—a good sign that my appetite is returning to pre-breakup.

I fetch my laptop from under the coffee table. Loading it up, I bite my lip nervously in anticipation of what might be waiting in my Soul Mates inbox. It's all so new and weird and well out of my comfort zone.

I go straight to Soul Mates' site and find five messages in my inbox. I clasp my hands together in nervous excitement, then click the envelope icon.

1. *Hi honey, how are you?*

2. *Your free trial has six days remaining. To renew after this time, please click on the link below for special rates.*

3. *Holla hot stuff, where ya from?*

4. *Alreet, I'm Duncan. How's yi doin sex-ay? Got any pics like?*

5. *Hello K-30. You sound like a lovely woman. Would you like to chat?*

I put my hand over my mouth, stifling a giggle. Scanning over the messages again, the only appealing one is number five. I click on the profile of the sender 'Mr Blue Eyes'.

'Agghhh.' Bloody hell, he looks like Bob, the pensioner down the street. He's a lovely man but not someone who makes my heart skip a beat. 'Mr Blue Eyes' certainly isn't under forty-five. Dirty old man and a bloody liar at that, I think, then immediately feel bad. Everyone deserves love, no matter their age. Plus, my profile gives nothing away about myself other than a few interests.

My mission has been identified: I'm definitely going to complete the profile. Perhaps leaving a photo out for now. I need to narrow down who can contact me and who I can search for.

But first, pizza. After cutting my pizza into slices and getting some orange juice, I take my plate and glass into the lounge and place my laptop on the space next to me on the sofa—Liam's space. Another brief, unexpected moment that takes my breath away a little. I shake my head and grit my teeth, determined to stop those thoughts encroaching into my mind.

Refocusing on the laptop, I click onto the search profile criteria and start where I left off yesterday.

Height: 5'11 and over.

For 'Appearance', I can click on a range of options around hair colour, eye colour, facial hair. I scroll through, laughing to myself at something Henry always says, 'Anyone you've ever dated looks like the roughest impersonator ever of Jamie Dornan.' It's true; they all look akin to the handsome actor. In all fairness, I've only had a few boyfriends. At least I know my type. So, I select Jamie-Dornan-like traits.

Appearance: Brown hair, tall, facial hair.
Smoker: No.
Drinker: Social. (Which could also include borderline alcoholics, but I will take the chance. A teetotaller isn't for me.)

I raise an eyebrow at 'Marital Status', wondering why 'married' is even an option on this. I also don't trust 'separated'.

Marital Status: Single and divorced.

'Children' is another tricky one. Although I don't want to be anyone's baby mama, I also acknowledge that people often get to thirty plus years old with children. Hell, if I had a child for every time an insensitive person asked when I was going to host in my womb, I would have over 100 myself.

Children: Optional.

An option that I'm not bothered about is 'Education'. I know some dreadfully stupid people who have multiple degrees. Common sense can't be learnt, and although I don't want to date *Mr Bean*, I also don't want to date Jeremy Paxman.

Education: None specified.
Employment Status: Employed.
Interests: Travel, theatre, live music, cinema, eating out, museums, fitness, reading, cooking, walking. (I avoid the generic 'socialising', as it makes me think of the *Geordie Shore* crew, which is a turn off.)

Distance: Within a fifteen-mile radius. (A long-distance relationship isn't something I want or have the energy for at my age.)

Save.

Excellent. That part's now done and means at least I won't get messages from sixty-three year olds in Cornwall. I add a little to my own profile—interests and some information about myself. I still have five days left of the trial, so after searching through the type of men on the site, I could always add a photo or two if there's any merit in being on Soul Mates.

My search begins, with pages upon pages of hopefully eligible men. I scan over the first few pages. There are a few blatant Google Image cut and paste jobs of men in modelling poses or coming out of a pool with a toned body and strategically placed wet hair. There are also a few who look genuine on first glance, so I click on their profiles. Some have smiling photos of nights out with pals, playing sport, their pets. A few even have poses with their arms around women on what look like nights out. Other profiles have nothing but night out pictures—something I'm keen to avoid. Beer boys need not apply.

There are so many profiles, it's like dating bingo. I let out a sigh. Is this even the right thing for me? Profiles are one thing, but online dating has a whole lesson in etiquette, safety, communication and emotional protection that I'll need a semester of lectures about. I decide to call it a night on Soul Mates and instead speak to Sophie about her experiences of internet dating; after all, she met the love of her life, Chris, online. Surely she will have some advice that will help me make this possible gigantic step on the best footing.

Chapter 9

'Here you go, my little Kit.' Sadie puts a steaming plate of heaven in front of me.

I look up and smile, grateful for the plate of goodness. Her leek and cheese mash is bliss and the exact comfort food needed on an autumn night.

Sadie pours me some juice, knowing I don't drink on a school night, and squeezes my hand as she takes her seat. I didn't see her at work today apart from a quick hello, which happens once or twice a week due to our timetables being so different. My day always seems a little less sparkly when I don't see her cartoon-like face across the corridor or hear her dirty laugh entering the staffroom.

'I was talking to Stu last night about you, love,' she says as she watches me tuck into the food, like a proud mother.

'Oh yeah?'

'Yeah, I was reminding him of that time we did the open day for the transition students last year and we played the game of how many Queen song references we could get into the conversation with parents.' She laughed, her bright red, manicured nails going towards her mouth.

'Yeah, asking them if they "want to break free" was a bit much for teenagers before announcing you "don't want to ride your bicycle, but Brian May" and pointing to a random person was likely to have the poor kids wondering what the hell was going on.' I grin, reminiscing the memory with fondness. 'Eeeh, you were so competitive, it got ridiculous in the end. They must've thought we were right weirdos and probably didn't even know who Queen are.'

'We are, love.' She howls, beaming with pride at our escapades.

I look at my friend's face, filled with warmth and exactly the right level of sass. I know with all my heart that Sadie will always be here for me. We've only known each other a short time in terms of friendship, but sometimes when you meet someone, you just know that whatever the circumstances, they'll be around. That you will forever be connected. Your people, your hive. Swallowing the lump forming in my throat, I look at Sadie. 'I'm so lucky to have you,' I say as I start to well up.

'Hey, hey, come on, my little one, it's okay,' she says, getting up and coming round to my seat.

'I'm sorry, Sade. I'm really sorry. I just feel so up in the air, like I'm trying to bury a feeling and it won't stay down. I keep thinking I'm doing okay, then something else hits me unexpectedly and winds me. Then I just feel lost and lonely again. It feels like a train travelling through me, snatching my breath and leaving me wobbly.' I wipe my face on the serviette.

'I know, Kit, I know. You're grieving for Liam, your relationship, your future. It's understandable. You have to let yourself hurt, cry, be angry. But you also have to realise you are loved and you'll be okay.' She strokes my hair, her love and friendship soaking into me.

I nod and manage a clumsy smile. 'I know, I just have these moments of struggling. But you're right. Jane said the same. I don't know what I would have done without you two the last few weeks.'

Two hours later and with a full belly and full heart, I'm home. I shower, get my pjs on, make myself a cup of tea and settle into bed with my laptop. Logging into Soul Mates, I have a few messages. It appears people aren't great at opening dialogue and really need to pay more attention to the 'first impression' rule. One of the messages is from a 'MaxT'.

Hello, how are you? Your profile sounds great. I went to Northumbria uni a few years ago as well, although my degree was in Marine Engineering (sounds much more exciting than it actually was!) Max.

The message has me raising an eyebrow with a flutter of interest, but his profile is the same as mine in that it has no photo. The grey-blue outline of a head peers blandly back at me. It automatically puts me off and makes me think he's either married or looks like *Shrek*. Then the penny drops. Perhaps people think that of me also. It may explain why most of my few messages seem to be from faceless folk, the Google Image brigade or possible bots. I learned that term from research. It's basically robots/not real people. Sophie also texted me some online dating basics, some of which made me laugh, some of which terrified the life out of me.

I have a few men in the 'Favourite' section of my profile from the quick search last night, none of whom have messaged me—maybe the lack of photo is a deterrent. It would be hypocritical of me to think it isn't, given my feelings on 'MaxT'; after all, the men I have categorised as 'Favourites' drew me in with their photos. It isn't even shallow. Surely physical attraction is the first thing people see and feel. If I'm in a bar, I can't look around the room and tell someone has a great personality. I've met some beautiful people, men and women, who have a personality like cow pat, but still, it's definitely looks first. I can't expect men to view it any different to me.

So, on day three of my Soul Mates journey, I upload a photo of me from a holiday last year and the one of Jane and me on our night out last week. Clicking upload, I feel nervously sick, but I know I have to give it a fair shot. Love isn't going to come knocking on my door, so I will have to go and knock myself, even if the door doesn't open.

Chapter 10

I decide to have a quick look at Soul Mates on my laptop before breakfast, excited to see if adding some photos has made a difference. I've resisted downloading the Soul Mates app on my phone; I'm not in the type of job where it's acceptable to be on my phone all day. A quick look in between lessons and on lunch break but that's about it. Mobile phones are like the pinnacle of communication and a communication killer at the same time. I dislike that life is spent on them, but I understand the need. There always seems to be someone to respond to, and the frantic nature of personal admin demands, returning emails, texts, calls and social media wears me out. Another app to check is the last thing I need.

I can't believe the number of messages I've had overnight since uploading some pictures—twenty-four. Wow. I click into my inbox, scroll through, half going straight to the delete pile. The photoless profiles, the 'Hi baby, how r u?' and 'Hey Sexy, whatcha up to?' ones, which I really don't like. I loathe text speak, especially when not texting. But there seem to be a few that could be worth at least checking out, if not replying. Clicking away, I read a few of the messages. Some seem friendly, polite and respectful but not my cup of tea at all once

I check out their profile. I talked to Sophie about this during our phone call the other day.

'Kit, *do not* under any circumstances start a conversation with someone you don't find attractive. You can't get rid of them, and fifty percent of the time, it turns nasty. The other fifty percent of the time, you end up their counsellor.'

'Surely not, Soph. Can people not just have a bit of banter without expecting to marry you?' I asked, making light of it.

'Well, it's just part of the dating world. The amount of grief I got. Seriously, hun, don't even go there, or you will definitely be put off internet dating,' she sternly warned. 'One creep kept sending me messages. Firstly, it was the old "beautiful eyes and smile" line. So, I politely replied with a thanks and good luck message. Then, it was the whole "Why are you on here? You could have any man you want" eye-rolling crap. I ignored it. After work, I had like fifteen messages from him, becoming more and more angry and calling me a prick tease. I mean, jeez, if a "good luck with your search" message gets him horny, he needs some serious help.'

I sniggered at her comment, but fifteen messages with no reply and nastiness sounds more than off-putting.

'I blocked the moron and put it down to him being a lone maniac, but then I had a Facebook request from him a week later. Haven't a clue how he found me, but I deleted it, then got one of those weird hidden messages about a day later. He said he was sorry but that I had led him on, he really liked me and he'd like to meet. Led him on by one thanks but no thanks message? Seriously, Kit, don't even bother with those who don't make your stomach do the slightest of flips.'

With my snippets of internet dating advice, or should that be health warnings, I decide to ignore the messages I'm not drawn to, despite feeling a bit of a cow. I skim over a few more messages. Some of the profiles look nice, intriguing even, and there are some good-looking blokes in my inbox. A boost of confidence flows through my veins, and a portion of hope is served up before breakfast. Both of which I absolutely need, given the events of the last few weeks.

I have the gym after work tonight with Jane—my favourite Metafit class. I'll come home and return to my inbox after. With a little buzz of happiness, I begin getting ready as I sing along to Alexa.

'Jeez, my legs are like jelly,' I say to Jane as we leave the gym class and begin walking towards the gym exit. My legs tingle with the pulsating of my glutes, the sensation making me walk like an elderly woman.

Jane sniggers as I huff and puff. 'Mine too. Doubt I will be able to get up off the toilet seat tomorrow,' she replies, hobbling alongside me as we walk to our cars, red-faced but invigorated. 'Exercise shouldn't be this brutal,' she says, rubbing her thigh. 'Fancy a night out next weekend to make up for all this calorie burning?'

I smile but don't reply yet, partial reluctance after what happened last time. Instead, I take the conversation back to online dating. Jane has been a great support and, except for seeing Sadie at work and dinner at her house, I've had the most contact with her this week. She's offered a number of distractions to keep me from thinking about my breakup with Liam, including a night out, shopping and dinner. Jane isn't looking to date at the moment and has never tried internet dating, but she's entertained by my stories, asks questions and encourages me to enjoy the process.

'Be careful who you give your number to mind, Kit; you'll be showered with dick pics,' she warns.

I twist my face at the thought of seeing any genitals land in my inbox. 'Gross, but sadly, I think you're right,' I reply as we chuckle before reaching our cars.

'Let's have that night out,' I finally agree. 'It was such a laugh last weekend and did me the world of good. I just don't want my neighbour having to put me to bed this time, so I'll be less of a gin pig.'

'Sounds like a plan, Kit,' she says, hugging me. 'See you Saturday morning for some cardio? If I can walk after that beast of a class.'

'Yeah, see you then but will text before.'

Driving home, I think about what I'll have for dinner. I usually go food shopping on a Friday from work, but I opted to go clothes shopping instead last week, so the cupboards and fridge are starting to look bare. On the plus side but not such a plus side due to the lack of food, my appetite is back. I decide that I'll batch cook and freeze it at the weekend. I always enjoy cooking—curry from scratch, ratatouille, soups and casseroles. Even my own bread. I'm getting my motivation back and will spend the weekend getting back into routines and reading. I'll make a list of what I want from the supermarket and head there after work tomorrow, like I usually do each Friday.

After arriving home, examining the cupboards and fridge for what I can make a meal out of, I end up with beans on toast. Which is actually one of my favourites. I'm sure I have some custard in the cupboard and think about banana and custard for pudding. Sadie always playfully mocks me for some of my food choices. Whilst I can cook a tasty casserole from scratch, I sometimes eat things a seven-year-old would want. Maybe it's the comfort of my youth, when Mam would make me soft-boiled eggs and toast soldiers, with Angel Delight for pudding. The nostalgia of a lack of responsibility and being tucked in at night. I eat my tea as I catch up on the news. More doom and gloom from incompetent governments and global warming. I switch it off and clear away my plate. I don't want to become addicted to my laptop and Soul Mates, but I'm itching to log on.

Opening my laptop with anticipation, I log into my account. Wow. More than twenty messages have flooded my inbox. I get comfy on the sofa, smirk to myself and make a start on looking through. Delete, delete, possibly reply, definitely reply, block, delete. I go through all the messages, leaving only the ones whose profiles I want to know more about. Looks are definitely the first thing, but I have to have common grounds and values with any potential suitors. After scrolling through those who got to the second round, I filter it down some more to around ten men I will reply to. I don't want to start messaging umpteen people at once and get confused over what's been sent to whom—another tip from Sophie, who said to not be 'attention greedy'.

There's a nervous excitement tumbling around in my stomach. I don't know what will come of it all, but Soul Mates is absorbing my boredom and loneliness for now. I reply to the messages, trying to make them personal. A few stand out as intriguing profiles, mainly those with more than one photo and a bit of personality in their description. Sophie also warned me about the 'one photo' guys, these being men with a fifteen-year-old profile picture that looks nothing like them now. She so eloquently termed these men as 'golden deceivers'.

I only have a few more days on the free trial of Soul Mates. I'm not massively keen on having to pay for a subscription, but I guess it would be cheaper than a night out, and I'm limited on where I can meet partners, like most single people. At the gym, I look like a perspiring space hopper on legs, and at work, it's mainly middle-aged and retirement-aged people. Plus, I'm not a fan of shitting where I eat, so to speak. I don't have time or the mental capacity to join a college night class, and I don't think joining a club related to a hobby I have, such as reading, would draw in the Jamie Dornan type.

I re-read the conversation with 'MC-32'.

MC-32: Hi K-30, Happy Thursday! How's your week been? Your profile sounds great and some really pretty photos there. I'd love to talk more. Mark x

Me: Hi, Mark, happy Thursday indeed! I've had a good week so far, thanks, have you? I'm new here, on a free trial, so kind of just finding my feet, or maybe that should be fingers?! Have you been on here long? Kitty x

'Crap.' I re-read the 'finding my feet' line, which clearly makes zero sense, and consider facepalming myself.

I've also replied to another man called 'Modster'. While I'm not keen on someone stuck in the late 1990s, I love indie music, and as long as they don't think they're a Gallagher brother, I don't mind a bit of a barnet and some Adidas Samba.

Modster: Hi Darl, how are you on this crisp autumnal day? I see you like live music. What's the last gig you went to?

Me: Hi, I'm good thanks, how are you? Yes, it's definitely getting chilly in the North East! I do love live music. The last gig I went to was Paloma Faith—she was brill. What was yours? Your profile says you play an instrument? Kitty

I decide to only return kisses if they're sent. All of this etiquette and the rules are a lot to absorb, but I'm starting to learn the best way to navigate from my few days of experience and Sophie's wisdom.

A potential replied to a message and immediately got himself deleted.

ScottyNUFC: I'm good baby, do you want to FaceTime?

I have no interest in dropping my mobile number all over the place, like autumn leaves falling from the trees.

A few more inbox shortlisters message back over the course of the evening, and as the new messages continue coming in, I delete the ones that are okay but don't impress me with their profile. I feel a little harsh but also empowered by my decision-making. I begin getting a sense of intentions from most of the messages after two or three exchanges, if not beforehand. I tut aloud a few times at the boringly predictable and at those definitely trying to enter dick pic territory.

I download the Soul Mates app on my phone so I can shut the laptop down, and then I head to bed.

Chapter 11

'Late night, you internet harlot?' squeals Sadie after I finish a big yawn. She plonks down next to me in the quiet corner of the staffroom, where I'm trying to be discreet. 'Tell me aaaaaaall about it.'

'You're mad as a box of frogs, Sade,' I reply, jokingly rolling my eyes.

'Any fitties been shortlisted?' she enquires, clasping her hands with delight.

'Well, I was talking to three or four last night for a while,' I say as I rub my face and stifle another yawn. 'I'm knacked, Sade; it was after one by the time I turned my phone off.'

'Ooooh, you dirty stop out.' She winks.

'You know, it's not as bad as I thought, this online dating lark. I think as long as you're savvy and don't put up with any rubbish, it's okay, and the blokes I've been chatting with seem lovely on the whole.'

'Zero tolerance, Kit, that's the way. And I don't want nice, I want tasty.' Sadie pouts her lipstick-covered lips. 'Seriously though, love, don't let anyone take the piss. Enjoy it, okay?'

'I will. I'm not looking too much into it. My free trial ends at the weekend. I might not even renew it. I'm just seeing how it goes, and it's filling time for me, if nothing else.'

She nods, and we get up to get ready for the day full of lessons.

The last lesson eventually finishes and I head out of work feeling lighter and knowing next week is half-term, so I have a little break. It's the first time I'm going to be off work and single, and I have a creeping anxiety on how I will fill my days. Jane will still be working in the prison as usual. Sadie and I have planned a day with a picnic in a local nature spot, which I'm looking forward to. I will go and see my mam and dad one day and then perhaps do some of the deep cleaning and house sorting I've been putting off. The gym and cooking will also provide me with some much-needed routine, and hey, you never know, I might even end up on a date.

It takes twenty-five minutes to get to the supermarket near to my housing estate from Richardson High. I have my list and bags for life ready. Browsing the shelves, I start getting all my usual items and a few more staples for cooking and baking, as well as some treats. The middle aisle has the usual random items strewn across it: hiking boots, cat igloos, American cereal, writing sets, slippers and crochet-your-own-flamingo sets. This crap is addictive to look at, and as I walk slowly past the piles of bizarre stock, I wonder if every customer can't help but get distracted by the weird and wonderful items.

I scan the other crochet-your-own-animal boxes, for no valid reason I can work out, as it's something I would never actually create, yet I can't help but—

'Oww.'

I look up at the man in front of me rubbing his calf, and my eyes widen. I can feel my face reddening as I continue to gawp. The man is still rubbing his attacked calf but he's half laughing. I notice he's even more appealing to look at than the middle aisle, and I touch the back of my neck before clearing my throat.

'I, I'm so sorry,' I stammer. 'Are you okay?'

'Yeah, of course, I just got a shock as you tried to steamroll me.' His tone sounds serious, then he smiles. The fact he can still joke around is at least a little comforting.

I nervously let out a laugh. 'Honestly, are you okay? It's this rubbish in these aisles, like some kind of hypnotic jumble sale,' I explain.

'No worries at all; I'm messing. Well, half messing. And yes, the middle aisle has a certain charm.' He raises an eyebrow, glancing into the metal crates filled with colourful randomness.

'Well, erm, sorry again. I'll keep my eyes on where I'm going in the future. It will save me money from buying things I don't need, like a glow-in-the-dark face mask.' I start to make my way down the aisle.

'One can never have enough glow-in-the-dark face masks,' he replies as I walk away, still not looking where I'm going.

I manage to do the rest of my shopping without incident whilst trying to get out the shop as quickly as possible before assaulting someone else. Back home, shopping unpacked, I jump in the shower as I put some pasta on low to boil. Cosying up with my bowl of pesto pasta, I check my social media, reply to a few messages and then go on the Soul Mates app. There are a load more messages, new ones and some from conversations with men I've been chatting with. One is from the site admin, reminding me my trial is running out. One of the messages is from 'MC-32', who I now know to be called Mark. Another is from 'Modster', real name Tom.

Both messages are sweet and have open questions. I feel no alarm bells ringing. I look over their profiles again—the photos are attractive and the profiles interesting. I make my mind up here and now that if Mark or Tom ask me on a date, I will say yes. I won't ask them first; I'm not confident enough. A few of the others have potential, and I will keep my options open.

I chuckle to myself. 'Kitty Cook, who the hell do you think you are?'

Chapter 12

Jane and I met for cardio at the gym this morning, where I updated her on the dating progress, to reactions of shock, disgust and intrigue. Hours of lazing on the sofa to recuperate energy, boredom and mental pushing have motivated me to organise my spare room, which I've been avoiding tackling since Liam left.

Standing at the doorway, I take a deep breath and slowly reach for the door handle. Just as my fingertips reach the metal, I pull my hand back, as if the handle is on fire.

'Urgghh, bloody hell.' I shake my hands, as if to shake off the invisible scorch marks from the handle. I'm reluctant to confront the memories I know are going to hit me smack bang in the face on the other side of this door.

I count to three and try again, this time not pulling away from the door handle. I step inside the little box room and look around, half-expecting a monster to jump out. I hurry to the window and open it, letting some fresh air in, putting my head out the window and deeply inhaling. It smells like him. The whole room. And not just his fragrance, his actual smell, drifting from his belongings after being shut in here ever since he left, no ventilation to dull the scent. I rest my elbows on the windowsill, head in my hands. It's just memories, it's not him. And I can't hold on to something that doesn't work, someone who doesn't make me happy, irrelevant of how much I hurt.

I internally pull myself together and focus on the task I've set myself, opening the storage chest placed against the wall. I immediately come across some of Liam's old DVDs and books. Books he won't be missing, as he never reads, spending all his bloody time on his phone.

The burst of anger spurs me on as I open the wardrobe. At the bottom sits a pair of tatty trainers, and I spot one of Liam's hoodies hanging up. I push the hangers aside so the print of the top is visible. It's a Hard Rock Cafe one that he bought on a holiday to Tenerife. Despite bickering at home, we never seemed to argue on holiday. That's when I had the Liam I'd fallen in love with. I take the hoody off its hanger and pull it towards me, sniffing it. A wounded sigh escapes my mouth as I wrap it around myself, the feeling of needing the smell of him to escape now replaced with longing. I shake my head and tug it away from myself, knowing I can't let the upset overwhelm me, and I stare at the logo that held so much promise when he bought it. My hand goes to my chest as I take a deep breath and place it in a storage bag along with his other items. I zip up the belongings of my past along with the crushed dreams of what could have been.

An hour later, the room looks de-Liam-ed. I place the storage bag inside a wooden chest that's sitting neatly under the bedroom window. Liam obviously isn't missing them, or me for that matter, but I want them out of sight. The less reminders in view and in my head of my failed relationship, the better. Despite the emotions, I know it's onwards and upwards from here. Another step forward. I run my hands through my hair as I walk out of the bedroom and shut the door firmly.

Back downstairs, I instruct Alexa to play some dance music as I get on with doing some batch cooking, singing along and doing the odd dance moves as I create some homemade goodness.

I'm okay. The realisation washes over me that even after being with someone for so long, and knowing them even longer, life does indeed go on. I eat some of the delicious tomato and basil soup I've made with some pitta-style bread I have also made. One of my favourite things about autumn, along with the lipstick-shade leaves and cosy knits, is soup. In particular, homemade soup. I even sit at the table, alone, without the distraction of my phone or laptop. Yeah, I'm doing okay.

After a productive few hours, it's time for Soul Mates. I'm logging on a few times a day but trying not to get sucked into the vortex of the app, obsessing over who's messaging me or why men aren't replying. I know female friends who've fallen in love with men quicker than a kettle boiling, but that's not me. I'm not emotionally hard—quite the opposite most of the time, and I get on with all types of people—but finding a man attractive, physically and mentally, then feeling that all-consuming sensation of falling in love... I dunno. I guess it just takes a long time for me. It isn't me to have a different future husband each month. I try to keep my emotions in check and, perhaps a little like my work ethos, smart.

With the void Liam's left, the cracks in my heart, the body missing in the bed, all the aloneness and sadness, it would be easy to jump straight into a relationship with the next man on a conveyor belt of dating CVs, but it won't help, and in the long run, won't be fair on anyone. A rebound relationship isn't the answer. I'm still healing from the breakup, no doubt about that. I'm proud of how far I've come in a few weeks and that I'm getting my routine and confidence back, but I'm not going to emotionally invest in or possibly emotionally hurt someone as part of my recovery.

I get cosy on the sofa and log on. There's an array of messages in my inbox, and I filter them out as usual. Some of the men I replied to have come back with lazy responses—one or two words or no attempt to stimulate any conversation. If they can't be bothered to ask me anything about myself or show any humour, kindness, something appealing about their personality, then I won't reply. I'm pretty sure many do a mass copy and paste to multiple potential dates. I have to remember I'm likely to be compared to other women by any possible date, but I'm certainly not going to chase men. Boundaries are really important to me and something Sophie has mentioned several times that I need to have.

I respond to a few messages from men I've been chatting with and several new ones. Mark and Tom have both messaged, as has a man called 'LewisT&W', who seems really nice and is absolutely gorgeous. He's very much my type, with a look of a younger Gerard Butler about him. Henry, of course, would probably tease that Gerard is too good-looking and too old for me. But hey, I don't scrub up too bad.

The rest of the afternoon is spent chatting with a few people. Tom is working, so can't message much, but alongside Lewis and Mark, there's the odd message from others. I still haven't messaged anyone first, which feels ridiculously old-fashioned, but maybe it's confidence. I won't rule it out. Maybe I just need to get more used to the site and the internet dating vibe. Mark's messaging about his day.

Mark: We lost at the football, but it doesn't matter cos it's always a good laugh. I'm probably not competitive enough to be on a football team, even if it is just a local lads one! Ha! Do you like sport? x

Me: I think exercise would be pretty mundane without the laughs, so I think you've got the right idea, and I'm sure you're brilliant with ball control! Yeah, I guess I like more exercise than sport as such. I love the gym, classes mainly that leave me feeling like I've been steamrolled the next day and unable to put my shoes on. I like cycling, walking, a bit of tennis (very competitive at it, as left-handed and always felt at a disadvantage) x

Mark: Haha I can just imagine a game of tennis with you. I think I would be terrified! Those lefties have a mean backhander. I like cycling as well and walking. There's nothing better than wrapping up in the cold weather and going for a long walk, then having a nice coffee and sarnie. We live in a lush part of the world, don't we? x

Me: We do indeed, and yeah, it's so nice to be in nature. Our coastline is so stunning, and I think we're really lucky living next to such amazing green space and historical landmarks x

Mark: So maybe we have just chosen our first date? X

My stomach churns as I look at the screen. Crikey. I'm not sure if I'm ready for this. What if he's really some weirdo, or what if he doesn't like me? I'm completely frozen, the chat still open in front of me. I can't bring myself to give an answer either way.

Mark: Have I scared you off, Kitty? X

I tap my legs. I feel like an awkward teenager, and I don't know what to say but know I have to answer quickly. I can't hide behind a computer screen forever.

Me: No, not at all. Sorry, just nipped to the loo. Yeah, possibly! I'm always cold, mind, so I would probably look like a human quilt. X

Mark: I would hold your hand to keep you warm x

Oh God. I'm not sure how to react. I mean, it certainly isn't on the dick pic level, but I guess I'm just not used to flirty intentions, even if it is only a hand hold. Is a hand hold even considered flirty? Probably not, but I'm feeling beyond prudish after being out of the dating game so long. I've spent years practically married off but without the ring. I bring my hand to my mouth and bite on my thumbnail. This is so new, so strange. I've found myself wavering on Soul Mates between feeling as confident as a catwalk model to feeling like I want to hide in the corner like a timid mouse.

But I have to get back into the game or at least learn what the game is about.

I reply with a smiley face and say I have to pop out to the shops and will chat later. I need some space to think about meeting up and to reply in a way that doesn't make me sound like I'm overanalysing, which, of course, I am. This is what dating apps are about, I know that, and he seems lovely, but am I really ready for this step? The lack of reality from the screen is my safety blanket. I can sit here in my pjs, chatting and flirting badly without wondering if my breath smells or if my lipstick is smudged. Meeting in reality... well, perhaps that's just a bit too real.

After giving myself a lecture, then having a chat with Sophie, I pull my big girl knickers up and make arrangements for a first date with Mark. As a physio, he has a flexible work diary and is off on Monday, so we have chosen to meet at a local nature reserve at 11 a.m. It's convenient that it's half-term, meaning a week off from Richardson High for me.

Arranging to meet in the daytime in an area that will be filled with families and dog walkers feels safer, and I don't want any first dates to involve alcohol. Pubs are fine, but

I've decided I will always take my car. Sophie gave me an extensive safety lecture. Even though daylight could be intimidating for the first date, my nerves wouldn't take stretching my first date in five years out another week or to somewhere where I would have to wear four-inch heels and false eyelashes. I will still make the effort for myself, if not Mark.

Chapter 13

My trial ends on Soul Mates today. I bite the bullet and subscribe for longer. The deal is five pounds ninety-nine a month if you pay for three months or nine pounds ninety-nine for one month. I pay for the former, hopeful that I won't need more than three months to find my much-promised Soul Mate. Hell, I might have already found him, but I want to keep my options open until I meet Mark in the flesh at least.

I continue to chat with the other men I've been communicating with, feeling a tad guilty when I see Mark online. The etiquette is a minefield, but I'm sure he'll still be talking to others. We haven't even met yet. I'm curious about his dating past and current conversations. He's alluded to previous disastrous dates but not in great detail. There's also the issue of chemistry in real life, standing next to someone and seeing them in the flesh, speaking to them and exploring their personality will be very different to typing crap on a screen and sending emojis.

I go to my parents' for Sunday lunch as per usual. Sarah is here with Henry today. She's a lovely woman, and it's nice to see Henry settled and grown-up.

'Any news from knacker Ned?' Henry asks in the kitchen.

I burst out laughing. 'No, Henry, I've not heard from Liam.'

'Good, I hope you don't hear from him. Sarah's brother said he's all over Facebook plastering nights out like he's on a bloody Ibiza holiday. Topless and everything.' He screws up his face in disgust, and Sarah nods.

I feel a kick to my stomach that he's moved on already and probably never gives me a second thought. 'It doesn't surprise me, to be honest, Henry. He'll be thinking he's worthy of being on *The Batchelor* and is no doubt hanging around with the twenty-year-olds he works with. Let him get on with it; I don't give a shit,' I reply, trying to sound convincing. I don't give a damn deep down, but there's still something about him getting on with life seemingly so carefree. I would never wish bad for him though. Even with all the times of real love with Liam, we're such different people now from when we met all those years ago, and the gap between us just got bigger and bigger. He had no consideration for us as a couple and didn't want to grow up.

'So, you're doing okay, Sis?' Henry asks, concern etched across his forehead.

'Yeah, yeah, Henry, I'm okay thanks,' I reply, just as the living room door opens and Mam's voice enters the room.

We sit down together as a family for our Sunday roast. My mam has given me extra sprouts—my favourite.

'Phawww, you'll not be getting any dates after eating all those, mind, Kit; you'll be frigging stinking.' Henry laughs, wafting his nose animatedly.

'*Henry*. Don't be cruel to your sister.' Mam giggles, tapping Henry's arm playfully.

'You stink without them, love,' Sarah says, looking at Henry, then nodding loyally at me.

'Well, actually,' I begin, a slight smug expression on my face, 'I have a date tomorrow, so maybe I should take it easy.' I wink as I happily shovel another leafy delight into my mouth.

'A date, darling? So soon? Who with?' Mam asks, apprehension surfacing in her voice.

'So, I'm trying internet dating,' I announce as I glance around the table to gauge everyone's reactions.

'Good for you, hun,' Sarah says, an encouraging smile on her face.

Dad looks up. 'Full of perverts and murderers, those things, Kit. If you're meeting blokes off there, I hope you've got one of those rape alarms or some of that CS gas. Can you get it on eBay?' Dad nods to Henry for confirmation.

I almost choke on my water as I begin to laugh. Dad is always trying to protect me, even with his extreme preconceptions at times. 'Jeez, Dad, I'll never leave the house at this rate. I guess there are some fruit loops, but they're everywhere. Pervs and murderers walk amongst us and probably live in this cul-de-sac, not just on the internet,' I reply.

Mam straightens her back. 'Eric, are there any pervs or murderers on this street?'

'How the hell would I know, Liz? Maybe quiet Winnie down the road is a cannibal, or perhaps Frank and Cleo are into swinging.'

'Urgghh, Dad,' I exclaim, chuckling. Henry is having a full-blown laughing attack and Sarah is trying to compose herself with a mouthful of veg.

'Bugger off,' Mam replies in jest as she gets back to tackling her Yorkshire pudding.

'Well, just be careful, darling. These wrong 'uns hide behind a screen, a false identity and prey on people, Kit.

Why can't you meet people the normal way?' Dad says, his shoulders dropping with the long breath he lets out.

'Normal way? Dad, it's not the 1980s. I won't meet someone at the local dance or community centre like you did.'

'*Darling*, local dances were more 1950s,' replies Mam. 'Your dad and I, well, we aren't quite that old yet, thank you very much.'

'Well, you know what I mean.' I shrug defensively. 'Where am I meant to meet someone? Pissed on a Saturday night in town?'

'Alright, alright,' Henry interjects. 'I can't eat me scran with all this drama going on.'

'Listen, pet, just be careful. Your dad's right that there are perverts around. I know it may sound like we're being killjoys, but better to be safe than sorry,' Mam says, affectionately grabbing my hand across the table.

Dad stares at me, raising an eyebrow.

'Okay, okay, I get it. Dad, Mam, Henry, Sarah, I'll be careful, alright?' I say, looking at each of them in turn, as if I'm a child. 'I'll tell Jane where I'm going and when, and I'll have my car and mobile. I draw the line at CS gas, mind, Dad; I don't want to be struck off from teaching.'

There's a round of nods from my family and a snigger from Henry as I wonder why I opened my mouth. Niggling deep down, however, I know they have a point.

Chapter 14

I wake up on Monday morning at my usual work time, even without my alarm. I hate that my body clock won't let me lie in, and I yearn for the ability to sleep for hours and hours like I did a decade ago. However, today is the day I'm meeting Mark, so I have to be up early to steady my nerves and get ready. My bowels are screaming at me already, my guts churning. Maybe the mass consumption of sprouts wasn't the best idea. At least the date is outside. I reluctantly gave Mark my personal email so he can let me know any issues with our date plans. I'm not ready to give out my mobile, and he's understanding, which earns him another point in my mental tally of possible potential.

After breakfast, I begin getting ready, creeping nervousness crawling over me. Extra deodorant applied to hopefully compensate for me being an anxious sweater, I look at my outfit for the walk. Blue skinny jeans, a red woollen jumper, my black hiking boots and my black DKNY puffer coat with cosy faux fur hood. I have a cute knitted headband to put in my Ralph Lauren messenger bag alongside my gloves, in case it gets cold. For now, I will shower, then do my hair and makeup in my dressing gown. I wish almost daily that it was acceptable to wear dressing gowns outdoors.

Pottering about in my bedroom, I think about the newness of dating. The exciting parts but also having to get comfortable with someone again. Not the comfortable lazy that can happen with some couples and what definitely happened with me and Liam, more the comfortable where you can just put your hair back in a bun without feeling you look like a horse or putting your dressing gown on and being cosy rather than having control pants cutting into you. All those new things to get used to, to discover and to share. So many things are taken for granted when you're in a long-term relationship and at that comfort point. But I guess there's also something exciting about the newness, the effort and anticipation. I want to feel the stirrings of new connections, romance, love eventually. The same butterflies that flew away long ago with Liam and died somewhere cold and unhappy.

After getting out of the shower and back into my dressing gown, I sit at my dressing table with morning TV on as I start to get ready. I can enjoy taking my time now I'm not clearing up after another adult. I relish the slower pace of life and I learnt the importance of it during the pandemic, wanting to keep hold of the small positives from such a worldwide trauma. I have another cup of tea by my side as I put some fresh nail varnish on whilst my hair is piled up in a towel, the soft material absorbing some of the dampness. I opt for an opal pearl with a glimmer of sparkle in—great for daytime but also a little glitzy. Drying and straightening my hair is next as I glance at the TV advising me of the most recent money-saving tips and winter kitchen delights.

At 10:20 a.m., I leave the house, feeling I look okay and suitably confident I'm not going to have nervous diarrhoea in the next forty-five minutes. Well, hopefully anyway. Even though the date destination is only around twenty-five minutes away by car, I want to get there early and calm any nerves. An achievement for someone who's usually always running late.

Mark told me he has a gunmetal grey Nissan Almera, so when I park up in the small car park at the nature reserve, I do a quick scan. No grey cars, which means I can begin a desperate ritual to compose myself. The nerves and thoughts whirling in my head have started again. How do I greet him? I talk rubbish when I'm nervous, and I'm worried about what random cack will pour out of my mouth. What if he doesn't find me attractive or if I don't fancy him? How will we leave it? I don't want any more friends; it's dates or bust. Then I realise he probably feels the same.

I take deep breaths, count to ten, then pull the visor down to check my makeup. I reapply my lipstick, which normally I don't wear a lot of. My lipstick is a beautiful autumn shade of Soft Berry, a Bobbi Brown lipstick that was a generous gift from Sadie for my thirtieth birthday. Another spritz of Jour d'Hermes perfume. Christ, I'm almost flammable.

I check my phone as a grey car pulls into the car park. Agghhh, is this him? I pop another chewing gum in my mouth, convinced that my breath smells of sprouts or bins or something else undesirable. He gets out the car. He hasn't parked close enough for me to see his face properly, but the person looks vaguely like his descriptions.

An email pops up on my phone: *I'm here, just looking for your car. M x*

I smile and quickly shove my phone in my bag and get out the car. He looks around as I try to make sure I don't step on a big rock or slip on my unsteady legs and twist an ankle before I even stand up properly.

I walk, slightly wobbling, towards where Mark's stood. I keep my head up and shoulders back as I try to muster some confidence in my body language despite feeling like blancmange inside. A second later, he notices me, waves and starts walking towards me as the shaking in my legs ups itself on the Richter scale.

'*Sadie*, it's not funny,' I exclaim.

'Oh, my Kit, it really is.' She almost deafens me with her cackle down the phone. 'I love you dearly, my little fuckwit, I really do.'

I start chuckling. We often refer to each other as FFs. Whilst people fondly use terminology such as FFs as Friends Forever, ours is Fuckwit Friends, as we're both prone to heavy doses of stupidity, clumsiness and general misadventure.

'Okay, so it is quite funny, but it was awful at the time,' I protest.

I explained my first adventure into the bold dating world to Sadie for a full ten minutes as she gasped and howled down the phone. Walking across the car park, I had gotten closer to Mark and begun to panic ever so slightly. The closer I got, the more I realised he didn't quite look as I'd imagined he would from the photos on his profile. As we reached each other and had a few nervous seconds of how to greet before he went in for a relaxed hug, I wondered if my face covered the sheer shock. Saying hello to me, I noticed his teeth, or should I say lack of teeth. Now, I'm not one to gnasher discriminate but Mark's teeth resembled 1800's gravestones and were about as spaced out. I wondered what the hell had gone on to be a man in his early thirties with less teeth than an eighty-year-old and realised all of his photos must have had a closed-mouth smile.

As shallow as it may sound to some, it was the beginning of the end. Mark's my height in my not even one-inch sole hiking boots despite claiming to be six feet tall. It made him five-foot-nine at best. Again, not a problem for some, but not what I would normally go for. Along with a mouth like a row of wooden pegs, it was too much for me to see past. Nevertheless, we went for a walk and had a good chat, then a lovely cup of tea and carrot cake in the on-site café. Mark told me about his hobbies more, his job in physio and his marriage breakdown. I can't say the date wasn't pleasant and the chat wasn't nice, but I fancied Mark about as much as I fancy retraining to be a mechanic—beyond zero. I don't want to be unkind, but I also don't want to lead anyone on. When we said goodbye and he said, 'Maybe do this again?' I said, 'Perhaps', knowing that I would message him in the evening, diplomatically reflecting on the date.

'You know what, Sade?' I say, starting to laugh again. 'I remember thinking his name sounded familiar but couldn't place it. He mentioned it on the date and made a joke of it, the poor bugger.'

'Mark. Mark who? Is his surname Penis or something?' Sadie squeals.

'It's Mark Chapman, as in the name of the guy who assassinated John Lennon.'

'Oh my God, you are something else, Kit. You'll be meeting that Freddy next week, you know, Freddy West.'

My mouth drops open. I now need to add getting their full name to the criteria before saying yes to a date. 'Stop it, Sadie,' I shriek.

'Well, love, you've given me a great Monday. Keep me updated with your bizarre dating diary, please.'

'Will do. See you later in the week.' I hang up and then walk through to the kitchen to make a cup of tea.

I sit with my tea and message Mark, thanking him for the date but saying I didn't feel a connection. It seems a sensitive yet truthful line and one I personally wouldn't be offended by. It doesn't take him long to reply.

That's a shame, but you're a great woman and I wish you the best x

I make a mental note to look at mouths of possible dating candidates in their photos more thoroughly in the future for any clues. I exchange a few messages with Tom and Lewis and reply to a few new ones before switching off for the night to watch a new three-part drama on TV. I text Jane snippets of information about the date. We're meeting for dinner at the local pub tomorrow, so I'll update her in more depth then.

Chapter 15

'Why do people lie on the internet about things like appearance? I mean, fair enough if they aren't ever gonna meet someone, although morally it's still shady, but knowing you're meeting people and lying about obvious things. What's wrong with people?' Jane asks, completely perplexed as we sit opposite each other in the pub.

'I agree, hun. It's bizarre, pointless and a waste of people's time. He was a pleasant guy and maybe lots of women wouldn't be bothered about his height. I mean, I'm tall, so for a woman shorter, that's great.'

We tuck into our food. I've opted for bean burger with chunky chips and salad and Jane has Hunter's chicken. It's nice to have a meal cooked for me, other than by my mam, who in all fairness would cook for me every evening if I wanted. I pop a fluffy, crispy chip in my mouth.

'What did you tell your mam?' Jane asks.

'I didn't go into detail, just that I didn't find him attractive. I don't want them worrying about me.' My shoulders slump. 'I get it, I'm always going to be their baby, but I'm okay at adulting most of the time. Dad thinks every bloke on the internet is Jack the Ripper. I don't want them stressing me, so I'm gonna just keep things on the down-low unless I actually meet someone I like and it progresses, which I'm not filled with hope about after yesterday.'

'Just arrange to meet people and strike them off if they're not for you.' Jane shrugs and picks up her drink to take a sip.

'You say it with such romance,' I jest. But Jane does have a point. I don't want to waste time messaging people for ages who turn out to be nothing like I imagined. But at the same time, I don't want to just meet people without chatting much. That feels risky, even with my robust safety planning. In all honesty, I don't want to waste my energy, time and money getting ready for date after date only for the potential of progressing to a relationship having as much chance of success as Tyrannosaurus rexes making a comeback into the food chain.

Maybe I'll just go along with the idea that if I've been messaging a man for a few days, a date can be arranged within the next week or so. I ask Jane what she thinks of this.

'Sounds like a good idea to me, hun, but I think you're gonna need a personal assistant.'

'You might be right. Or maybe when we go out on Saturday, I'll meet the man of my dreams. Hey, you might even meet yours.'

Jane rolls her eyes.

It's evening when I log onto Soul Mates to more messages. It's nice being popular, but it's also proving a time-intensive task, and for each seemingly genuine message, there's a message that evokes a negative emotion. I'm fully aware there are many morons around, in both male and female form, but there seems to be a concentration on the internet. There's something about the keyboard warrior and hiding behind a screen that clearly appeals to all types of weirdos and deviants. Blatant misogynists, perverts, liars and so many pity-story sad sacs. I've felt my own sadness at times in life, and although grateful to have not experienced any clinical mental health issues, I've experienced anxiety and know so many people who have all levels of mental ill health. Some of these people need actual psychological intervention and aren't going to get it from a dating site. It saddens me. At the same time, it feels like some people are exploiting past vulnerability or experiences and even lying to try and get numbers and attention.

Some messages are making me feel like an unpaid counsellor. That's me all over—I'm one of those people in life that folk gravitate to. A massive compliment much of the time, but it also means I'm often a madness magnet. Strangers will pour their souls out to me, in real life as well as on the internet. If colleagues at work have any problems, I get a call from the Head of Pastoral team to see if I can be a 'Buddy'. For my friends, I'm their go-to for advice. Which, of course, is a compliment on my skillset as a friend, but when everyone needs advice at once, there's been times I've drowned in my own worries whilst keeping others afloat.

Even in the fullest of training rooms, I'm always the arsehole magnet. It's a running joke now. Sometimes it's nice to get out of the office, away from teaching and learn something. To not have to tell the kids off for having their mobile phones and not think about lesson plans. Get the old grey matter going and eat multiple biscuits that are always available at break times. However, in my case, each and every single training course I've attended, in the history of time, the arsehole in the room has gravitated towards me. Like the proverbial fly to shit. These people are always on my training course, they always sit next to me and by 11 a.m. I feel I know them so well that I've given birth to them.

As per every other realm of my life, Soul Mates has become a place where undesirables gravitate towards me. A week and a half into my online dating journey, I'm getting my eyes increasingly opened to etiquette, expectations and the grim side of the phenomena.

I start replying to a few people. I haven't heard back from Lewis since my last message, but Tom has messaged.

Hey Kitty, how's your week going? Enjoying being off? Any dates yet?

I like that he's remembered I'm off work, as we haven't talked in a massive amount of depth.

Me: Hi, Tom, great thanks, and yes, it's lovely having a break. How's your week going? Any gigs? Well actually, yes, I had my first date yesterday. He was a nice bloke but not for me.

Tom: Whaaattt? So I didn't get the chance to pop your online dating cherry? Not good enough, Kit.

I laugh. Tom has good banter, although I guess most performers do. Liam can orchestrate a room, he has charisma and is entertaining, just not really to the level of a real Hollywood actor.

Me: Well, Tom, you know what they say: 'If you're not fast, you're last!'

Tom: Yeah yeah, you snooze, you lose. I understand. I better get in fast then, how about a date?

I have a little rush of excitement, like opening a new, big box of tasty chocolates. Tom seems fun, a bit rogue and can make me laugh. He's handsome in his photos and has me intrigued. On those grounds, he's definitely worth a date.

Me: Sounds a good idea, before I'm swept off my feet by the next person trying to date me

Tom: Well, talking of gigs, I have one on Thursday night. You could come along, VIP? I'll only be on stage for an hour, as it's a two-band gig. We could have a drink before and after? I might even dedicate a song to you.

My hand goes to my heart, my pulse racing at the thought of it. Wow, who wouldn't want someone dedicating a song to them? Although, I bet he's been through a bloody baby name book's worth of dedications. Tom seems a cheeky chappy, and I like it.

Me: Great, sounds like a plan. Mind you, I expect more than a dedication of song. I'm thinking more the Courteney Cox/Bruce Springsteen stage dedication

Tom: I like your confidence, Kitty, I like it a lot! X

We talk a little longer and Tom confirms he's put my name on the guest list for his band, Presto's Project, on Thursday night at a local bar in town. Although I'm nervous about going to a gig alone, it also feels exhilarating, and it will be another achievement on the bucket list. I'll take the car and not deviate from the blackcurrant and sodas, but it's something different and, I hope, full of potential.

I'm also messaging another guy, someone from earlier this week, 'StubblyIan34'. His name made me smile. In some of his photos, he does indeed have stubble and, in fact, a full, handsome beard. I love beards, and I'm starting to gather a list in my head of possible non-negotiables that will help narrow my search and message replies further, saving time and energy, of which both are starting to deplete. Facial hair is definitely on the wish list. Not a Freddie-Mercury-style moustache, but a nice, neat beard. A non-negotiable, I'm not sure, but at the moment, a definite plus. I'm becoming Soul Mate savvy, and I give myself a metaphoric pat on the back. Sophie would be proud.

'StubblyIan34', or just 'Ian', lives in the next borough to me, about a twenty-minute drive. He's an engineer and lives alone, divorced and with an eight-year-old son, who he sees through the week. I'm pleased he's upfront about his commitments to his son, showing me he's hopefully honest and hopefully a good dad. From what he's said, he gets on with his ex, which I think could terrify lots of possible partners. For me, it shows he respects the mother of his child and probably indicates he isn't a psychopath. Always a bonus.

As we chat, he asks questions, which gains him more bonus points. Ian's messages have good depth, and he seems articulate. His messages don't result in me rolling about laughing, but he definitely has potential, and I feel a connection is worth exploring. Lewis has also popped back into my inbox, albeit for only a short period. By 10 p.m., I've agreed to a date on Sunday with Lewis (I can't deny I was expecting more a date ask from Ian than Lewis, but not much shocks me anymore in the world of Soul Mates) and I have my date on Thursday with Tom and his band.

I smugly log out of Soul Mates, feeling like I'm definitely upping my internet dating game. I have to make the most of my week off, after all.

Chapter 16

Thursday comes around quickly, but before my date with Tom and Presto's Project, I'm meeting Sadie for a cuppa in town at one of our favourite cafés.

After a quick but tight hug, Sadie pulls away and holds me at arm's length. 'You look tired, Kit. Are you okay? Too busy internet flirting to get a decent night's sleep?'

'I think I just still have the odd night where I feel a bit lost in the king-size bed.' I hope it's my eyes fluttering every now and again and not the black bags under them I spent ages trying to cover this morning that she's noticed.

'Well, I'll send Stu round. I would love a night starfishing and not listening to him snoring like a bullmastiff,' she jokes as we stand in the queue, browsing the menu.

'Aw, poor Stu. He's a darl. I want what yous have. You're total couple goals.' My attention is quickly swept away by the cake display. 'Oh look, they have those caramel brownies back,' I say, almost salivating.

'Caramel brownies it is.' Sadie rubs my arm. 'He's a keeper, my Stu. He really is a good 'un, even with his obscene snoring,' Sadie says with affection.

'What's the dating goss, then?' she asks a little too loudly as we find a seat after ordering.

'I'm getting the hang of it, I think. There are some crackerjacks, Sade, there really are. But there are also some seemingly nice blokes, and I'm getting a bit savvier with who I'll respond to and all that. It's bloody time-consuming, but I'm kinda enjoying it,' I say triumphantly, shoving a piece of brownie into my mouth.

'Who's your next date with, then? Which lucky stud?' There's a cheeky glint in her eyes.

I cover my mouth and quickly swallow the mouthful of brownie. 'I have a date tonight with a guy called Tom and one Sunday with a guy called Lewis. I'm also talking to someone called Ian, who I wouldn't mind asking me on a date.'

'Oooh look at you, I love it. Hey, it's not Ian Brady, is it?' Sadie asks, a smile trying to crack through her serious face.

'Bugger off, not this again.' I chuckle as the people at the table next to us look over.

'Just steer clear of anyone called Adolf, will you?' Sadie laughs as she pours the tea from the pot into our cups. 'Love, I'm proud of you. It's just what you need, serial killer aside. Just don't put up with any shit. I know you know this and you're a tough cookie, but be careful, eh? Else they'll have me to answer to.' She holds my hand over the table and stares into my eyes, face completely straight. 'But seriously, now I've mentioned Ian Brady, if he asks you on a date, maybe I should come along and hide behind a plant or something. I could bring binoculars? Or you could say you're a fuckwit and need adult supervision at all times?'

'Sadie, I think you would end up on some undesirable register if you did that and you would terrify my possible suitor into a life of celibacy.'

We both howl with laughter before I cover my mouth, conscious that most people in the café are looking over at the guffawing at our table.

I'm home from meeting Sadie by lunchtime and not due to go out until 7 p.m., so I decide to go to the gym and do some cardio. The plan is to then return home, have dinner and not rush getting ready for the date. The gym is quiet, being midweek, so I'm able to take my time on the machines and enjoy the peace. I check my messages. There are a few off Tom confirming the process for this evening. He told the PR staff I'm on the guest list and he'll come and find me for a drink before Presto's Project performs. He's being considerate, which is nice. I think back to when Liam used to get involved with local drama productions. They would dominate our lives for months on end: lines, rehearsals, him talking about nothing else for weeks before. It soon took the excitement off. Even the pride and admiration I had for him dissolved, as it became the only thing he considered important.

Ian has messaged wishing me a nice day. There are a few more messages, some men I've exchanged a little communication with and a few new profiles. Nothing from Lewis. I reply to about ten before taking my book out of my gym bag and getting stuck into my latest Chevy Stevens thriller.

A few hours later, I'm back home. Having showered and eaten scrambled eggs on toast, it's time to get ready as Alexa plays me some music. It would be easy to get an Uber and have a few alcoholic drinks at Tom's gig and going alone makes me feel I need a drink even more to steady my nerves, but I'm still determined to not drink on any first dates. I need to keep my wits about me, and I also don't want to make a prat of myself. Anyone can pretend over the internet; meeting face to face is completely different. I have to be sure that not only do I find someone physically attractive, but the personality and mental attraction is also essential. Alcohol would just cloud this judgement and possibly make me feel vulnerable.

I sing along to the music as I look in my wardrobes, hair in a towel and wearing my cosy dressing gown. It's cold in the evenings now and I'm not one for flashing much flesh, so I decide on black skinny jeans, a leopard print T-shirt and my black faux leather biker jacket. A pair of small-heeled boots and my Gucci belt and handbag will complement the outfit perfectly. After drying and straightening my hair, I put some bubble gum pink nail varnish on and start applying my makeup. I finish it off with a pink lip gloss and a heavy squirting of my signature Hermès perfume before reluctantly peeling off my dressing gown and getting my evening outfit on. I've given Tom my phone number, the first man on Soul Mates I've shared it with. Although I felt wary at the time, I guess it's as easy to be pestered and to block someone on a mobile as it is email. Tom seems laid-back and not needy, in fact, the opposite. I haven't heard from him since this morning, so I text to tell him I will be leaving in fifteen minutes and let him know what I'm wearing, just in case it's busy or he doesn't recognise me from my photos on Soul Mates.

My stomach does a little churn as I check the timer light in my lounge and pull my jacket and boots on before setting the alarm and leaving the house. It doesn't feel long at all before I'm pulling up into the car park of Che's, the trendy bar and restaurant where Tom's band, Presto's Project, are playing this evening. There are posters for the band and the other band playing plastered on the windows and doors. When I googled Presto's Project, I noticed they have quite a following. There are a number of impressive, live music videos with loads of views. I couldn't help but feel excited about going on a date with a musician as I watched them eagerly, moving my head to the beat. I spotted Tom immediately, who looks so confident. He also looks as handsome in the videos as his photos on his dating profile, which is something I'm grateful for after my date with Mark. The music is modern-day Indie with a bit of a David Bowie feel. Tom is one of the two singers in the band and also plays guitar. There's already a queue to get into Che's despite the bands not being on for over an hour.

Following Tom's instructions, I nervously edge towards the entrance. On the other side of the queue that's formed, women are moving on the spot to keep warm. Laughs and cigarette smoke floats into the evening air.

'Oh, hi, erm, I should be on the guest list. For Presto's Project. My name's Kitty Cook,' I say nervously to the door supervisor, smoothing my hair down.

The door supervisor turns and looks into the bar, nodding towards a colleague for confirmation.

'Yeah, she's on the list. Let her in, Ange,' says the distant voice.

I thank Ange and walk on in. It's a trendy bar, styled in 1970's décor, which I love. Prints of some of my favourite vintage art adorns the walls. I've been to Che's before, and it has a feel of luxury mixed with the lounge of your great aunt or grandma's house. The stage area is massive and there's a restaurant upstairs. I'm so busy absorbing the atmosphere that I don't notice Tom approaching until he's right in front of me. Standing less than a metre away, my eyes widen and my heart beats a little quicker. He's gorgeous. Even better than his photos and the videos I watched online.

'Hey, you,' he says, leaning in for a kiss on the cheek.

'H-hi, Tom,' I say, a little taken aback at how attractive he is in real life.

'I'm so pleased you came. It's brill to meet you.' He beams at me with beautiful, dive-in eyes. 'Let's get a drink and have a sit down before the show starts.' He ushers me to the bar area. 'What d'you want, darl?'

He hasn't called me babe, which is good. Darl is just about acceptable from a man I've just met. Although, looking at him again, I realise he could probably call me pumpkin or even snuggly wuggly right now and it wouldn't knock more than one percent off how gorgeous he is.

Tom orders me a blackcurrant and soda water and a Polish beer for himself. He carries the drinks to a nearby booth, with a confident swagger. As he sits opposite me, I look into his ocean-blue eyes, encased with eyelashes women pay good money to try and achieve. With such a flawless complexion, I wonder if the band has a makeup artist. Tom has black, thick, shiny hair and a neat beard. He's tall, like promised in his description, and although definitely a slighter frame than his profile, he looks in good health and shape.

We chat away, and it's natural and easy. Tom asks about my week off, my interests and job. As we talk, people keep walking past and saying hello. He remains polite, shaking hands and exchanging nods and waves. It's like sitting with a celebrity and feels a tad intimidating. There's still just over fifteen minutes until Tom's band go on stage and I'm sensing no sign of nerves from Tom. He's calm and self-assured, like he was born to perform.

'I'm going for a ciggy, darl, then I'll get another drink on the way back. Same again?' Tom asks, getting up and nodding towards my glass. My mouth opens but nothing comes out for a second or two. *A ciggy? Yuk.*

'Erm, yeah, please, thanks.'

He walks off, and I sit knowing I put non-smokers on my profile. I know lots of people smoke, some of my friends even, but it's something I personally hate and really don't want in a potential partner. I check Tom's profile quickly—there's definitely no mention of him being a smoker. Maybe it's just social smoking or maybe he's just started. Plus, I know people can stop smoking with the right help, if they want to. I'm thinking too far ahead anyway. I'm certain Tom is way out of my league and surely can't fancy me.

I watch him come back in and head to the bar, chatting to people on the way. He's so charismatic; it's understandable why he's a performer. He stands at the bar with style, wearing double denim and with body language that oozes controlled confidence. Bringing my drink back, he drops some crisps onto the table.

'I remember you mentioning you love a bag of crisps,' he says, grinning. I wonder if he also remembers it says 'No' under 'Smoker' on my profile.

'I have to go now, darl. I'll come and see you after our set.' He picks my hand up from where it's resting on my leg and kisses it. In any other circumstance, I may have felt it a little cringey, but with Tom, I beam back at him like a dog waiting for a new toy.

'Thanks. Enjoy. You'll be great,' I say as he winks and meanders into the crowd. He eases through the people waiting patiently for the show, like a cool breeze on a summer day, knowing its direction of travel. Sitting with my pop and crisps, I feel like an overgrown child, but I'm here, sober, alone, and I've been pushed far out of my comfort zone. For this, I'm definitely proud of myself.

Presto's Project come on stage to a loud cheer ten minutes later. A crowd has gathered around the stage. My seat is at the side of the stage, still with a great view.

Tom looks over as he walks on the stage and smiles. The music starts, and the crowd soon get into the groove. Their music is catchy, funky, and the band are excellent. The fans love them, clapping and singing along as they soak up the atmosphere like sponges. Presto's Project plays mainly their own songs, with the odd cover. After about six songs, Tom takes the microphone and thanks everyone for coming.

'This next song is for a woman called Kitty.' He points at me, and I blush as everyone turns to take a look. I do a pathetic little wave, then immediately regret it.

I hear the first few chords of the guitar and know it's one of my favourite songs. "Last Request" by Paolo Nutini. My hand goes to my mouth in nervous surprise as the crowd clap and sway to the song. Tom is no Paolo on the vocals, but he's a bloody good second. A little firework of excitement explodes in my stomach, and I absorb the song as I drink my pop.

A few songs later and the set is complete. There's a break before the next band. I wait for Tom as he chats to people in the crowd. He owns the room, his presence big, magnetic and vibrant. I watch him weave in and out of the crowd, stopping to say hi and for photos until he eventually makes his way over to me.

'You were amazing, Tom, and thanks so much for the dedication.' I get up to give him a hug, in awe of his talent and reeling a little bit from the public dedication.

'Did ya like it?' He has a big smile on his beautiful face.

It was one of the most romantic things anyone has ever done for me. Romance seems to come so easy to Tom, and his attention and gesture make me melt. 'It was lovely. Very sweet,' I reply. 'Let me get you a drink.'

Tom shakes his head.

'I insist.' I walk to the bar and look back to the swarm of people now in the seating area I was in, crowded round Tom. He's full of energy and theatrical body movements, proud of the band's performance and rightly so. Returning with his drink, I battle through the growing crowd around Tom to hand him his beer. I'm introduced to another band member, Kavan, who I chat to as Tom continues talking to his friends and fans.

Soon, the next band comes on and the crowds are dancing again. Tom tries to keep me involved in the chats and I also chat with Kavan and the other members. They seem a nice bunch. It's soon 10:30 p.m., and I'm ready to leave. Everyone is in high spirits and the drinks are flowing, but if I have another blackcurrant and soda, I know I'll be farting or burping enough air to blow up a bouncy castle. I want my dressing gown, some toast and a cup of tea.

I find Tom and thank him for a great night. Tom says he'll text me, and I nod as he kisses me gently on the cheek. I walk back to the car. Driving home, I already know I won't see Tom again. He's gorgeous, talented and energetic, but I don't want to be a face in the crowd or always waiting in the wings. We're at different stages in life, and I'm not a performer's pair of slippers, needed at the end of the night. I wouldn't be able to cope with late nights through the week and sharing attention with the whole of Newcastle and beyond. And on top of all that, I distinctively got the feeling that Tom doesn't fancy me, which is fine, even if it's scratched a layer off my ego. Such is life in the world of Soul Mates.

Chapter 17

I wake up the next day feeling a little deflated from my date with Tom (and half of Newcastle's music fans). Although Tom is gorgeous and seems lovely, I'm not prepared to be low down on anyone's list of priorities. I had enough of that during my relationship with Liam, especially the last eighteen months of it. I decide I won't text Tom and just see if he gets in touch, given I didn't get the impression it was love at first sight for him. Thinking about the app, I roll over, grab my mobile and log in.

There are a number of messages. As per usual, many just get deleted.

Want ma numba sexy?

I roll my eyes as I delete it.

No message from Lewis. We have a date planned for Sunday morning, a cuppa at the coast, but he isn't the best at communicating, and I feel I know very little about him. Not a bad thing, I guess, it means plenty of conversation points on the actual date, and him not messaging all the time could mean he has a life outside of Soul Mates.

I decide to do some housework. I plan on going to the gym before my usual Friday afternoon food shop later in the day. Jane and I have our night out scheduled tomorrow. I'm looking forward to catching up, having a gin or ten and a dance in town. The last few weeks and being on Soul Mates have definitely perked up my confidence, and more importantly, I'm starting to heal from my breakup with Liam. Maybe I'm ready for love again after all.

After a few hours of cleaning, I head to the gym and decide to reply to a few more messages on the app before I head inside.

'CharlieCheekyChap' has been messaging me sporadically this morning. Whilst his user ID name reminds me of something you would say to a toddler, he seems a nice bloke and, although not in line with the usual 'Jamie Dornan' look, is handsome and interesting. He lives local, is a quantity surveyor, has his own home and doesn't smoke. Tick, tick, tick, tick. After a few more messages, he asks, *Fancy a coffee sometime?*

Me: Definitely not a coffee, but certainly a tea .

I can't stand coffee but can drink cup after cup of tea.

Charlie: This weekend?

Ooh, he's keen, but as I continue on the elliptical, I consider that maybe Charlie has the right idea and doesn't want to waste time himself. Carpe diem and all that. I'm aware I have my night with Jane tomorrow and a date with Lewis on Sunday morning. I chuckle to myself, thinking I now need a PA to organise my dating dairy, like was suggested at the start of my internet search for love.

Sod it.

Me: Tomorrow lunchtime?

Charlie: Yeah, great. How about Cozy Coffee in Jesmond at 12?

Me: Works for me .

As simple as that, date number three has been scheduled with Charlie. Perhaps it will be third time lucky.

I leave at 11:30 a.m. to meet Charlie at Cozy Coffee. I'm wearing jeans and a T-shirt with my sherpa jacket for the winter chill and a little pair of studded boots. Finding a parking space is a nightmare, and although I set off in plenty of time, it's after twelve before I've paid for parking, reapplied my lip gloss and walked the few minutes to the café. I sporadically pull my hair away from my lip-gloss-drenched mouth as the autumn wind blows it into my face.

I see Charlie sitting in one of the window seats as I approach. My stomach rumbles—I've been here before and know they have the most delicious cakes. Walking into the café, I feel suitably relaxed. Charlie gets up, and as I get closer, my heart sinks a little as I realise on initial physical appearance he just isn't my type. It becomes absolutely concrete that 'CharlieCheekyChap' most definitely isn't my type after what happens in the thirty seconds following.

I approach the table he's now standing next to, smiling pleasantly. Charlie moves round towards where I would naturally take a seat. I assume he's going to greet me casually or even give a light, friendly embrace. No, none of that happens. Instead, in something he must have seen and hoped for in a Romcom based in the city of love that is Paris, Charlie grabs me, pulls me into him and pushes his lips on mine in what he clearly thinks is a sweeping-me-off-my-feet snog. I don't quite register what's happening until his tongue darts into my mouth like a slug bullet. I quickly pull away, certain my face looks like an award-winning gurner.

'Wow,' he exclaims.

Bloody wow, indeed. I stare in disbelief, other customers looking over as my cheeks turn an autumnal shade of red. I'm in one of those fight, flight, freeze or flop moments, or to put it another way, a 'what the actual hell just happened?' moment.

Charlie, who has since sat back down and is grinning like a Cheshire cat, is clearly in amazement of himself for assaulting me in a public area with his wet, rubbery mouth and mollusc tongue.

'Sit down, gorgeous.' He gestures towards the seat with bold confidence.

I'm amazed he's managed to actually look at me and assess my level of 'gorgeousness', given he pounced like a tiger on an antelope as soon as I was in a three-metre radius.

I muster a weak smile, speechless, as I wonder what I'm going to do next before Charlie mounts me.

'Can I get you guys anything?' comes the welcome, gentle voice of the waitress.

'I'll have a cappuccino and a slice of red velvet, please,' Charlie replies confidently.

I feel the urge to add, 'And some salt, please, to shrink the big, fat, wet slug inside his massive gob.'

The waitress looks at me, smiling. 'And yourself?'

I cough, realising I haven't said a word and need to clear my throat of the contents of Charlie's that he plopped into mine. 'An English breakfast tea, please, and a caramel shortcake.'

'Coming right up,' the waitress almost sings as she happily glides away.

'So, gorgeous, lovely to meet you. You're even hotter in real life,' exclaims Charlie.

Hot. Does anyone actually say that anymore? It sounds very late 00s, but he's right in some way—I'm bloody steaming that he thought he could molest me with his dripping sponge mouth as soon as I met him. No wonder he's single.

I don't know what to say and really want to leave, but I'm still in shock. I decide to make the date as quick as possible. I don't find Charlie attractive to look at and I find his wet bottom half of a face even less attractive. The St. Bernard drool look is most definitely not for me. I make awkward small talk as I scoff my caramel slice and gulp my scolding tea down as quick as possible. He fails to notice my record-breaking eating speed as he tells me how long he's been single and what he's looking for in a mate, winking as he says it and looking me up and down. My skin crawls.

'Well, it was, erm, lovely meeting you, Charlie.' I get up quickly and throw ten pounds onto the table.

'What? You have to go already? We've only just got here,' he says, clearly disappointed and wounded.

'I'm sorry, I have to pick my brother up from football,' I lie, smiling and starting to back off before he can jump up and have a go at round two of slug archery.

'Oh, okay, I see. Erm, that's disappointing, but maybe we can do it again?'

'I'll message you. Bye.' I walk away from the table and out of the café door, not looking back.

As I scurry away, I vow to never return to Cozy Coffee, and if a date ever does that again, to leave immediately, preferably after throwing a drink in his face.

Chapter 18

I brush my teeth and tongue twice, then swill mouthwash. Bloody hell, what's wrong with folk? I go downstairs and sit on the sofa. I'm certainly no prude and love a good snog. Although not a fan of public displays of affection, I'm happy for a little peck on the lips or cheek. But jeez, Charlie must have thought he was in Pacha in Ibiza as he tried to Pash on with me. I laugh a little to myself at the sheer audacity of him. Sadie and Jane won't believe this one.

I decide to get the elephant in the room—or should that be the slug in the room?—exposed quickly. I message Charlie on the Soul Mates app.

Hi, Charlie, it was nice to meet you today. Sorry I had to rush off. I didn't feel a connection between us but wish you all the best in your dating journey.

Polite but definite.

Jane's coming round at 5 p.m. for some snacks and pre-drinks, so I decide to pop to my parents' now for an hour instead of the next day. I'll keep the dating update on the down-low. I'm pretty certain my dad still thinks I've never been kissed, and the term kissing a frog to turn into a prince most definitely didn't apply to Charlie, despite the slimy similarities.

'You've gotta be kidding me?' Jane howls as I update her on the date. 'That's so gross. I wouldn't have been able to eat my cake.'

I raise an eyebrow at her, knowing she licks cake crumbs from paper bags at times. 'Not even that can put me off cake, Jane,' I exclaim as we pour ourselves a grapefruit gin and lemonade.

'Eeeh, your dating stories are so funny, but they're doing nothing to make me want to join the site,' she says as we carry our drinks upstairs to start getting ready.

I put some red nail varnish on that will match my Mac Ruby Woo lipstick. I've decided to wear a black jumpsuit with red roses on and black strappy sandals, along with my Mulberry Daria clutch. Jane's wearing leather-style trousers and a teal, lace off-the-shoulder top, which complements her green eyes and almost black hair.

'Selfie time,' I say once we're ready. We pose for the camera, Jane with her heels on to match my height a little better, both of us pulling silly faces and moving our heads to get our best angle. No Snapchat filter for us, but we still want to look good.

Finishing off our drinks, we shove lipsticks, perfume and some mints into our bags as we rush down the stairs for the Uber. We're soon in town after Jane shared my dating disaster with the Uber driver, who was in hysterics until he had a coughing fit. We go into the bar on the stylish Millionaire's Row, as it's named in Newcastle, near the train station. Of course, it's far from a Millionaire's stomping ground, someone has clearly named it once at the end of the night when they were skint and couldn't afford the cheesy chips in the nearby takeaway, but it's definitely classier than the famous Bigg Market, which was filled with Stag and Hen dos and drunks having pees against lampposts in its heyday.

Jane and I get our first drinks in and sit on some stools a little distance from the bar. The place is getting busy, and it's only 7 p.m. There's been a Newcastle United home football game on, which always enhances the atmosphere. As long as the topless, beer-bellied hooligans keep away, which, of course, they do on the whole in Millionaire's Row.

As we chat and catch up on the week, a few groups of men walk past us, some giving a nod and smile. It feels strange but nice noticing men acknowledging me. At thirty years old, I'm at the age most people are settling down while others are breaking up and divorcing. A breeze of sadness comes over me as I wonder if I'll ever find someone I could love again. Someone who'd love me back and accept all my faults. A man who doesn't mind that I fart like a trooper or want spaghetti hoops for tea sometimes. Who wouldn't care that my natural hair is like a burst mattress and I wear my dressing gown as much as humanly possible. Someone who would get my sense of humour and my insecurities. It feels like such a big ask. I sigh, defeated, as I stare momentarily into the distance.

'What's up, Kit?' Jane gently clutches my hand.

'Ah, nothing, lovely, just deep in thought. I'll get another one in, eh?' I reply, taking a deep breath as I get off the stool and head to the bar. I wait at the bar, relieved to have a few minutes to get my head back to the here and now.

'Alright?' says a male voice next to me.

I look to my left and smile, replying with a not so enthusiastic, 'Hi.' I feel slightly annoyed that someone is interrupting my thoughts. I don't want a night where I feel sad, missing being in a relationship, but it's threatening to pull me under, like a ferocious wave, and for some reason, I keep letting it nearly drown me.

The guy interrupts my thoughts again. 'I could ask if you come here often, but I think we would both fall into a pit of cringe.' He looks curiously at me, clearly waiting for a response to his attempt of humour.

I laugh, liking the silly comment, mentally climbing into the life raft he's just offered. 'Yeah, well, you would for sure.'

'So, do you?' he asks, raising an eyebrow and smiling. 'Come here,' he clarifies.

I shrug. 'Actually, no, not loads. It's getting busy though with the match.'

'Who's next?' The bartender looks up, towards me, and I place our order.

'Yeah, it's going to be a bustling one. Where you headed later?' he asks.

I hesitate, unsure if I can be bothered with men tonight. Plus, I'm yet to decide if I find this particular man attractive. Bugger it. 'Erm, I'm not sure, probably just around here. Maybe Danza.'

The bartender passes over my drinks, and I pay him the extortionate price.

'Well, I hope I'll see you later,' the guy says with a sprinkling of hope as I gather the drinks and make my way from the bar back to Jane, smiling to myself.

'I think I've just been tapped up,' I tell Jane as I put our drinks down.

'Oooh really? Who by? Where is he?' She looks to the bar.

I describe where the bar stranger was, but it's impossible for us to see as the crowds descend.

Thirty minutes later, we're ready to move on. We meander to the bar next door, where we guzzle another gin before moving on again. A group of men chatted with us, but most were married and it was innocent banter. Jane and I have a little dance in the third bar, Warehouse, as the drinks flow and the atmosphere thrives.

An hour later, we head to Danza. It's before midnight, so we get in free. The place is jam-packed, music booming, strobe lighting and pop-up bars in place to help keep the queues down. We head to a pop-up bar, decide on a bottle of fruity cider rather than more gin and travel straight for the dancefloor. My feet feel like I'm squashing a loaf of bread into an envelope, but I'm determined to continue with the good night. Jane and I take more selfies as random people photobomb. I have that not a care in the world feeling that's rare in adulthood. It's a magnificent sensation, and Jane and I hug, laugh and sing to each other. The song ends, and Jane and I slow our wannabe breakdancing down. I look around the dancefloor and notice the man from the first bar at the side of the dancefloor with a group of friends. He's looking straight at me and lifts his glass and nods, acknowledging me. I give a weak smile back, and he turns to chat with his friends.

'Jane, there's the guy from the first bar over there. Look.' I point. 'He's got a grey jumper on and a mate in a white shirt.'

Jane looks around, trying to spot him amongst the fellow partygoers. 'Over there, near the pop-up bar?'

'Yeah, there,' I say loudly over the music.

'I can't see him properly, Kit, I have beer goggles on,' she says nonchalantly as she knocks back some more cider.

Another great song comes on, and we begin dancing again, thinking we're the best on the dancefloor but no doubt looking like a pissed auntie at a social club engagement party.

I'm pulled from my moment by a tap on my shoulder. I swivel clumsily around and end up face to face with the man from the first bar, alongside his friend in the white shirt.

'Hello again.' He laughs. 'Come here often?'

I smile and say hello to him and his friend.

'My name's Adam. This is Ryan.' He gestures to white-shirt man.

'I'm Kitty, this is Jane,' I say back, touching Jane's arm.

'Do yous want a drink?' Adam asks.

Adam is growing on me. He seems to have a silly sense of humour, and I'm leaning against being intrigued to find out more. I decide to give him a chance.

'Erm, yeah, please. I'll go with you.' I look at Jane, and she nods. We never take drinks off men without going to the bar with them, just to be safe, and we're also happy to pay our way and buy rounds.

I walk to the bar with Adam. He says a few things on the way, but I can't hear a word, so just do that nod and smile thing. Once we reach the bar, it's a little easier to hear away from the speakers of the dancefloor.

'I was hoping to bump into you,' he says, a handsome grin on his face. Did I say I wasn't sure about him earlier? Yep. Definitely growing on me.

'Well, here I am,' I announce, gesturing up and down myself, my nerves dissolved by the drinks I've had so far.

Adam tells me he lives local and he's thirty-five years old, separated from his wife. I tell him a little about myself too, then we head back to the dancefloor, drinks in hand. Jane is kissing Ryan, and I giggle to myself like a schoolgirl. It isn't like Jane, but why not? At least it's not in a café with someone who houses slugs in his mouth.

After we finish our drinks, Jane and I decide we've drunk over our limit and our feet feel like they're giving out. We say goodbye to Adam and Ryan. Jane refuses to give her number to Ryan, taking his instead. I know damn well she has no intention of calling him—she's happy single. Adam takes my number and gives me a cheeky kiss before we leave. It's nice, gentle and not slimy.

Jane and I get in our Uber, and I'm content the neighbour won't have to put me to bed when I get home. It's been a great night. A little flirting in real life as opposed to online has done me the world of good, and perhaps it might even lead to a date where I know what I'm expecting. I have high hopes.

Chapter 19

I wake up Sunday morning feeling less ropey than I anticipated, thanks to the water and cheese on toast I shoved down my throat when I got in. I don't have those awful post-drinking blues that can happen at times; instead, I'm motivated and rested for the day ahead. I get up, make a cuppa and cereal, and log into Soul Mates. I'm meeting Lewis today and hope he's messaged. He has.

Lewis: Morning. See you at Beach Bun at 11am?
Me: Hi, yes, see you then x

Lewis is good-looking on his profile and probably the man I have now been messaging the longest, but I've had the least communication with him. I'm intrigued to find out more about him.

I choose a nice floral midi dress and my wool coat. I'm going to wear them with tights and ankle boots. It's cold and the coast is always colder, but hopefully the café will be cosy, and I'm hoping my date will have a little more decorum than Charlie.

Walking into Beach Bun thirty minutes later, Lewis is nowhere to be seen. I take a window seat and order myself a tea as I wait. Traffic and parking are a challenge around the area. The town attracts locals, visitors and tourists alike with the quaint coffee shops, quirky gift shops and seaside charm. I scroll social media for a few minutes until I'm interrupted by a 'Hello'.

I look up. Lewis is towering over me like an Adonis. I can't help but glance for a moment too long at the impressive sight. He's got to be popular on Soul Mates.

I clear my throat. 'Hi, Lewis.' I stand up nervously and lean in for a friendly semi-embrace.

'Hi, sorry I'm late. What you having?' he asks, pointing to the table.

'Erm, a tea, please?'

'Anything to eat?'

'No, I'm fine, thanks.' To be honest, I'm always hungry and usually eat more than a wrestler, but I think a cup of tea will do for now.

Lewis nods and strolls off to order. I can't help but look at his bum as he walks to the counter with a sexy swagger. I pull the neckline of my dress, trying to get some air in as my body temperature rises. He is almost too good-looking.

I watch him as he waits in the queue, holding his phone, tapping away. He doesn't look back at where I'm sitting, instead waits calmly to be served. Lewis is either very chilled or dates *a lot*, as he shows no smidgen of nerves. Unlike me, as I sit and my knees bounce up and down.

Eventually, Lewis reaches the front of the queue and orders.

'You're prettier in real life,' he announces bluntly, sitting down opposite me.

'Thanks, I think,' I say, smiling. He's rather pretty himself and has a swag about him that makes me think he knows it.

His phone starts to ring.

'Sorry, I have to get this.' He walks quickly away, goes outside and strolls into a crowd of people hanging about.

It's like a Lewis version of *Where's Wally?* as I move my head about, trying to see what's going on.

He comes back in just as the server comes over and places our drinks on the table, alongside a full English for Lewis.

'I'm starving,' he states, tucking in. 'So, when did you join the site?'

'Only a few weeks ago. It was a free trial, then I paid for a few months. What about you?'

'I've been on a year and a half. Had a decent amount of dates, nothing too serious.'

I wonder if he is really fussy, not ready to settle down or just not met the right woman. 'Wow, that's a long time. Have you just not found what you're looking for?' I ask curiously, hoping it's this option.

'Nah, not really. You women are mental, to be honest,' he says without so much as a smile on his face, indicating he's not saying it in jest.

I'm taken aback a bit but assume he's perhaps being a little sarcastic. Plus, he does have a point. Some women, just like some men, are more than a bit bizarre, and I have encountered a few of those men already in my short time on Soul Mates.

'A load of first dates, then?' I enquire.

'Yeah, mainly. Some a few more dates, some hook ups, friends with benefits and all that. I've not found a woman I think deserves my commitment yet, you know?' Lewis winks as he chews on a bite of sausage.

I cradle my cup of tea, knowing this date is sliding into the reject bin. He's a fuckboy. Sophie told me about them. Only interested in how many women they can get into bed and always on the search for the next. The internet provides a much easier way of doing it than putting in the effort on a night out.

'So, you aren't after anything serious?' I give him an opportunity to perhaps redeem some appeal.

'Well, if the right bird came along, of course. But she would have to be something fucking exceptional,' he says boldly, continuing to shove half the local butcher's stock into his gob.

An older woman looks over to our table, an air of disgust floating across her face. I can swear like a construction worker but not in public and not with regards to demeaning sentences about people.

I shake my head. I can see he's a prick, but a tiny part of me also thinks at least he's being honest, even if there are more diplomatic ways to express it. There are so many men on the site with fake photos and who would make a politician look transparent with heaps of integrity. I can't help but to begrudgingly slightly admire his honesty, despite not liking his viewpoint or delivery.

'You lot are just as bad, mind. The women on that site, woooahh, they're filthy perverts. I've had old wives asking me to sort them out and everything. Desperate, they are,' he exclaims, laughing loudly as he mops some egg up with his bread. Air of Disgust Woman looks back over and tuts. I nervously smile in her direction.

Dear God, please don't tell me any more about your dating propositions and conquests in this tiny café, filled with pensioners, pinnies and cake stands.

I take a direction turn and ask him about his weekend, desperate to change the subject. Wrong move again.

'I had a date yesterday with what I thought was a tasty tart. She was all over me in the bar, but I didn't fancy her. She was a bit, well, fat, to be honest, and a bit past her sell-by date.'

My eyes widen. 'Erm, sell-by date? People aren't packs of mouldy cheese, Lewis,' I can't help but snap. 'Did you not know her size and age through the site?'

'She said she was thirty-four, but she was clearly forty, and she said curvy, so I assumed a nice rack and arse, you know? But she was out of shape and flabby, and I ain't into fat chicks.'

I look over at the pensioners on the table next to us, who sit in the opposite direction of Air of Disgust Woman. They glance back with empathy for me, and one shakes their head gently. I'm sitting here with a fuckboy who's ageist, fattist and clearly isn't keen on females apart from in the bedroom. Wonderful.

'Forty isn't old, Lewis, and not everyone can be super thin. I'm sure you're not perfect,' I say, trying to make him reflect. It doesn't work.

'See, I am though, and I won't compromise, and that may be why I'm single, but the women who get me... well, they are more than happy with the arrangement, you know?' He smiles, tapping his nose.

I roll my eyes and let out an exasperated sigh. Lewis is clearing his plate. Not only does he have little respect for women, he eats like a blind pig—there are food splatters all over.

'So, do you fancy a stroll back to mine, then? I only live round the corner.' He suggestively raises an eyebrow.

What the actual hell goes through people's heads?

'Erm, no thanks.'

'You sure? I reckon we could have a good afternoon together now I've got some fuel in me.' Lewis taps his stomach and lets out a quiet burp. The only quiet part about him so far.

'I think I'll decline that invite, Lewis, as appealing as it does sound,' I reply sarcastically.

We both get up and head out of the café, the eyes of most of the café following us.

'Well, if you change your mind, message me. I guarantee you won't regret it.' Lewis walks off, oblivious to his revolting attitude.

'Oh, I won't change my mind. I'd rather bathe in horse piss,' I mumble as I walk in the opposite direction, mouth open in absolute astoundment.

Chapter 20

'You should've had some fun, Kit,' Sadie says, laughing when I tell her about Lewis and the aghast pensioners. It's the first day of work and the new term, and Sadie is wanting full details of my dates.

'I don't want that type of fun. I just want to meet some normal men who aren't players, megalomaniacs, named after murderers or have big, wet mouths,' I whine.

'Aw, I do love you, my little fuckwit.' She pulls me in for a cuddle. 'Now, it's a new week, Kit. I think you need to start being a bit firmer with these freaks and have your list of non-negotiables ready. Draft them this morning once you set the little turds off working and then we can discuss at lunchtime, okay?'

I snigger. 'Yes, Mrs Flitcroft.'

Thirty minutes later, the 'little turds', as Sadie called them, are working away on research around youth crime prevention measures in the UK and US. I get my notepad and think about what I want from a potential partner. So far, I'm not sure if anyone has been truly honest on their profile, so perhaps I need to start asking more questions in any communication and weed out the maniacs and game players. I can check against my initial message criteria this evening but will start to have more conversation with people before meeting them.

Non-negotiables

1. *Must be over thirty years old and under forty-two years old.* I don't want a man-baby, nor do I want to have a future with someone who's older than what feels a comfortable age gap for me personally.

2. *Non-smoker.* Tom has solidified this. It repels me, and there's enough illness and disease to worry about without the fear of lung cancer shadowing a relationship.

3. *In Employment.* I'm not prepared to financially support someone from the off.

4. *Homeowner or renting alone.* Someone living with friends in their thirties gives me party house or *Peter Pan* vibes; likewise, someone living with parent(s) feels a bit Mummy's boy.

5. *Driver.* I don't want to be a taxi, and I also want to be driven at times.

6. *Intelligent, including emotional intelligence.*

7. *Personal qualities: must make me laugh. Must demonstrate empathy, kindness and compassion. Must talk about family and friends with positivity and love. No discriminatory views.*

8. *Looks.* Sticking to what I like and not deviating unless the guy seems perfect in every other sense.

9. *Must like animals.*

10. *Must not be afraid of planes/travel.*

I decide ten is enough for now and wait until lunchtime to show Sadie.

'Well, I think that's perfect, love, just perfect for you, and you should settle for nothing less,' she says with conviction as she passes me a Curly Wurly. 'Now, get on the case tonight and find your Mr Kit.'

For the rest of the day, in between lessons, confiscating phones, breaking up a fight between two male students and marking a few assignments, I think of questions I will try and ask each potential man on Soul Mates. The site is entertaining and has done wonders to heal my broken heart, but four dates in, two of which were average and two disasters, I need a new game plan. A decade ago, I may have been happy sailing along for a few years, dating, not committing and flirting as a way to inflate my ego, but I'm a softie, even when I try to be emotionally strong and in control. I want to fall in love again, and I want someone to fall in love with me again. To sit on the sofa together in blissful comfort, holding hands and a cup of tea each. I want the first Christmas together, birthday and Valentine's Day. I want the exploration of personalities, bodies and mind. I want my soul mate, and I have to put the lessons I've learnt into practice; after all, I am a teacher.

Chapter 21

It's Friday already, and my week has been productive, both inside and outside of work. We have an Ofsted inspection due and then some student teacher placements. Headteacher Mr Dryden completed a spot audit through the week. My lessons were observed with great feedback—syllabus and assignments were excellent, and the students gave good feedback on my teaching. I've been to the gym twice, caught up with my auntie and Jane, and I've arranged a date on Saturday night and possibly Sunday night.

I get into my car, ready to brace the Friday traffic to get to the supermarket for my usual food shop. I could do the shop with my eyes closed, knowing where every regular item is and not often deviating away from my usual purchases. I'm a creature of habit. But dating is pushing me out of my comfort zone. Right out of it in some cases, without a life jacket.

I enter the shop and look at the fruit and veg on offer this week. I pick up a melon and pineapple in addition to my usual bananas, apples and plums. I'm trying to eat healthy as the winter encroaches and I want to just eat tiger bread and Sadie's cheese and leek mash. I avoid the fresh pizzas, opting instead for some pre-mashed sweet potato and carrot, which I'll have for tea, perhaps with a little homemade bread. I'm soon at the middle aisle, which is full of the usual randomness. I pick up a ceramic hanging bird feeder, shaped like a cactus. Reduced to three pounds ninety-nine. Cute. I place it in my trolley. The birds are my only pets. I really want a cat, but it feels like a lot of responsibility, especially now I'm single.

Moving on, I go to the cleaning aisle. There's something about cleaning I find therapeutic, which is a good job, as in the year Liam lived with me, he did very little. There are some new fragrances of disinfectant. I happily steer the trolley over and pick the first of the new bottles to smell.

'Oooh,' I say as I put the open bottle under my nose. Passion fruit and peach. I reach for the next one, Grapefruit and geranium. 'Mmmm.' I put both bottles in my trolley.

I turn around to continue, happy with my new cleaning additions, and some man walks past, smiling. I smile back, wondering who he is. Then I panic in case he's on Soul Mates. I give my head a wobble for being so ungrateful at a stranger just being kind, finish the rest of my shopping and head to the checkout.

Once home, I unpack and put my sweet potato and carrot mash in the oven for tea. After showering and getting my fleecy pjs on, with my dressing gown on top, I crack open a beer and tuck into my dinner whilst browsing social media, then Soul Mates.

My date for tomorrow, 'BigBen', has messaged. After confirming he's called 'BigBen' because he's six-foot-one and not because he thinks he's porn star material, we've been chatting for a few days. He hasn't given away too much but has been complimentary about my photos. We've arranged to meet at a stylish bar in Jesmond tomorrow at 5 p.m.

Another guy I've been chatting to, 'MarkTheMan', has also messaged. He's a local mechanic and has his own home. His photos are a bit grainy, so he could be a golden deceiver, but he makes me laugh and we have lots in common. We chat for a while and confirm to meet on Sunday evening, at a bar down the coast.

Some of the names on the site are more embarrassing than childhood photos. I struggle to understand some of the names that have messaged me, the majority of which haven't received a reply, including 'Dog'sLipstickLee', 'Bond069' and 'DongaDon'. Then there are the ones who've had that opportunity to be creative and alluring without being seedy, but no, their names are things like 'MalcolmFranks', 'MichaelJohns', and 'PeterDennis'. Although, I'm sure they're perfect for the right women.

A message pops up from 'Garyliftsweights'.

Garyliftsweights: Hi, nice profile, what's a pretty girl like you doing in a place like this?

Me: Hi, thanks. Well, I could ask you the same thing. Shouldn't you be lifting weights?

Garyliftsweights: Very good! Cheesy name, I know. But I used to be a right tubster, and instead of finding God, I found weights!

Gary and I talk for a few hours. He's at uni, teacher training after working in support with young offenders for six years. We have things in common and he seems fun. I eventually say goodnight, in favour of an early night so I can get to the gym in the morning and catch up with Jane whilst doing some cardio.

Chapter 22

'Wow, you're an actual serial dater,' Jane says, impressed, as we march on an incline on the treadmills.

'I know, it's like a part-time job. Honest, Jane, I'm not sure how long I can keep it up for,' I reply. 'It's good company and an ego boost, but I don't just want a hundred first dates.'

Jane focuses on me as we walk. 'Well, you've got three months on the subscription, see how it goes, and by that point, you might have progressed something with someone.' She shrugs. 'Or you may have just had a solitary date with seventy-five percent of the North East single men.' She grins.

'Bugger off,' I say, chuckling. 'Ben sounds nice, who I'm meeting tonight, and he's good-looking.' I show her the photos on his profile.

'Very nice. Let's hope they haven't been cut and pasted from Google,' she jokes.

I look at her with terror, grasping my jaw. I hadn't even thought of that.

'Relax, Kit, I'm sure they aren't,' she says, seeing the fear in my eyes.

We soon finish our workout and make plans for next week's exercise classes before going our separate ways.

I have plenty of time to eat, do some housework and take my time getting ready for the date. As time is on my side, I decide to add waves to my hair for a change and try a new eyeshadow palette. I watch a video on YouTube of ideas using the eyeshadow palette, which turns into an hour of watching techniques on creating eyelid creases and blending. It's an addictive rabbit hole to go down.

My research pays off, and although it takes ages, I'm loving the finished look of my eyeshadow of rich browns, a sparkle of gold and red hues. My hair is subtly volumized and my nails varnished. I pull on my leather-look skinny jeans and a black, sweetheart neckline top. Finishing the outfit with a leopard print belt and kitten heel boots, I look in the mirror, happy with the slightly 'Sexy Sandy' from *Grease* look. It's a cold evening, so I take my hot water bottle to keep me toasty in the car for my journey. I may have had the 'Sexy Sandy' vibes with my outfit, but I'm most definitely comfort first where possible.

I arrive in Jesmond at 4:45 p.m. It's already dark. I manage to get a parking space off the main street with the bars and reluctantly leave my hot water bottle behind. I walk to meet Ben, checking my messages and seeing he's sent one saying he's in the bar. I walk in and look around, spotting him as he raises a hand. He smiles and gets up from his seat to greet me as I approach. I notice he doesn't have a drink. Now, I've never been one to expect a man to pay my ways. On the contrary, I've lost count of the amount of times I paid for things for Liam despite being a student at times and Liam always working full-time. I don't like the expectation that men have to pay for everything; equality is a fundamental for any relationship I want in the future. I expect, given we're in a bar, there will be more than one drink, but there's no suggestion of going to the bar from Ben, so after an awkward few minutes, I ask what he wants.

'Bottle of Bud will do,' he says.

'Coming up,' I reply, walking away, slightly annoyed that he didn't say please.

I return a few minutes later with his Bud and a soft drink for myself. I don't receive any thanks.

Ben tells me I'm stunning, which is lovely, and I thank him. He's clean-shaven, which isn't my usual type and in contrast to his photos, where he has stubble or a full beard. He is indeed tall, attractive and has kind eyes. I'm hoping to get to know more about him, as he hasn't disclosed much in his messages and we haven't had great depth of conversation.

An hour later, I've long realised I should be careful what I wish for after now knowing so much about Ben that I could write his eulogy. I'm getting increasingly irritated as the minutes tick by. Ben has failed to ask much about me, only really referring to me when he says how attractive I am. Ben seems to have some bizarre view that he's saving people's lives and runs some form of emergency service; in reality, he works for a gas company. There are some embellished beliefs that he makes a transformational impact on the lives of everyone the gas company touches. Whilst I appreciate the need for central heating and gas, I'm failing to put that on par with a paramedic, a firefighter, carer or police officer. However, according to Ben, his company, and him in particular, are above all these critical workers. Teachers, of course, are nowhere to be seen in his list of valuable workers in society.

To add insult to injury, I've just gotten up to buy round three, after already buying round one and two. I'm not sure what to do, so I go to the toilet for some respite from

Ben's incessant, deluded superhero talk, to plan my next step. Sadly, it seems he's quite keen on me despite me being certain that Ben could never put anyone on a pedestal above himself. He's even tried to pull down the scientists involved in developing the Covid vaccine and all the NHS staff who worked throughout the pandemic. This guy is a different breed of narcissist. I wonder whether I should ring Jane or Sadie for advice, but I know time is of the essence, or he'll end up thinking I have diarrhoea. Then the lightbulb goes on in my head.

It really isn't in my nature to be nasty, and I can't bring myself to tell Ben what I really think of him—that he's a self-absorbed narcissist with an insanely distorted perception of the world. That, in fact, his job is pretty average and I have more admiration for the people working in my local supermarket. So, instead, I do something I think will put him permanently off me, therefore getting me off the hook from the truth and hopefully closing the chapter with Ben. It will be a challenge sober and without laughing, but if I'm dramatic enough, I'm confident it will secure the needed outcome.

I leave the toilets, heading back to where 'the plaster that holds the world together Ben' is sitting. Once within sight of him, I pick up my pace, hurrying over. He looks over, and I practice my best worried face from afar. He reads my body language the way I want him to.

'Are you okay?' he says quickly, reading my anxious expression.

'No, Ben. No, I'm not. I've shat myself, and I need to go,' I announce, touching my forehead for added drama. I look at him, keeping my concerned expression and gently crossing my legs for effect.

A grimace etches over his face as his body goes from leaning in to stiffening up. 'Urgh, God,' he says in shocked disgust.

'Yes, it's a right mess and I stink, so I'm going to head off. It was nice to meet you,' I say as I turn to go, leaving Ben to digest the information.

I rush out the bar and laugh to myself once clear. My shit-gate outburst is a first and I'm hoping a last.

As I head to my car, I quickly look at my messages on Soul Mate. 'MarkTheMan' has messaged saying he's going on a spontaneous night out later and asking if we can change our date to Monday night.

Screw it.

What time you meeting your mates? Maybe we could meet up for a quick drink before?

I've spent ages getting ready, so there's no way I'm wasting my efforts for an hour out with a call handler who thinks he's *Superman*. Given I actually don't have soiled underwear that requires changing, meeting another potential date seems a good use of time. I get in the car, placing my still warm hot water bottle on my lap. I wait a few minutes to see if Mark will answer.

I like your way of thinking, Kitty. Sounds good. Tynemouth in 30 mins work for you?

Chapter 23

'Oh my dear God, Kitty, I can't take it. Wait a minute. Wait right there,' Sadie squeals down the phone, laughing hysterically.

I wait patiently until a minute or so later "Another One Bites the Dust" by Queen starts playing in the background. Stu's laughing as well as she comes back to the phone.

'Well, I'm ecstatic I've entertained you,' I say sarcastically but giggling.

'Tell me again, Kit, please, tell me what happened. I'm going to put you on loudspeaker so Stu can hear.'

'Bloody hell, man,' I say playfully as I rub my eyes.

'Right, *go*,' she replies, full of eagerness.

Feeling like a performing seal, I start the stories of the night again, almost visualising Sadie and Stu sat on tenterhooks as the tale unfolds.

'Okay, so I met this guy at teatime. He was really dull and tight, and I bought all the drinks. Fair play, it was only two rounds, but he was about to let me buy the third.'

'The tight shit,' Stu says with disgust.

'Well, talking of shit,' Sadie says before howling with laughter again.

'Can you calm down so I can tell the story?' I joke, tutting. 'So, he was tighter than Ebenezer Scrooge, and he had some mad distortion of reality that made him think working in a call centre for a gas company was more important than being a scientist who developed the Covid vaccine or working in emergency services. He was totally serious and literally thought he deserved an OBE or something.'

Sadie sounds like she's about to pass out with all the amusement as she guffaws away, knowing what's coming.

'So, basically, I had to get out of there, as he was a narcissistic knob and I couldn't bear to hear him talking about himself and his superhero fantasy land any longer.' I put my hand to my head, thinking back to what happened next. 'But I think he fancied me and I was too nice to tell him what I really thought, so, Stu,' I continue, 'I went to the toilet to hatch a plan, and I came back and told him I'd hatched a load of shit in my underwear and had to leave.' I begin chuckling as I finish, then grimace as to how gross the whole thing sounds. Sadie starts having a coughing fit from laughing so much and Stu sounds like he's just about holding himself together.

'I love you, Kitty. You are my ultimate fuckwit friend.'

'Gee, thanks.'

'But, Stu, love, it gets better. Go on, Kitty,' Sadie instructs.

I shudder as I begin to recount the next part of the evening of doomed dates. 'I had put some lovely new makeup on and spent loads of time getting ready, waving my hair and everything. I didn't want to waste it, so I messaged another guy and I drove straight to meet him for a drink.'

'Time management,' shouts Sadie.

'I met him, and he was about a foot shorter than me. Well, maybe not that much shorter, but very short, and he literally had the same face as my brother, Henry.'

'Incest is not in for this season's fashion, Kit. Not a good look,' Sadie states.

'No, Sadie, it's certainly not,' I agree, laughing at the whole debacle.

After providing Sadie and Stu with their Saturday night entertainment, I get my pyjamas on and make a pot of tea and some crumpets. It's funny, I have to admit it, but somewhere inside, there's a pang of disappointment and my old enemy loneliness. How is it so hard to find someone who's right for me? A kick of sadness is in my stomach, and for the first time in a while, I wonder if I'll ever find happiness again.

The next morning, I still feel the void of love, harder than I have since Liam and I first broke up. I'm always the one who has a smile on their face, who props others up when they're struggling. The person who hides their feelings and soldiers on. I'm basically rubbish at talking about my own feelings to people in my life who care, and in most of my friendships, I take the role of the supporter. Forever being commended on my resilience and perceived ability to get on with things, it isn't always the reality, but I never let on to the world. This morning though, I'm utterly deflated and entirely alone.

I turn over and cuddle into the pillows that have lain vertically next to me in the bed since the day Liam left. It doesn't fill the missing human-shaped jigsaw piece, but psychologically, it has helped a little. Until now, when I'm sobbing into a pillow, wondering if my destiny is to be alone.

In reality, I know it's only been two months since I split with Liam; however, two months of coming home to a cold, empty, quiet house each night has started to play on my mind. The increasing queries about the dating site were a great distraction and source of entertainment at first, but now they feel like pressure, and I'm increasingly feeling like a failure. Maybe it's me. Maybe I'm not good enough or attractive enough. Maybe men want younger women, who they can travel the world with, party with and still have enough time to plan a family.

I heard enough of the incessant queries about when Liam and I were planning on having babies. The constant cross-examining at any social event as to why I simply hadn't hosted a growing embryo in my womb yet. Even in the 2020s, women still get quizzed about why they aren't prioritising popping out babies over everything else in life. Women are consistently told that their body clock is ticking and they'll soon be past it or left on the shelf.

It seems even after years of study and self-development, I'm nothing without my eggs and my use of them. It bothers me, much more than I've ever expressed. Because unlike the people basically calling me a failure for not wanting my womb to be an oven for a doughy little baby, I've never turned around and called them rude and insensitive. I've never turned around and told them I will have a baby when they sort their big nose out or I'll consider procreating when they get a decent job. Or that perhaps I can't conceive or have experienced miscarriage and they should really be more sensitive making such comments. Nor have I said that even though I work with teenagers, I actually don't really like kids and think I would make a rubbish mother. Because of course that one's always met with looks that you are either Myra Hindley or need sympathy. Then you get the whole 'it will kick in, the urge to have babies. It's human nature' type of bullshit. It's exhausting. Other people's agendas, beliefs and pressures are exhausting.

I let out a little scream and put my face back into my attempted human pillow mould as I start sobbing again.

I reach for the most comforting, cuddle-like thing in my life at the moment—my dressing gown. It will do until I get a hug later today from my mam at Sunday lunch.

I'm going to have a day off Soul Mates. My own soul feels wounded from my catalogue of depressing and disastrous dates. I will re-evaluate tomorrow, when I'm feeling less sorry for myself.

When I pull up at my parents', Henry's car is here, and I hope Sarah is here as well.

My mam greets me at the door, beaming and with her usual cuddle, which feels even more like home. 'There's news,' she exclaims, pulling me inside.

'Alright, everyone?' I ask as I kick my trainers off and go into the lounge. Everyone is sitting down, Sarah included. The fire is blasting and everything's all cosy. I take a seat next to the fireplace.

'We've got some news, Sis,' Henry says, holding Sarah's hand as he taps his leg with his free hand. 'We're pregnant,' he shouts in delight before letting out a laugh that teeters on the brink of tears.

My mouth drops open, and I look at Henry, then Sarah, who both have the biggest smile on their faces and tears in their eyes. With my hand on my chest, I start screaming with joy, jump up from my seat and rush over to hug them.

I don't care about anything else in the room. I don't care if I never find love, if I never date again or if any future dates are as crappy as the ones I've experienced the last month. I'm not bothered if my destiny is to be an old spinster with too many cats and hair like a mad professor. I don't give a hoot about any of it. Because I'm going to be an auntie. The greatest gift I could ever wish for.

Chapter 24

As I arrive at work, the adrenaline of being an auntie is still pulsing through my veins. I meet Sadie, who hands me an extra gingerbread to celebrate the news.

'It's Sarah eating for two, not me, you know,' I comment as she gives me one of her incredible cuddles.

'You'll be the most perfect auntie. You'll give the best advice and support but still be a little rogue,' she says. 'Just the most perfect auntie.'

We rush off to our lessons but promise to catch up at lunch. It soon comes round, and we both sit in our usual corner of the staffroom. Sadie asks about my dating plans, giggling again about shit-gate.

'That's one to tell your niece or nephew, love.' She chuckles as we eat. 'Maybe you should buy extra nappies for yourself?'

I roll my eyes. 'I'm disenchanted with the whole thing, Sade. I'm not sure it's for me.'

'Give it a little longer, love, for my entertainment if nothing else. Seriously though, just give it time. I know so many people who've met their partners online. There are good guys out there, and at least you have a conveyor system going to not waste your makeup.' Sadie playfully nudges me. 'You will find someone, Kit. I promise. Just enjoy the, erm, ride, until then.' She raises an eyebrow.

She's right. I have to pull, and keep, my big girl knickers up and just continue trying. Surely there's someone half decent out there for me?

'Eeeh, Kit, it sounds a right nightmare but rather funny. Maybe give it a few more weeks but start thinking about other places to meet men?' Jane suggests at the gym.

'Like where?'

'Well, how about here? There's some good-looking men. Actually, there was a right fittie the other night in here. I was hoping to see him again tonight,' Jane replies, glancing around as she steadies herself on the treadmill.

'Ah, I see.' I'm shocked but also excited that someone's turned her eye. I even wonder if they have potential to change her mind about staying single. 'That's why you have extra eye makeup on?'

Jane grins like a naughty child.

'I hope he comes in, and hey, he might have a friend.'

Jane's gym crush doesn't come in, but we have a catch up, our mouths working out more than any other muscle. Still, it's better than sitting on our backsides somewhere, at least.

I get home and decide on an early night with a book, still not in the mood for Soul Mates.

I gravitate back to browsing on Soul Mates as the week goes by, but it still doesn't have as much of my attention as before. 'Garyliftsweights' has messaged a few times. I've not had the energy to message back to anyone for a few days, but I decide it's time to at least answer back to him.

Me: Hi, sorry, not been on for a few days. How are you?

Gary: Hi there Kitty, I thought you must've met your Prince Charming and rode off into the sunset.

Me: Haha, chance would be a fine thing

Gary: Well, you haven't met me yet! So how about the weekend? Before you disappear again?

Me: Perhaps, but I'm not going weightlifting!

Gary: Funny and beautiful, eh? How about Friday night? Could go for something to eat and a few drinks?

I know it will be soft drinks for me but eating out will guarantee no cooking that night, with the added bonus of a possible decent date. The chances are slim, given my recent record, but I'm not quite ready to cut the dating cord completely.

Me: Yeah, that sounds good. What type of food do you like?

Gary: I'm not fussy, only fussy with who I ask on a date . I'll be the gent and let you pick. What do you fancy, apart from me? x

I laugh at Gary's humour and confidence. I hope they aren't just the type of lines he delivers to anyone, as if he's a postal worker on his rounds. Gary and I chat some more and settle on a new Italian restaurant just outside of the city centre, in an area with a few more bars. There's a happy hour from 6 p.m. My usual Friday after-work food shop will have to happen on Thursday this week. I don't mind changing my routine as a one-off, especially after looking online at the menu and photos of the new restaurant.

I have a few other messages in my inbox that I sift through. I half-heartedly answer a few that could have a bit of potential. Finishing my last reply, I log off, opting to spend the rest of the night with a cup of hot chocolate, a few ginger nut biscuits and my latest read. I need to put less pressure on myself and Soul Mates, then maybe, just maybe, everything will fall into place.

Chapter 25

It's the start of the first weekend in December, and places have begun erecting Christmas decorations. The eye-catching sparkles and flashes of colour are spellbinding. There's something romantic about Christmas that I very much crave. A magical distraction to my lack of romance was gifted yesterday when Sarah had her first baby scan. Even though the photo looks like some bizarre alien, we're all in love with our latest family member, who's the size of a plum, according to Henry. I'm certain it's a girl and can't wait to meet her already.

I rush in from work and start to get ready for my date with Gary. I've chosen to wear my favourite shirt dress with thick tights and stilettos. It's pretty, classy and leaves a little room for my own baby of the pizza variety, which I'm planning on accommodating in the next ninety minutes.

I drive to the new restaurant, where there's parking on-site, and see who I hope is Gary getting out of a car. He looks over, waves and begins walking towards me as a flush of panic rushes over me.

'Kitty?' he says, coming closer, arms out in an open gesture.

'Hi. Hi, Gary,' I exclaim, trying to sound casual and focusing on moving my wobbly legs.

Wow, he's so handsome, with a look of a younger James Franco. I immediately feel inferior as he leans over to greet me, kissing my cheek and stroking my arm.

'You look stunning,' he says. 'Shall we?' He gestures towards the entrance of the restaurant.

I feel like a jabbering wreck as I nod and say a quiet, 'Thank you.'

Inside, Gary takes control of the reservation, and we're directed towards a table. I immediately think I can't eat the pizza I want for fear of looking like a glut despite being starving and always the one who clears their plate.

He pulls my seat out for me, and I nervously smile as my bag clatters against the buttons on my coat.

'So, how's your week been?' he begins, taking a seat as I try to get to a position on the small seat that makes me look elegant and not like a mannequin. I stare at his perfect face and rich brown eyes. He leans forward slightly, his body language indicating he's waiting for a response as I just gawp. I snap out of it before a slither of drool begins dripping from my open, fly-catching mouth.

'Not, not bad,' I stammer. 'How about yours?'

Wishing I didn't bring my car, as I definitely need a glass of anything alcoholic for courage, I order a blackcurrant and soda, wondering if a side order of Valium is appropriate to joke about. I'm ridiculously nervous from the combination of his good looks and confidence.

Pull yourself together. I take a deep breath and start to feel less like I'm on an audition for *Love Island*. The talking seems to flow as we look at the menu. I even order the pizza I originally saw on the online menu and have my greedy little heart set on. Luckily, Gary talks about loving his food and having a massive appetite as he orders a pizza and a side of fries for himself. We patiently wait for our food order and continue to chat about fitness, food, movies, travel and hobbies. I relax as our meals are served and the atmosphere of the restaurant soaks in. But each time I look at Gary, there's a quiver of nerves. He's way out of my league, and I'm certain he must have interested women queuing up to go on dates with.

I decide to enjoy it for what it is as we look at the dessert menu. I don't want to order more and look greedy, but Gary orders a chocolate brownie sundae and asks for two spoons. We share the dessert, laughing at the noises we're making as we indulge in the fudgy, chocolatey lumps of brownie and the luxurious vanilla ice cream.

Gary requests the bill, scooping it up as it arrives and insisting on paying despite my protests. I finally graciously accept and send a quick text to Jane as he goes to pay.

He's bloody gorgeous xxx

I send the same to Sadie.

Gary and I then stroll to one of the bars across the road, where we sit for a few hours, absorbed in chat and banter. We both order soft drinks, and although I'm still nervous, there are no awkward silences. Gary is funny and interesting, with an adventurous outlook and a fun, childlike spirit. He's doing teacher training, like I did a few years ago. We talk about uni, the course and his future plans as well as my career path and school-aged kids.

It's soon last orders even though I could stay longer—a first so far in my dating history. Gary walks me back to my car.

'Kitty, it's been a pleasure, thank you. I hope we can maybe do this again?' he asks, tilting his head.

'Yeah, definitely. I've had a lovely night, Gary, thanks.' I'm a little shocked that he's boldly asked to see me again. I still feel he's out of my league and I'm not convinced he finds me attractive. I guess if the second date doesn't materialise and he dissolves like ice in the sun, it will be another lesson in 'what people say to be polite' in the labyrinth that is dating school.

He leans in and kisses me on the cheek, giving me a light hug. I inhale Gary's aftershave. His scent of citrus fruit and bergamot dances around my nostrils, making me want to press my nose against his neck.

'I'll message you,' he says as I get in my car and he shuts my door behind me.

I belt up and start the engine. As his delectable scent leaves my nasal passages, I begin to drive past Gary and out the car park.

I smile all the way home, wondering if my luck is changing.

Chapter 26

'There he is,' says Jane as we're building up a glistening of sweat on the ellipticals.

I turn around.

'*Don't look*,' she quickly exclaims, ducking, as if that won't draw more attention than me turning.

'Jeez, you've got me dizzy,' I complain.

'Look in the mirror.' She points to the wall-length mirrors in front of us, which I usually try to avoid in order to minimise seeing the movement of my bingo wings synchronising with the stride of the elliptical.

'He's the one with the chestnut, wavy hair and blue vest on.'

I look in the mirror and spot the man Jane has a crush on. He's setting up by the free weights, chatting to another guy. 'Well, I can't really see much, but nice legs.'

Jane tries to focus on the mirror whilst lamely striding on the cardio machine. 'I wonder what he's called?'

'I hope he's called something like Barney or Ezra or Floyd.'

She playfully glares at me. 'Kitty, those are the names you would call your future cat. He will be called Adam or Ben or Steve, like every other man.'

'Do you want to go and hover around the free weights, like two glistening, greedy pigeons?' I ask.

'Bugger off,' Jane snorts. 'Hey, I wonder if he's going on the gym's Christmas night out?'

'Sounds about as exciting as constipation.'

'It might be okay? They are going down the Fish Quay. There's some trendy new bars opened this last year. We could just go for one and scoot off and do our own thing if he's not there?' Jane looks at me pleadingly. I haven't seen her interested in a man for ages, so know I have to be the supportive friend with this serious crushing going on.

'Okay, when is it? And if he isn't there, you have to promise you'll try and spark up a conversation in here, even with your hair scraped back and limited makeup.'

'Promise. Let's check the poster over there. I think it's next Saturday.'

We dismount the ellipticals and stroll over to the wall. Jane almost falls over the rowing machines as she twists her head to see her new interest. She's right—the night out is next Saturday. Luckily, I have no dates arranged or any other commitments.

'Hey, just think, this time next month, you could be in a relationship with Barney Boy and I could be in one with Gary,' I say, smiling.

'What a Christmas present, eh?' She laughs, picking up a pen from the desk near the poster. Jane glances over to where Barney Boy is free weighting. It isn't clear if he can see us.

We scan the list of names of the people who have signed up to go so far.

'I don't see any Barneys down,' I say.

Jane chuckles. 'No, but a few Steves and Adams. He's bound to be one of those.'

We scrawl our names and leave the gym.

'When you going to see Gary again, then?' Jane asks.

'I don't know, he might've just been saying it. I'll have to see if he gets in touch, or maybe he's had a better offer.'

'Kitty, stop putting yourself down. I don't care how good-looking he is, he'd be the luckiest bugger in the world to have you on his arm. You'd be any bloke's lottery ticket.' She looks at me lovingly. It's just what I need to hear.

'Keep me updated,' she says, giving me a cuddle before we go to our own cars.

Gary: Hey, had a great night yesterday. Wondered if you want to exchange numbers?

The words I've been waiting to read have finally reached my inbox. Well, the first part. I've been cautious about giving out my number, especially given my lack of dating success so far, but I've decided I'll probably share it with anyone I want to see again. I can always block them if any dating crumbles into disaster.

I send my number, and half an hour later, a message comes through to my mobile from him.

Gary turns out to be so charming by text. So normal and interesting, complimentary and mature but still with great humour. He's almost thirty, but he doesn't give off the vibes some men in their late twenties do who are single and want to hump anything that moves before 'settling down'. Gary was previously in a long-term relationship when at uni. He moved to Leeds, where he lived for five years, two years with his former girlfriend. They grew apart, but he was still heartbroken, wanting to make it work. She refused, moving out, moving on to another relationship not long after. Gary admits it hurt him and it's taken him a long time to want to open his heart again. I'm touched by his honesty and reflection on his emotions and vulnerability. There's little to dislike about Gary from what I'm discovering, even if his level of good looks is intimidating to me.

He tells me he'll talk to me soon, but he is going to his sister's. I decide to log onto Soul Mates, not wanting to put all my eggs in one basket quite yet.

I open the first message.

ManofURdreams: Hey sexy, you've got the sexiest come to bed eyes on here. So I'm ready when you are!

'Dirty creep.' I click on his profile, and I'm met with an image of someone who looks like Jabba the Hutt's child. I block 'ManofURdreams', who is anything but.

There are a few more messages, one from 'FirefighterPhil'.

Hello, well aren't you a sight for sore eyes?

I can't decide if I find the message sweet or sleazy, so I decide to give 'FirefighterPhil' the benefit of the doubt and message him back.

Moving on to the next one, 'BigBalls84'.

I'm looking for a sweet honey to satisfy.

For God's sake, does this crap work? Surely not.

Me: Well, look in the opposite direction to me, please!

Send, block.

It must be sleazy Saturday, as there is another message from a man who looks like a rat asking if he can send me a picture of his scrotum. I wouldn't want to see his ball sack even if he looked like Tom Hardy.

I call it a night on Soul Mates, which is repulsing my soul, and watch some TV. It's stupid but part of me is waiting for Gary to text.

Eventually, I go to bed and doze off at midnight, cuddled into my human-shaped pillows.

Chapter 27

'Ooooh, you little minx,' Sadie squeals in the staffroom as everyone looks round.

I start to blush as I playfully elbow her.

I was messaging Gary on and off yesterday and have been telling Sadie all about him on our Monday lunch break.

'He's positively delicious, Kitty. If I didn't love my darling Stu so much, I would eat him up myself.'

Will, our ever-disgusted colleague, gives an appalled glare. I stifle a laugh. Sadie and I are great at our jobs, but together, we're like characters out of *The Beano*. Always up to some sort of trouble, then using our charm and intelligence to get away with it. Most people love our quirkiness, but some, like Will, clearly think we're morons.

'Shh,' I say quietly, nodding towards Will.

'Ah, bugger 'em, Kit,' Sadie announces with the confidence of Lady Gaga. 'Now, tell me, when are you seeing Gary again?'

After more innuendoes and attempts to make Will think we're creeps, I update Sadie on my plans for a mid-week date at a local coffee shop. She's positively delighted that someone, at last, has made it to date number two.

'I'm going to make him a certificate. I'll laminate it and everything. You can give it to him on the date,' Sadie teases.

'Maybe on date four or something, Sade.'

Disappointment flashes momentarily over her face before she smiles again, and her face lights up like a firework.

Gary's already sitting inside when I arrive at the café. I'm wearing a tartan dress and thick tights—casual but festive and pretty, being almost Christmas. I didn't have much time to get ready after rushing home from work.

He stands up to greet me, kissing my cheek and complimenting my outfit before asking how I am. He's attentive, and although I know that happens when you start dating, it's upsetting realising how little Liam said in the way of compliments or checking up on me. I guess I just got used to one-way conversations.

Gary gets up to order our drinks and a slice of cake each.

'No.' I fish around hastily in my bag for my purse, trying to get it before he heads to the counter. 'It's my turn, Gary.'

He places his hand on my shoulder, letting me know it's okay. 'I insist.'

'Please, I want to pay. I like things to be fair. I wouldn't feel comfortable you paying again,' I respond, getting up from the table, purse found and in hand.

He smiles at me and nods. 'Well, it's my turn next time.'

I walk to the counter to order our drinks and cake, basking in his last comment. I don't want to get ahead of myself, as things seem so fickle in the world of online dating, where people come and go like they're travelling through a McDonald's drive-through. For all I am an independent woman, even when I was with Liam, I still have a fragile heart, and I need to protect it. Returning to our table, the drinks and cakes are soon brought over, and we continue chatting.

Gary tells me about his family, his closeness to his grandmother and how he helps her around her house in exchange for a never-ending supply of sweets. I talk about my family and Sarah and Henry's pregnancy. We have drunk three cups of tea by the time the café starts to close.

It's freezing outside, the December breeze whipping my face and hands as soon as the café door creeps open. As we walk to the car park, Gary puts his arm around me. I breathe in his aftershave, the same scent as last time. Even though it's only the second time we've met, the smell is starting to feel familiar and safe.

'Well, here we are,' I say as we reach my car.

I turn to face him and gasp as he leans in, his mouth tenderly touching mine, like warm silk against my cold face. His kiss is soft and gentle, his lips moving in synchronicity with mine. For the first time in many years, butterflies flutter around my stomach as he holds my face with his warm hands. The cold can't touch me in this moment as I'm transported to a blissful bubble.

Gary slowly pulls away. He looks at me with tenderness, and smiles. 'So, you're amazing, gorgeous and a good kisser.'

I hold his gaze, mouth slightly agape as I focus on my breathing and my heart tries to go back to its normal rhythm. 'Takes one to know one.'

I'm beaming as I drive home. I try to remind myself to keep my head in check above any excitement that could easily lead me off into a fairy tale land of unrealistic expectations. It's been so long since I've experienced the excitement of attraction for someone. Most of the men on Soul Mates struggle to ask questions, are too intense, display maniac tendencies or there's about as much attraction to date them as there is for me to count grains of sand on a beach. Finding a balance seems rare, being attracted to them even rarer. Maybe all my first dates have been for a reason. Maybe all the rubbish messages and fake profiles of pretend doctors with fake Rolexes were meant to be, to lead me to Gary. Just maybe.

Once home, Gary and I arrange date three for Saturday afternoon, a trip to the pop-up ice rink in town. Another opportunity to fall into his arms, literally.

Chapter 28

I've been thinking about what to wear for my ice skating date with Gary for the last two days. My outfit has to be attractive but practical. I know how cold it will be on the ice rink, as well as how uncomfortable those ice skates are. I'm not great at ice skating; in fact, I'm actually pretty rubbish and struggle with balance, a bit like an elephant on a tightrope. But it will be a good excuse to cling on to Gary and hold hands.

Both Sadie and Jane can't believe I'm going on a third date tomorrow. It feels like a monumental achievement. They're ecstatic for me and both did the usual lectures of keeping safe, keeping a wise head and not letting Gary into my home and my bed too quickly.

I haven't been on Soul Mates since my mid-week date with Gary. I know I will have to get to the stage with him where I mention not dating other people at some point. Right now, it feels too soon to ask him, even if I've already got it in my head that I don't want to date anyone else whilst dating him. I have to play it cool. There's nothing worse than a needy, clingy person. I've been there, in both roles.

After work, I head to the supermarket for my usual shop. The traffic is terrible due to flooding on one of the main roads. Bloody British weather. I take another route, adding thirty minutes to my journey time.

The rain has stopped but I'm in a foul mood once I arrive at the supermarket. I grab my bags and head over to the trolley bay. Someone toots their horn as I cross the zebra crossing. I look up, a scowl on my face at the man driving, who I slightly recognise through the glass. Shooting him a look that says 'don't mess', he raises a hand and lets me across the crossing.

As I push my trolley round the supermarket, I'm annoyed that I'm late to get the week's food. I soon cheer up when I spot some cute slipper socks in the middle aisle, which I treat myself to along with some pastel highlighter pens.

The next morning, I go to the gym to meet Jane, who surprisingly hasn't missed a gym session in the last two weeks, albeit she's spent half her time looking around the gym for Barney Boy.

'He's over there,' she says quietly, indicating with her head as we sit on the exercise bikes. There he is, Barney Boy on the free weights again.

'He's in such good shape,' she swoons.

'Are you ever going to talk to him?'

'And say what, Kitty? Do you come here often?'

'What about asking about free weights or something,' I reply, ignoring her sarcasm. 'If he isn't on the gym Christmas night out next Saturday, I'll say something to him on your behalf.'

Jane ups the resistance on her bike and swiftly changes the subject. 'So, another date with gorgeous Gary, eh? He will be wanting to get you into bed soon.'

'Well, I'm not rushing into anything. I want to be certain, and I need to have the awkward conversation about the dating site before anything else.'

'Some of these men are already married. Gary seems genuine, but just check where his wedding ring would go in case there's some smooth skin and it looks a bit thinner.' Jane half laughs. 'Maybe even a lack-of-tan line.'

She's looking out for me, like Sadie, and she's right. The site's an easy pathway to cheat, fabricate and conjure up a complete fantasy life. I have to bear that in mind. It's just so hard to do when it feels so genuine with Gary.

I've chosen dark blue jeans and a jumper with a bit of glitter in, to try and feel Christmassy for my date with Gary later. I've opted for my DKNY puffer, knee-length coat with faux fur hood and a hat to keep cosy.

I rub argan oil into my face and use my jade facial roller in a desperate attempt to rid me of the start of a wrinkle line on the left-hand side of my jaw. I'm certain it's from sleeping on that side and that it looks like a ventriloquist's dummy. Two things are making me anxious about dating Gary in general. Actually, scrap that, there are about fifteen things. My main concerns are he's so good-looking and men age so much better than women. Although still young at thirty, it only feels like a heartbeat ago that I was twenty. Time goes too quick, and the last few years, including the pandemic, have felt quicker than turning the page of a book.

Women have such different pressures. Not only about popping out a baby or two, but it seems a never-ending quest to stay young. Don't get me wrong, I'm not drawn in by all the surgeries available to freeze my youth. I have concerns about the women who end up looking like cats from too many procedures instead of addressing possible underlying mental health issues. Neither am I impressed by people who look like their mouths have been stung by a colony of angry wasps and those with fingernails so long I forever wonder how they wipe their bum. Nor do I have any desire for breasts that look and feel like bowling balls. Although, fair play to anyone brave enough to do anything that makes them feel better, as long as it's psychologically sound. I just don't want to end up with lines in my forehead that could match Gordon Ramsay's.

I ponder how I've never been able to eat quite what I want and even looking at cheesecake makes me gain a pound in weight, but now I'm almost thirty-one, shifting weight feels like flying to the moon on a paper aeroplane. I've been a comfy, baggy jumper to Liam and he's been mine, even when the tag rubbed at my neck. I didn't have to worry about body image pressures that left me feeling inadequate. Liam loved me for me, my personality, my faults. Then it stopped. The thought of being enough for someone else has never really escaped my consciousness since the day we broke up.

Chapter 29

Gary is waiting by the ice rink, standing with radiating confidence. As I walk towards him, I still feel the slight nerves of insufficiency. As if leaving a job interview knowing you could have done better. He turns and looks. A smile brighter than a lighthouse beacon emerges on his face as he heads in my direction. As we meet, he embraces me and kisses me on the lips. I blush. It's daytime and I'm self-conscious even though it wasn't a full-on snog. After saying our hellos with actual words as well as body language, we pay for boot hire and an hour on the rink. I'm dreading the uncomfortable boots and have two pairs of socks on, prepared for the pinching and aching of the stiff footwear. The boots haven't changed in the many years from when I used to go to the local ice rink sporadically. It's beyond my comprehension as to why someone would design something so damn uncomfortable that it could almost be used as a form of torture.

I make a mental note to add ice skating boot designer to my ever-increasing list of possible career paths for when I eventually get fed up with working alongside hormonal teenagers or when the Ofsted regulations make it impossible to be creative and do the job I'm trained to. Ice skating boot designer can go alongside librarian, book shop/cake shop manager, kitten handler and travelling gelato/gin slush seller.

Gary holds my hand as we get onto the ice, and I immediately think I might fall like lumpy potatoes tumbling out of a bag. Crikey, I'm certainly never going to be Jayne Torvill with my balance. I have to concentrate hard to stay up and not fall onto my backside. There's pressure to impress Gary and not pull facial expressions like I need to do a massive fart or where my tongue's out to the side like always when I'm concentrating on a task. Gary is a natural. I should have known. I wonder if there's anything this guy's rubbish at. We skate round, me trying to look casual but looking as awkward as a priest in a strip club. My body is sweaty, but my feet, hands and nose remain like icicles. Even Gary's hand in mine doesn't do much to warm my numb fingertips. Despite this, as I get into it, I actually have a good time on the ice, managing to not splat to the ground like a water bomb or knock any children over. Win-win.

Once the hour slot is over, I'm knackered and Gary looks as if he could manage three triathlons and still not break into a sweat. Putting my boots back on, I do that spaceman-type walk where your legs don't quite feel your own. Gary pulls me in and gives me a gentle kiss that almost makes me collapse to the ground, when I've tried so hard to stay upright. The softness of his cool lips, his mouth dancing with mine like they're meant to be united. I don't care that it's the middle of Newcastle and only beginning to go dark. He pulls away, kisses my forehead with gentle tenderness and suggests we go for a drink. I nod, slightly lost for words and just wanting to savour the taste of his lips and imprint the kiss in my memory forever.

The rest of the date with Gary continues to be wonderful as we chat non-stop and get to know each other more over a few soft drinks.

'I've never met anyone like you, Kitty,' Gary says, looking at me as he turns a coaster on the table between his fingers.

I feel a gentle warmth in my cheeks, or maybe it's the heat of happiness radiating around me. He seems so genuine, and it's refreshing to meet someone who can be honest and complimentary without coming across as creepy. I tell him about Jane and Barney Boy and the plans for the gym night out.

'Well, I hope he hasn't got a friend,' Gary says, winking.

Again, the heat rises in me as I smile. 'I'm purely being her chaperone.'

We talk about Christmas, my plans with my family and his plans with his, alongside a Boxing Day night out with the lads. I can't help but wonder if we'll see each other over the festive period. Luckily, in my line of work, it means I have two weeks off, but I'm anxious it will leave me at a loose end being single.

'Are you off work much over Christmas?' I ask, trying to sound casual as I tuck my hair behind my ear.

Gary works in a mobile phone shop part-time to support his PGCE at university. It's admirable that he studies for an intensive degree but still wants to work and have an income.

'Yeah, I've only picked up a few shifts. I kinda need some time off, to be honest, to chill. It's been a heavy semester, and we'll be sorting out placements in the new year. My aim is to recharge a little and perhaps spend some time with this gorgeous new woman I've met.' He looks at me intensely, and I smile nervously.

The hours pass, and we end up grabbing a pizza from a takeaway to share. Gary lets me choose—another point for his ever-mounting list of positives. As we sit in the takeaway on hard bar stools, sharing a veggie pizza, I'm content at the excitement of a possible blossoming romance.

'I want to see you again soon. You're gorgeous, Kitty, and women like you don't come around very often.' Gary touches my cheek gently.

I close my eyes momentarily and soak in the attention. It could be us in the world in these few seconds, but then the chef shouts from the kitchen to his staff and my bubble of private romance is popped.

When I open my eyes again, Gary's are warm and welcoming.

'I want to see you again too. And you're not visually offensive yourself.' I tap his leg as I continue to look at him.

Gary touches my hand and strokes my hair with his other. His touch feels almost electric and so right. I don't want to get carried away, but it's difficult not to, and for all my nerves and anxiety about not being attractive enough, Gary actually seems to like me just the way I am.

Gary walks me to my car after we leave the takeaway. We kiss for what feels like forever but not long enough. Eventually pulling away, he takes my hand, squeezing it affectionately.

'Text when you get home,' he says as I slide into my car, and he shuts the driver's door behind me.

I nod, starting the engine, hopeful that Soul Mates may just have done its job.

'It's so nice to see you happy again, Kit,' Jane says as we chat over tea and biscuits at mine. 'You were with Liam so long, and yeah, you had ups and downs, but it was still a long time. I know how much you loved him and wanted it to work.'

I always act like I'm okay, but those closest to me get to see my vulnerability, and Jane has forever been there with a tissue and a cuddle. When my heart feels irreparable, Jane, Sadie and my family provide the medicine of love and nurturing that helps soothe my soul and knits the cracks in my heart back together.

'When are you going to see him next, then?' Jane asks, dipping a biscuit into her tea.

'We haven't arranged anything yet,' I admit. 'I think he is waiting to see his shifts at work and his family commitments over Christmas, but hopefully soon.'

'As long as it's not Saturday,' she says, referring to the gym Christmas night out.

'If we see Barney Boy at the gym on Thursday night, you have to ask him if he's going, mind.'

'Stop calling him that.' Jane laughs.

We talk about our outfits and plans for Saturday night before Jane leaves.

I message Gary, the last few days having been saturated with text conversations between us filled with flirtation, future and promise. We haven't discussed coming off Soul Mates, but I haven't logged on since the last date. Right now, Gary is absorbing my thoughts, and I have no interest in communicating with anyone else.

Chapter 30

Saturday comes around quickly, and Jane and I are getting ready for our night out. I'm trying to hide my disappointment that Gary and I haven't arranged a fourth date. He's been quieter the last few days after intense texting. He has text saying he's out with his mates but will text later. I don't want to keep texting him. I know it's a turn off for people. I have to try and remain cool and calm even though I'm desperate to ask about us being exclusive.

Tonight, however, is Jane's night, and I can't make it about me. My dating disasters and now Gary have dominated conversations for over two months. She's been single so long, disinterested in relationships, so it fills me with hope that she now has a sparkle in her eyes. I just hope Barney Boy is out tonight, that he's single and interested in women.

I have to admit we look pretty good. Jane is wearing an off-the-shoulder lace midi dress that shows her toned figure, and I'm wearing a black sequin above-the-knee dress that has the right level of glam and Christmas sparkle. Teamed with black heels and my Gucci clutch that I bought in New York with Liam a few years ago, I feel celebrity chic. Bobbi Brown lip gloss and smoky eyes finish my look. Despite feeling a little flat inside, I present as a confident, carefree woman.

'You'll have to do a load of your stinky farts tonight to keep the blokes away,' Jane says, laughing.

'Well, I did have some homemade soup earlier.' I make a fart noise.

Our Uber driver soon arrives and takes us into the Fish Quay part of town, where the gym group are meeting. Jane and I have the odd pleasantry with some of the gym folk, but we don't know anyone in great detail, always talking away to each other. It's going to feel a bit strange seeing people usually sweating over the stepper all glammed up. But hey, it's a night out.

There's already a crowd, and we spot two of the instructors, who are lovely and who Jane and I usually speak with.

'Hey, ladies, you look great,' Donna, one of the instructors, says.

'So do you,' I reply, thinking how different Donna looks glammed up compared to in her usual gym leggings and vest.

After exchanging pleasantries, Jane and I go to the bar.

'I didn't see him, did you?' she asks, disappointed.

'I don't think so, but it's hard to tell when people aren't wearing gym clothes.'

We order drinks, two Southern Comforts and lemonades, and return to the group, which has a number of small groups chatting away. Some are sat down, some are stood hovering around. We smile at a few regulars as we sip our drinks and feel a bit school dance-ish. As more people arrive, Jane and I begin to relax.

'If he doesn't turn up, we can just shoot and go and do our own thing or get a taxi into town?' Jane suggests.

'Sounds good.'

We get another drink in as the bar begins to fill. It's always busy in most places in December with staff parties and friends catching up before Christmas. The vibe in the area is friendly and chill, and the odd Christmas song comes on, getting people in the mood. Although, I draw the line at eggnog or mulled wine.

Jane keeps glancing to the entrance of the bar, hoping for her gym crush to turn up. She seems to be between getting irritable to leave and a reluctance to go somewhere else just in case. After looking over at least twenty times, each look getting more impatient, Jane's mouth drops. I turn to the entrance and spot Barney Boy in the doorway. He looks smart, dressed up, and immediately spots one of the instructors, Anthony, sauntering over to him. There are no more glances from Jane now, her eyes firmly fixed to her crush instead. I have to admit he looks good in his shirt and chinos, and luckily for him, he isn't wearing bad shoes, which is a massive turn-off for Jane. I elbow her gently to knock her out of her trance. She looks at me, giddy with excitement as her face lights up. She has a cute pixie face and a beautiful smile.

Barney Boy and friend go to the bar as Jane watches. She reapplies her lip gloss and waits for his return to the group. We move a little closer into the congregating gym goers, smiling at randoms who we can't quite place. Barney Boy soon returns to the group and sets about chatting with Anthony. I don't recognise his friend.

'We're moving bars,' Donna bellows in her broad Geordie twang.

We all gulp our drinks and follow like she's the Pied Piper.

'Hang back,' Jane says, grabbing my arm as she studies Barney Boy's every move. As he starts to walk to the exit, she pushes me along.

'Bloody hell, easy does it.' I laugh as she kicks my heels to get going. We then slow down the pace in line with him and his friend.

Barney Boy smiles at us, my arm pretty much touching his. 'Hi there, yous okay?'

Jane lets out a giggle that sounds half whoopee cushion and half cartoon.

'Hi, yeah, I'm Kitty, this is Jane,' I say enthusiastically, taking control.

'I'm Dominic, and this is Christian,' he replies, glancing at his friend and then back at us.

Christian lifts his hand in a small wave. He is short, with a baby face. I still don't recognise him up close, although he hasn't got the type of face that would leave an imprint on my mind.

So, Barney Boy is Dominic. I'm disappointed I wasn't right.

We all start walking, following the crowd. We move behind Dominic and Christian, the door only big enough for two at a time. Jane is doing some kind of calming technique, her lips counting to ten. I hope he doesn't look back and wonder what she's doing.

'Snap out of it, you little creep,' I whisper out the corner of my mouth, elbowing her gently.

She nods and looks at her feet instead. I'm not sure if she's making sure her feet are actually working or petrified of accidentally stepping on the back of Dominic's shoes.

We hurry along to the next bar. Most of the gym group are already queuing for drinks. We squeeze into a space behind Dominic and Christian, hoping we don't look like we're following them even though we definitely are.

Dominic turns to face us, hand gripping the bar to make sure he doesn't lose his space. 'What do you want, ladies?'

A grinning but still mute Jane eventually opens her mouth. 'Oh, are you sure?' she says, gawping.

'Yeah, no bother. What will it be?'

'Two Southern Comforts, please. Erm, that's not each, I meant between us. Two between us. One each,' she overexplains, her eyes widening.

He laughs. 'Coming up.'

'Shit, he must think I'm a right dick,' she mutters, sighing.

'Well, you are,' I joke.

Jane glares at me.

'He won't, hun,' I reassure her, realising now probably isn't the best time for my humour. 'He'll think you are endearing, because you are. Just try to talk to him and relax. Surely the drink is kicking in, and anyway, you're absolutely gorgeous. If anyone is going to be intimidated, it's him.'

Dominic and Christian finally get served before Dominic turns to find us, passing us our drinks. We say our thanks and all move to stand near the gym group. They begin talking about the gym, and Jane seems to relax into the conversation, avoiding sounding like she's in an awkward teen comedy. As the conversation and night goes on, we find out Christian lives with his partner, Ben, and Dominic is single after splitting with his last girlfriend in the summer. When they ask about me, I don't know what to say. I know I don't want to date anyone else whilst I'm dating Gary and I definitely feel like feelings have developed. I settle on that I'm dating someone. It seems the safest answer.

The drinks keep flowing and the group becomes more jovial, some dancing, some splitting away from the group to meet friends and join other nights out. We chat to a few people, but in each bar, it seems we gravitate back to Dominic and Christian, or they gravitate to us.

It's soon the end of the night. People are pouring into taxis, with sore feet and slurred speech. We decide to share a taxi with Dominic and Christian. They live in the same cul-de-sac, around ten minutes from mine, where Jane is staying. Chatting in the taxi, we have a laugh with the driver about his attempts to get online shopping for his wife without her intercepting and knowing what everything is even through packaging.

Dominic and Christian are dropped off first. Dominic keeps the taxi door open as we say our goodnights.

'It's been lovely to meet you both,' says Christian, nodding at us.

'Hopefully see you at the gym next week,' Dominic says, smiling and then looking directly at Jane.

'Y-yes, that would be nice,' Jane says, squeezing my hand to release excitement.

Dominic shuts the taxi door, and the taxi driver starts driving off. We wave until they're both out of sight, Jane straining her neck to watch Dominic as long as possible.

Jane slumps in her seat and shuts her eyes. 'Boom, I'm in love,' she announces.

'Crikey, well, this is big news from the woman who has no interest in relationships.' I chuckle.

It would be lovely to see Jane happy.

I check my phone for the fiftieth time tonight, hoping Gary has texted. There's nothing. I text him.

Hey, sexy! I hope you're having a great night. Xxx

We arrive at mine, down some water and then get undressed, taking our makeup off. I get into bed, Jane getting into the spare bed, and check my phone one last time. Gary still hasn't replied. Perhaps his phone battery has died. He'll be in touch in the morning, I'm certain of it.

Chapter 31

Jane and I awake the next day to synchronised head holding as we vow to never drink alcohol again. My lips are dry and cracked, and I'm immediately engulfed in a torrent of nausea. As I curse Southern Comfort, Jane laughs a weak laugh, then lets out a moan that it even hurts to laugh. Turning thirty has been the beginning of the end with regards to being able to keep up with drinking, or so it feels in my head. Putting the kettle on, we run through breakfast options.

I pick up my mobile phone for what must be the hundredth time this morning already. I put it on the bench and let out a childish whine.

'Still no message?' Jane asks.

I shake my head and lean against the counter.

'Maybe his phone just died and he's still asleep? You know what these lazy men are like,' she says as she gets the toaster out.

I nod and get on with making our pot of tea, trying to stir away the disappointment as I squash the teabags against the inside of the pot.

After we've munched on several rounds of toast, Jane gets dressed and leaves with the promise to catch up at the gym tomorrow and hopefully see Dominic.

I shower and attempt to tidy up a bit, feeling vulnerable in more ways than those inflicted by the excessive alcohol.

'Eric, our Kitty's here,' my mam shouts upstairs as I take my shoes off in the hallway.

After a soothing cuddle, I go into the lounge, where I'm instantly served with a piece of homemade fruit cake.

'How are you, pet?' she asks, touching my forehead tenderly. 'You look peaky.'

'I'm fine, Mam, just a little hungover.' I wince and exhale, trying to rid the poison from my body.

Mam tuts, stroking my hair. 'And what about the boys?'

'You mean men, Mam?' I snigger.

'Yes, pet. Have you found a man yet?'

'Mam, it's not a treasure hunt or something I take off the shelf in the supermarket,' I say grumpily, feeling like a failure.

'You know what I mean. We just want you to be happy and settled,' Mam replies in a jolly voice that has a distinct undertone of pity.

'I know, Mam, no one wants that more than me. It's just not that easy.' I can feel myself getting emotional about Gary, which is stupid in reality. I haven't really been single all my adult life, and I don't want to be single. I want companionship, a better half, a bloody soul mate.

'Mam, a lot of the men online lie as often as they breathe or, well, are only after one thing. It's hard to meet decent people.' I sigh.

'I know, pet, loads of pervs on that internet, just like your dad says. Maybe you need to meet someone somewhere else, love?' She reaches to the coffee table to pour from a pot of tea. 'When you do find someone, he will be the luckiest man in the world,' Mam comments, tapping my hand. 'Here, have another piece of cake.'

'Thanks, Mam,' I reply, trying to hold back the tears.

The doorbell rings, giving me a chance to wipe my eyes and compose myself as Mam goes to answer it. Henry and Sarah have arrived.

Lunch and pudding are dominated with talk of the baby, which is a beautiful distraction. Their second scan is scheduled for less than two weeks, where they'll hopefully find out the gender. It's the best Christmas present ever, and we're all excited about next Christmas and how wonderful it will be to have another addition to the family.

Leaving with food extras from 'Cook's supermarket', I drive the short distance home and decide on an afternoon nap. As I set my alarm so I don't sleep too long, I realise Gary has text.

Hi gorgeous, sorry phone died last night. Hope you had a good one? Missing you and hope to catch up soon? Xxx

I smile, all the anxiety I've been holding melting away.

Glad you're okay and hopefully not too hungover! Yeah, great night, fragile today but just been to my parents' and been fed . Miss you too, would be lovely to catch up before Christmas xxx

He replies a few minutes later.

Defo, I'll check my shifts and then we can arrange something. Can't wait to kiss those sexy lips again xxx

I bite my finger, putting my phone by the sofa as I pull the throw off the back and cover myself in it. I know I was being irrational before, but now I feel positive again that Gary and I have a future. I think about what we could do next week. maybe I will even invite him round here.

Chapter 32

'Sounds like an eventful weekend, love,' Sadie says as we sit in the staffroom. Our free period always matches up on a Monday. This free period, of course, is meant to be used for marking and lesson planning, but we always end up chatting, laughing and, more times than not, disturbing other teachers who are actually working.

'I'm pleased Gary got in touch. Mind you, any funny business from him in the future and he will have me to answer to. I might be small, Kit, but I'm mighty,' Sadie says boldly, tilting her head up to add to her drama.

'Don't I know it. You're like a Welsh, five-foot, big-boobed, glitter-adorned superhero.'

Sadie starts to guffaw, grabbing my hand and telling the staffroom how much she loves me. There are a few glances, a smile and an eyeroll. People are used to Sadie's eccentricities, but there are some colleagues who will never quite get it and some serious ones who see Sadie and me as their idea of hell.

'When will you see him, then?' Sadie asks. 'It's Christmas next week.'

'I'm not sure. I'll suggest something tomorrow if I haven't heard. I've been trying to keep it cool. It's him who starts with the deep and emotional texts. I'm just eager to see him again, but I know Christmas is a busy time for everyone and he has a big family and stuff.'

'Well, don't play it too cool. Get your sexy Mrs Claus suit out, you little minx,' Sadie says, purposely loud.

'Sadie, bugger off,' I say quietly, pretty much shrinking in my seat with a nervous giggle.

It's the last week of term, and the kids are in festive moods. Little work is always done around this time of year, but it's heart-warming to see the kids excited for Christmas and making crafts, preparing for the Christmas dance on the last day of term and getting gifts organised to deliver to the local refuge, which we do every year.

I sigh as I slump onto the sofa, phone in hand. I've just got back from the gym after a class with Jane. I had to wait around for an extra fifteen minutes so she could say hello to Dominic and then dissect their sixty second conversation. It's been over twenty-four hours since Gary last text. Although I promised myself I would wait for him so I don't look clingy, I cave and send a message.

Hey, you! Hope you've had a great Monday? Xxx

I spend the next two hours checking my phone. With no reply from Gary, I huffily pick up my book to read, knowing it will get me sleepy and hopefully switch me off from the escalating thoughts I'm having about Gary and the niggle in my mind that won't go away. Trying to think of anything but Gary, I instead realise that Adam never text me despite taking my number.

Young people can get such a bad name through the media, stereotypes and moral panic. It's wonderful to see fifty of our students wrapping presents and writing messages for the adults and children at the local refuge, who have left abusive situations. Many of the kids themselves have had experiences of this as children and even within their own relationships. They are sensitive, thoughtful and kind, working as part of a big team to ensure people in need have a present for Christmas day. My heart feels whole as I watch them and we sing along to Christmas songs. In this moment, nothing can spoil my high. Not even the lack of communication from Gary.

By the end of the day, both staff and students are emotionally spent. Heading out to the car park, Sadie skips over and puts her arms around me.

'Love you, my little Kit.'

'Love you too, my littler Sade,' I reply, cuddling her back.

Sadie has always insisted on cuddles since we met but more so since Liam and I split, after telling her the lack of human contact feels like a punch to my heart.

'Ring later if you need to chat,' she says as she walks to her car, knowing my vibes are a little off-kilter.

Despite knowing I probably shouldn't, I text Gary again.

Hi, gorgeous, hope you got my last text? Anyway, let me know if you want to meet before Christmas; I'm getting booked up with friends and family things xxx

The first part may have sounded a little desperate on reflection after sending, but sod it, I'm impatient waiting for a reply and need to make the first, or in this case second, move. Feeling a little happier, I put my phone in my bag before driving home.

After a comforting dinner of sausage casserole, mashed potato and crusty bread, I prepare for Christmas present wrapping. Pouring myself a little Baileys over ice, I look at the mammoth number of presents across my lounge floor. I've even bought something for baby 'Narna', which is its name this week, as it's the size of a banana. Henry and Sarah have their scan tomorrow to see if they can determine the gender.

Settling down on the floor, I grab my phone. It's almost always on silent for work and often just in general—something my parents often tell me off about. A smile spreads across my face as I notice Gary has messaged. I unlock my phone and open the text.

Hey beautiful, so sorry, been working long shifts at the shop—it's madness this time of year! I think we may have to try and meet between Christmas and New Year. My gran isn't well, so we're trying to spend more time with her and give her a little more care to get her well for Christmas. Will sort something soon though, can't wait to kiss you, and more! xxx

Tingles immediately spread through my body. I'm glad no one is here, as they would definitely have noticed me at least blushing. There have been some heated texts sent since we've met, and I know we're getting closer to sleeping together, but he's also been very respectful, making me like him even more.

I send a text back hoping his gran is okay. She's in her late eighties and lives alone, but she has mobility issues. It's nice Gary is taking an active role in supporting her care.

We send a few texts back and forth until bedtime, which soothes my paranoia and makes me feel appreciated by Gary again. I'm disappointed we haven't made plans to see each other before Christmas. It will take us into two weeks of not seeing each other, but I guess we have plenty of time together to look forward to, and I remind myself I want to be with someone who is a family man.

Chapter 33

I'm wearing my Christmas jumper, corduroy skirt and thick tights. It's the last day of term and the kids have just left. We had the school Christmas party from midday with buffet for the kids, a DJ and various activities in the rooms off the hall including a PlayStation, karaoke and reindeer piñata. With all teachers involved, there was enough staff to ensure health and safety but also for us to get involved with the festivities. It was an enjoyable afternoon, and the dance mat helped burn off some of the seventeen sweet mince pies I'm sure I ate.

Us adults were left to tidy up, but the caretaker is now finishing off and will lock the school up for two weeks after. Saying our goodbyes and wishing everyone a nice break, Sadie and I walk to our cars.

'See you Monday?' Sadie asks in reference to our traditional Christmas Eve cuppa, cake and present swap.

'Wouldn't miss it for the world,' I reply, giving her a cuddle before getting into my car.

I'm due to do my usual Friday food shop, which will be my last food shop before Christmas. Usually, I would buy a load of naughty, fattening food, but I feel like a stuffed turkey after all the buffet I've gorged.

I put my car into gear and go to set off when my mobile flashes. I grin, already knowing who it is and what the conversation will be about. I've been waiting for this moment all day.

'Hey, Henry, you okay?' I ask, almost dropping my phone in my rush to answer it.

'Yeah, all good, are you?' There's a tone of eagerness to spill and overwhelm in his voice.

'Yeah, just finishing work. So?' I ask impatiently, the fingers of one hand tapping underneath my seat.

'So, Sis, you are going to be an auntie to a little baby... *girl*,' he announces excitedly.

I scream and grab my jaw. 'Oh wow, Henry, that's amazing,' I say, my words an out-of-tune sound of voice cracks. 'I knew Narna would be a girl.' Tears fill my eyes, and I can almost see Henry beaming with pride. 'That's bloody brilliant, the best news ever. Is Sarah over the moon?'

'Yeah, she's ecstatic, Sis, we both are,' Henry says through chokes of emotion. 'I'm so proud of her.'

'It's just wonderful, Henry. I'm so pleased for you both, for us all. Now yous need to think of names.'

We chat for another minute before hanging up. I sit and wait for the scan photos to come through on my mobile. As I scroll through them, everything feels so surreal. Our newest family member, there on the screen, looking like an alien banana. But my heart is full. Still the best Christmas present ever.

Basking in my happiness, I head off to the supermarket for my weekly shop. I listen to the radio, playing Christmas songs, as I keep beaming about Narna. Even the usual road rage and idiotic drivers can't dull my shine. I eventually get to the supermarket, unleash a trolley and go inside. As I'm entering the shop, people are coming out.

A guy raises an eyebrow. 'Nice jumper.'

'Thanks,' I reply, smiling, a quick glance in his direction. I recognise him, but I'm not sure where from.

I stop, turn and watch him as he heads towards his car, trying to get a better view. Once he reaches it, he looks behind, back towards the shop, but he's too far away for me to get a proper look. I decide he's probably just someone from the local area I've passed before. This time of year is strange.

I enter the supermarket and push the trolley round the aisles. I look at all the naughty food, which I've been resisting most of December up until today. I pick up a sticky toffee pudding—one of my favourites. It says on the packaging it serves six, which I calculate to mean four maximum. It looks more like three servings to me. I could have it over three days or maybe one day. Breakfast, lunch and dinner. I laugh to myself, probably looking a bit odd, but I don't care. Placing the cake in the trolley, I make a mental note to get some custard and ice cream to go with it.

I add a Terry's Chocolate Orange into my trolley, one of my favourites, to devour with a big cup of tea. Next, some nachos and salt and vinegar peanuts, both of which I only have once or twice a year, as when I open a packet, I can't keep my hand out until the packet's empty.

Eventually, I'm shopped out, home and have filled the cupboards, fridge and freezer with an obscene amount of food for one person. Although, technically, I will be entertaining over the festive season with Jane, Sophie and probably Sadie popping in. I'll also invite Gary over. I rationalise I have enough to share or enough to last me throughout January if not.

Chapter 34

In true Sadie style, I hear her before I see her as we arrive at the same time for our Christmas Eve cuppa, cake and present exchange.

'There's my little fuckwit,' she bellows in her high-pitched voice across the café car park as strangers turn around. She's waving her manicured hand, and her bright red lipstick glistens in the frosty winter air.

I start to laugh.

Sadie always tells me I'm academically the cleverest person she knows but completely useless at most common-sense things. I struggle to remember my left from right, ask questions a five-year-old would know the answer to and get ridiculously excited about the most mundane of things such as sorting out drawers. Sadie, on the other hand, is one of the best teachers in the borough but has zero sense of direction and uses her Welsh accent to tell people asking directions that she doesn't live here, when, in fact, she's been a Newcastle resident for eight years. She avoids any paperwork and admin forms, and her mind is like a colourful and borderline seedy drag act.

Grabbing my hand, she ferries me inside the café, where we place our orders and then get a cosy booth.

'Any update on Gary?' Sadie asks, getting straight to the point as per usual.

'Sade, I've hardly heard from him. His gran isn't well but, I don't know, maybe I'm overanalysing.' I sigh, and she picks up my hand, squeezing it. 'I spoke to Jane at the gym yesterday when we exchanged presents. She said he's probably busy and being pulled in all different directions. I checked in to see how him and his gran are doing. Nothing.'

I didn't sleep great, tossing and turning and picking up my stupid mobile phone all night in the hope Gary had text. I'm annoyed with myself for feeling emotionally held hostage by a guy I hardly know. But I so want to get to know him more; he ticks so many of the non-negotiable boxes. Maybe I'm being paranoid. Maybe he's genuinely busy. Maybe he has doubts or is stringing me along. I gasp as it registers that maybe he's met someone else. Crikey, this is some form of mental torture.

'Love, you've been through a hard time, and it's all new to you. It's okay to feel anxious and apprehensive. But, Kit, never doubt your instinct.' She looks at me intensely, fist clenched and pressed against her torso. 'That gut instinct, Kit, it will be right. You're a special creature, for all the right reasons. If it lingers, listen to it and take back control.'

Our tea and cakes arrive, and my attention turns straight to feeding my face.

'What you going to do, Kit? Text him again?'

'Yeah, I'm going to have to, Sade. I'm not having this hanging over me, not knowing what's going on. I know it may be impatient, but surely, he has a few minutes a few times a day spare to text? It was nonstop for the previous month or so.'

The rest of our morning is soaked in laughter, friendship and reminiscing of the year. I leave the café and Sadie with a full belly and a full heart, feeling more in control of the situation with Gary and his distinct lack of communication.

I text Gary once I arrive home.

Hi, Gary, just wanted to know you're okay, since I haven't heard from you. I know you're busy but please let me know all is okay. Also, here if I can help in any way. xxx

I haven't been on Soul Mates for almost a fortnight, mainly out of respect for Gary. As the creeping sensation of doubt around his integrity grows, I'm curious to log on, even if just to clear my inbox.

As my laptop fires up, I boil the kettle, singing along to the Christmas tunes Alexa has selected. Settling down with my big mug of tea and three custard creams, I log into Soul Mates. There are almost eighty messages in my inbox. I scroll down, amazed until I reach the start of the messages in historic date order. On my screen, a few messages down, are a few old messages from Gary. I look to the left where his profile picture is and see a little green dot, indicating he's online.

'The absolute shit.' A mixture of shock and rage pumps through me. He can't answer my texts, as he's so busy caring for his gran and working, yet he's on here.

I pick up my phone and start typing out an angry message, only to stop myself. It isn't my style and it would make me look like a jealous, insecure, demanding woman (which I am partly, but I don't want him to know that). Instead, I sit seething and reading over some messages, most of which are deleted immediately. The messages are getting deleted at super speed as I curse Gary under my breath.

I feel like a fool; he's clearly just playing me and God knows how many more women. He could even be lying about his gran. I start to cry, more with frustration at myself. I'm not usually a gullible woman. I'm not usually a woman who would fall in love with a carrier bag if it didn't blow away in the wind. Who sits next to a guy on the train and immediately believes they're 'the one'. I feel used, lied to, cheated and hurt. Gary has made promises. He's talked about our future.

I place my hands together, wringing them as my pulse races with adrenaline. What is his bloody game? Gary let me think I'm special and desired. He's been respectful… well, until the last week or so. I like him, I really like him, and I started to see a future with us. He made me think there's a future for us.

I rub my eyebrows and place my hands over my eyes. It's too much. I'm not cut out for lies and bullshit. I've let someone into my prison cell of emotions, and this is what I've got back.

I look at the screen and see he's still here. It's clear Gary isn't just deleting his account.

I put my laptop to the side and get up, pacing the lounge. I want to message him, tell 'Full of guff Gary' that he can piss off. I'm shaking with anger as my body fights against crying. I've cried a river for the male species, and now I want to drown every last bloody one in it.

Maybe it's because I haven't slept with him, or maybe I'm not attractive enough after all. It's been months since Liam and I split up, and I haven't felt anything for anyone except Gary. Hours of internet searching and messaging, planning, dates. Nothing. I felt nothing until I met him.

'*Prick*,' I shout to the ceiling, as if it's going to agree with me.

I grab my phone and call Sophie. I can't wait a few days to see her. I need her advice now.

'Hey, Soph. How's you?' I ask as she answers the phone, doing everything to not immediately spill what's going on.

'Good ta, Kit, looking forward to the big man emptying his sack, and I'm not referring to Chris,' she says, laughing at her own joke.

'You're gross,' I say, trying to sound okay. Any other time, I would have been howling with laughter. 'Listen, I, I, I need to ask,' I add before my voice breaks and I start crying.

'Kit? Honey, what's up? What's happened?' Sophie says quickly, concern clear in her voice.

'It's, it's Gary. I'm sorry, I need some advice, Soph.' I take a deep breath in and wipe my eyes.

'Okay, hun, take your time. He hasn't hit you or anything, has he?' Sophie asks, alarmed.

'No, no, nothing like that,' I quickly respond, shaking my head even though she can't see me. 'Erm, my head's done in, and I don't think it can wait until I see you.'

I take a gulp of now cold tea, then start to explain. 'So, you know I've been seeing Gary for a good few weeks and our dates have been lovely? He was romantic, talked about our future and that. The texts have been the same—attentive, cute and making an effort and stuff.'

'Yeah, he sounded great.'

I let out a hummphh. 'Well, the last week or so, he's been evasive and not texting back consistently. For the last few days, he hasn't replied at all. He hasn't arranged to see me again, just said we'd sort something between Christmas and New Year. Then he said he's picking up extra shifts at work and his gran isn't well. So, I've text a few times and got no reply for a couple of days. It's been playing on my mind.' I pull at the cuff of my jumper as my shoulders slouch.

'Understandable, Kit,' Sophie says, her opinion reserved until she has the full story.

'I mean, I don't want to hassle him, you know, look needy, especially if his gran's poorly. But I text him just saying that I hope he's okay. I got no reply, Soph. I've logged onto Soul Mates tonight, really to check my inbox, and in all honesty, I feel a little wounded, so thought it would be a boost. He's bloody online on there, yet he hasn't answered my texts. I'm fuming, Soph, and really upset.' I don't want to cry again, but I'm becoming increasingly angry, and feelings of being pathetic are dancing around my ankles.

'What a dick, Kit. I think you've been ghosted, hun.' Her voice is quiet and soft.

I frown. 'Ghosted?'

'Yeah, basically when someone just disappears from your life, never to be seen or heard from again. I mean, I could be jumping to conclusions, but a dude saying his gran is ill, needing to work and turning distinctly cold, then popping up live on a dating site... it reeks of ghosting or juggling more women than one in my opinion.' She pauses, and I wonder what she's doing. Is she biting her lip at having to be the one to say what I bet others have been thinking? Is she trying to find the right words to make me feel better? 'Sorry, hun, I'm sure that's not what you want to hear. I'm so sorry there are massive idiots around.'

'No, it's absolutely what I want to hear, Soph.' I sigh and swallow. In the past two days, I've had Jane's optimistic opinion, Sade's neutral but hinting opinion and Soph's negative opinion. With Sophie's previous online dating experience, hers is the opinion I have a massive inkling is the right one.

'I won't allow myself to waste any more time on these fanny rats and bloody charlatans. My gut said something was wrong a week ago. I just put it down to being out the dating loop really and being paranoid. But you've helped me get some clarity, even if it's painful.' I scroll up on my laptop, desperate to not see Gary's online status anymore.

'It happened to me, Kit. It's not nice, but it did help with my dating boundaries. Morons like Gary don't deserve you. I'm sorry, hun, it's awful. I might be wrong, I hope I am, but sadly, I think I'm pretty spot on here.'

I know she's right. My instinct has been right— I just wanted to bury it and cover it in cement. Sophie isn't the type to push an opinion if she thinks there's no weight in it.

'Yeah, I think you're right too,' I admit. 'Even though it's not what I want to hear, I have to hear it and learn from it. I'm zero tolerance from now on.' An influx of determination is now battling my upset. I don't deserve to be ghosted. No one deserves to be ghosted. Why should I be upset over someone who probably isn't even thinking about me?

'It's crap and hurtful, but don't message him anymore, not even to give him a piece of your mind. You look the bigger person if your last communication is you looking out for his welfare. Sod him; the swine doesn't deserve you, Kitty.' There is grit in her words.

'Thanks, Soph, you always give the best advice. I'll let you get back to, erm, your big Santa.' I laugh, her joke now finally hitting me. 'Look forward to seeing you, and I have plenty of gin and snacks in.'

'Love you, Kit. Have a brilliant Christmas and try to forget about Gary the moron.'

'You have a fantastic one as well. Love you.'

I hang up the phone, take three deep breaths and return to my messages. I need a distraction from Ghosty Gary, so I spend most of the night messaging men on Soul Mates. It's hard getting into it feeling wounded and with some of my trust having dissolved like snow in the winter sun.

There are a few messages from *FirefighterPhil*, who I chatted briefly with before putting my eggs in the Gary basket, so to speak. We message back and forth, him talking about work and moving into his new home. I'm not set on fire by his banter, but he seems nice and mature. We pencil in a date in between Christmas and New Year. I figure I could always cancel, but I have to move on from Ghosty Gary, since it appears I have little choice in the situation.

Another few guys are messaging back and forth, one of which is called 'DuncanDoesLaw'. He has me laughing at almost every message, and although he isn't the most gorgeous of men I've spotted on Soul Mates, maybe that's what I need. Gary's attractiveness never really helped me digest the portion of insecurity I was served every time we met.

'StevenSUFC' has also caught my eye despite the football reference. Steven works as a paramedic and volunteers at the local food bank, which gives him two ticks in my checklist. I decide I'll keep chatting with both and see how it goes. I still have another month or so on my three-month subscription to Soul Mates, so I may as well make the most of it. I can't let the Gary situation tarnish everything—he simply isn't worth it. Well, that's what I have to keep telling myself.

I plan on some housework, last-minute wrapping and eating excessively whilst watching two of my favourite Christmas movies, *Love Actually* and *The Holiday*. I'm still smarting from Gary's rejection, and thoughts of him keep creeping into my head. Being Christmas Eve doesn't help my rejection levels, and stuffing my unwanted face and watching movies solo just adds to my self-pity.

My Christmas Eve plans were normally with Liam, after a walk at the local country park. Christmas Eve was really our day, as Christmas Day was a mixture of seeing families, me usually driving. We always enjoyed the peace and isolation of Christmas Eve. Sadness crawls up my throat as the pang of nostalgia suffocates. Even after all these months and knowing it was the right thing, I still miss Liam, partly for the good times and history but also partly for the intense and uncomfortable solitude I keep feeling. Liam and I haven't communicated, except for a text wishing him a happy birthday and him one back wishing my auntie a happy birthday a month ago. The texts didn't make me want to reconcile with Liam, but they made me want to fall in love again.

Lying on the sofa, ready to watch the second film, I scroll on Soul Mates and reply to a few messages. I know other people find this time of year hard too. Single or not, there always seems to be someone missing from the celebrations, from the present list or seat at the table. I often think of people alone, especially the elderly, and it hurts my heart.

Chapter 35

Thoughts of Gary soon dissolved over Christmas as I continued to not hear from him. After a wonderful Christmas Day with my family, I now have Jane round to keep me company. Or me keep her company. It's a mutual thing.

'I'm going for drinks with him, Kit,' Jane says as she puts her hands to her cheeks. 'I think he's a good 'un, you know, I really do.' Her eyes sparkle with the glimmer of excitement, and I can almost feel the happiness of potential breathing out of her.

'I think he's a keeper too, hun. There's something really natural about him, nothing seems put on and, well, he seems to be bloody normal and decent. Clearly a rarity these days,' I say, feeling hopeful for my best friend. I clutch a cushion to my chest and rest my chin on the top of it. I'm also hopeful for myself. All this luck around me must surely rub off on me at some point.

'He's as boring as counting envelopes by the standard of men you've interacted with,' she snorts, 'but I don't want any drama or to have to pretend I've shit myself.'

We both burst out laughing.

'Well, fingers crossed, or bum cheeks crossed, as I say,' I reply, and we howl again.

'That doesn't even make sense, you daft bugger.'

We talk some more about the plans for her date with Dominic, and Jane continues to glow with enthusiasm. It's a big deal for Jane, and Dominic seems so nice. I have high hopes for them.

'He might have a friend?' Jane mentions.

'Yeah, not at the moment. I don't want man-bus syndrome of none, then loads at once appearing,' I joke.

'What you like? I'm just pleased you're okay about Gary. He doesn't deserve you, Kit, and you can't have someone making you feel like that,' she reassures me as she takes a sip of her prosecco.

'You're right, and I appreciate your advice and support. You've been my spine these last few months. I'll never forget it, Jane.' I cuddle her, feeling emotional—a combination of the time of year, drink and the constant feeling alone.

'I'll always have your back, Kit. Always.'

The rest of our night is spent eating snacks, drinking prosecco and me showing Jane some of the people on Soul Mates.

'Bloody hell, look at that Google Image imposter.' Jane laughs and points to the screen.

I raise my eyebrows, joining in with her laughter. 'Oh, there are loads of those. Fake veterans, actors, models and doctors. It's very entertaining. They're always called Frank, as well.'

'It's a mad realm, this internet dating, isn't it? Imagine trying to explain it to your grandad. It would be a hoot.' Jane purses her lips at the thought of the hypothetical scenario.

'Yeah, he'd go mad and think I was going to get murdered. Which, to be fair, I could. But I think I'm sensible and would never go to anyone's home or even drink alcohol on the first date, especially not with anyone called

Frank,' I say, placing my hand on my forehead dramatically.

'Some of the stories Sophie's told me about one of her mates who internet dated the same time as her. She used to just let randoms come to her house or go to their homes, no consideration of safety.' I shake my head. 'She was lucky not to be raped or attacked. So silly and irresponsible. Granted, we shouldn't have to always think the worst of people and women are sick of being frightened. Men need to be educated and punished properly if they offend. But I wouldn't even let a random woman in my house, never mind a man,' I state, realising I'm going into teacher rant mode.

'You're spot on, hun. You have to be careful. Everyone does.'

It's soon time for Jane to go home, and I lock the house up and crawl into bed immediately after she leaves. I'm looking forward to the next few days, where I'll be back at the gym, doing some Christmas sale shopping and meeting up with Phil.

Time always seems to go so quick when on annual leave and drag so much when at work, but it's soon the day of the date with Phil. We've agreed to meet at a stylish bar in Jesmond, where the décor is quirky and the space is large enough to always have plenty of tables free. It's cold, so I've opted for my vintage leopard print wool coat that I'll take off once inside, with a chunky knit teal jumper and my black Levi's. I've added some knee-high boots for a little bit of effort and my favourite Bobbi Brown lipstick for a flash of colour against my pale, winter skin.

Parking up, I'm early. After checking my makeup, I venture into the bar in the hope of seats near the fire being free. I'm in luck, and I quickly shuffle over towards two armchairs with a little table between them, close to the wood-burning fire. There's still that Christmas vibe in the air, and the place looks cosy, rich in colours and scents. Phil approaches as I'm taking my coat off, looking very much like the imagined fireman and definitely handsome. I stand up to greet him. He towers above me as he leans in to peck my cheek.

'Hey, lovely to meet you,' he says, smiling quickly.

'Yeah, and you, Phil,' I reply.

'What d'you want to drink?' he asks, looking over to the bar. Off to a good start. At least I don't have to worry about paying for everything, like my date with a certain someone.

'Cup of tea, if you don't mind, please. A pot would be even better.' I rub my cold hands together.

Phil nods, then walks towards the bar. I can't help but admire his backside. He soon returns with his pint, followed a minute later by waiting staff with a tray of tea for me.

'You like your cuppas, don't you? I remember you putting about it in your profile.'

'Yeah, I'm a bit addicted. Tea is one of my favourite things.' I slide the tray towards myself.

'Hhhmm.' He flashes another quick grin. 'So, how come you're on Soul Mates? What's the craic? Cheat on your ex?' He winks.

I try not to visibly recoil as his words sound like a joke but don't hit like one. I look at Phil, hoping for the hint of a jokey smirk, but his face is deadpan serious.

'Erm, no. I split with my long-term partner. No cheating involved. Well, at least none from me. I've been dating since; nothing serious. What about you?' I'm already judging as I stir the tea I've just poured into my mug, unable to work out if he's trying to see if he can bed me easily or trying to rule me out if I have potential to cheat.

'How many you slept with from the site? It's like sex on tap if you want it, isn't it?' he asks, looking curiously at me without the weird flash of smile.

'Erm, I'm not really into that. I'm after a relationship. But yeah, I suppose it's definitely widely available if you are after that.' I shrug. I take a sip of tea, hoping the conversation will progress to feel less like an interview.

'Yeah, you say that, but women can't make up their thick minds at times.'

I twitch, wondering if I heard Phil right. I open my mouth to ask him to repeat it, but he starts talking again, raising his voice slightly, face expressionless.

'They say they want relationships, that there's no decent men out there, then when they do meet one, they end it or say they just want to be friends. You lot are worse than men.' He tuts and shakes his head.

'You know, sometimes I think women are called whores and sluts for a reason, because many of them are exactly that.' He sneers. 'Prick teases.' There's malice in his tone and quite possibly a spit onto the floor by his feet.

Bloody hell, I'm on a date with some insane misogynist. After picking my jaw up from the floor, where I'm certain his phlegm of disgust in the female species lies, I seize the opportunity to get a word in.

'I think you're being a bit harsh. Not all women want to sleep around, just like not all men do. I guess people, both men and women, go on sites like Soul Mates for all kinds of reasons. Maybe you've just met the wrong ones?' I already know Phil is the problem and not any woman on Soul Mates, but I want to at least try to make him understand and get off the one-way thought train.

'Why you on there anyway, then? How come you're single?' I ask, as if I don't know he's single because he's a creep who clearly hates women. I'll give him a chance to explain what he clearly needs to see a therapist about. I bloody know how to pick these freaks to date. Exasperated, I take a gulp of tea before waiting for what, no doubt, is more hate against women.

'I want love. I want a wife. I want a woman who is a real woman.' He says 'real' like he's gargling honey, which immediately makes me feel nauseous. I hope my animated face doesn't display the disgust I feel about the lump of lady-hating human sitting opposite me.

'No dirty sluts who just want attention from every man going,' he continues. 'You know them? Are you one of them?' His eyes bore into me as I look back, dumbfounded. 'I want someone genuine, devoted to me and who doesn't lie.' Phil looks to the ceiling and holds his hands up. Crikey, I'm not sure what he's going to do—pray for divine intervention to cleanse all the 'whores and sluts' he's convinced are walking around him?

'Why in God's name you lot cannot tell the bastard truth, I will never know. Leading men on. Claiming love.' Phil screws up his face. Christ, his eyes haven't blinked throughout this performance. I'm starting to think Phil's going to set me on fire with his women-need-to-burn-in-hell eyes, and he certainly won't be putting me out.

'Erm, well, I think you're very much generalising on your own bad experiences. You said in your messages you were in a long-term relationship but grew apart?' I enquire, not really sure what to say. I'm getting the sense Phil is the human version of a volcano—volatile and likely to erupt.

'Yeah, we grew apart cos she cheated and was sneaking around.' So, that's where the cheating question came from. 'I forgave her, but she just wanted to live the single life, you know, be out with her mates, gym and that.' Phil stares at the burning fire near our seats. 'I couldn't trust her. I wanted to spend all my time with her, I wasn't bothered about mates, and she should have put me first. But nah, she just wanted people in our lives all the time, interfering. She couldn't just fucking let it be us.'

I notice Phil's fists are clenched. This is too much. He's going to combust, never mind being a firefighter. He sounds distinctively controlling and coercive, and I'm uncomfortable in his presence.

'Excuse me, I'm just popping to the ladies.' I slope off, expecting a comment that they shouldn't be referred to as the 'ladies', but instead the 'whores' or the 'sluts' or something else derogatory.

I let out a massive, deflated breath once in the toilets. Shaking my head and wondering how I keep attracting these freaks, I ring Sadie, pacing the tiled floor as I wait for her to answer.

'Sade, I'm on a date with a maniac who hates women and sounds controlling and abusive,' I say the second she answers, giving her no time to even say hello. 'He doesn't blink and is going on intense, derogatory rants about women and his ex.' I lean forwards, one hand on the sink as I look in the mirror at my own expressionless face.

She gasps. 'Bugger me, Kit, get out of there. He sounds unhinged and dangerous. Are you okay? You're in public, aren't you?'

'Yeah, I am, but I need to get away. Call me back in ten minutes, will you, and I can say I need to leave?' I bite my lip impatiently, already assuming she'll agree.

'Kit, that's the oldest trick in the book. Psycho Norman will see straight through it,' she says, half laughing. 'Just say off you fuck to him or say you've cacked yourself like you did to that other guy.'

'Not helpful, Sadie.' I giggle, but it doesn't reach my eyes. At least they're blinking though, unlike Phil's. 'I don't even think claims I've dropped my bowels in my underwear will put this one off the need to dissect the female psychology. Just ring me, please,' I try again.

'No more dates without me vetting them, Kit. I mean it.'

I nod even though she can't see me. In this moment, I'd agree to anything just to get home and away from Phil.

'I'll ring you in ten, but have the poo line ready as back-up.'

I hang up and return to woman-hating Phil, expecting him to have filled the table with ripped-up photos of his ex and there to be a voodoo doll sitting in my seat. I try to avoid talking about women as I pray the next ten minutes go by without incident. I ask about his work, which brings him out of his rants and allows his eyes to blink. For a split second, he shows a bit of the banter I've seen in his messages, although clearly nowhere near enough to redeem himself.

'Hey, I have a wedding to attend on Valentine's Day; do you want to be my plus one?' he enquires. 'My mate has managed to snare one of the few women who isn't a slut,' he snarls, laughing.

Crap. I nervously smile and wonder what to say to such an insane request. But I don't have time to reply, as Sadie calls. I've never answered the phone with such enthusiasm before. As I fake a conversation with her, all I can hear is Sadie making the noise of *Jaws* coming towards his victims. I quicken my fake dialogue.

'So sorry, Phil, I have to go. My friend's locked out of her house, and I have a spare key. Erm, nice to meet you, take care.' I scoop up my coat and scurry out of the bar. Walking past the window, towards the car park, I see Phil's eyes following me. His mouth is formed in a sneer and there is no blinking in his eyes.

'Bloody lucky escape.' I shut and lock the car door behind me and start the engine with the intent of blocking Phil, aka Psycho Norman, as soon as I get home.

Chapter 36

'Crikey, you know how to pick 'em, Kit.' Jane shakes her head in amazement at the latest update on my disastrous dating life.

'I know, I'm a complete madness magnet,' I say back, giggling. 'I'm doomed.'

'No more communication from Gary, then?'

'No, not a squeak. Sod him,' I reply, trying to not sound bothered as we get ready for a New Year's Eve night in town.

'He doesn't deserve you, hun. Let's get on the flirt tonight.'

'Well, I will, but maybe not you, seeing as though you'll be on date two with Dominic next week.'

Jane bites her lip. I know how much she likes Dominic and feel she's possibly holding back from talking about him for my sake.

'You really like him, don't you?'

Her happy face is all the confirmation I need. 'Yeah, I think I actually do, Kit. But we'll see. I've... we've both been here before, and it went tits up. I'm trying to keep grounded.' There's apprehension in her eyes, and I know she's frightened to believe that she could be happy, that she won't be hurt and that Dominic, and the chance of love, is worth the risk.

I take her hand, squeezing it gently. 'I get it, Jane, I do. But don't be too grounded—your roots will stop you moving forward.'

There's a second of silence as emotion wells in her eyes, a vulnerability we all have despite age, gender and experience. The risk of heartbreak.

Jane leans in and hugs me quickly before pulling away and looking at me with a grin. 'Is that another of your bloody quotes from Instagram?'

'Bugger off. C'mon, the Uber will be here in five.'

We finish off our prosecco and touch up our lipstick before tottering down the stairs in our heels.

It's a freezing night, but for some reason close to stupidity, we both have knee-length dresses on and strappy heels. Jane looks stunning in a gold, sequin dress, and I have a black bodycon on, which thankfully holds in my sweet mince pie and sticky toffee pudding babies that are now attached to my midriff.

The next six hours fly by with lots of dancing and singing, too much prosecco and a few cheeky pecks on the cheek as the clock strikes twelve and the new year starts. I always feel a little emotional as the new year turns. It's full of promise and hope, which the world needs after a few turbulent years. But it always feels technically like another year of missed loved ones who have passed, and as the years go on, a reminder of my fading youth.

It's soon 2 a.m. and way past our bedtimes. We've been sensible and pre-ordered our Uber, so we leave the club we're in and head to a nearby takeaway for cheesy chips. Tumbling into the takeaway, we giggle as we browse the menu, which is always pointless, as we settle on cheesy chips with the only variation being mayonnaise or tomato ketchup every time.

There's a small group of men inside who look over due to our high-pitched laughter. Jane and I glance back at them, one seeming familiar. It can't be from Soul Mates though, as he's not my type. So, where do I know him from? We turn back and order cheesy chips. After collecting our food, we sit at a nearby table. The familiar guy from the group is still watching. Not being able to place men is happening more often from viewing hundreds of profiles on Soul Mates a week. All men's faces are blurring into a melting pot of masculine visions. I turn away, but each time I look opposite to Jane, I can see him out of the corner of my eye.

The man gets up and comes over. I slouch in my seat, as if he won't be able to see me anymore.

'Kitty?'

'Erm, yeah,' I reply, a bit sheepish.

'K-30?'

Oh bugger. I know who he is now.

'It's me, Duncan. Erm, "DuncanDoesLaw".'

Jane bursts out laughing, looks at me, then Duncan and then back to me. 'Sorry, it's just the name. Sounds like you "do" law, you know, as in have sex with law.'

I snigger, and Duncan stares at Jane without laughter or a smile.

'Jeez, serious much? Happy New miserable Year to you as well, law shagger.' Jane seems completely amused by herself as she stuffs chips into her mouth.

'Sorry, she's only messing,' I begin.

'Am not,' pipes a little voice next to me without looking up from her plate of carb delight.

'Hi, Duncan. Erm, how you doing? Happy New Year,' I say politely. I'm secretly aghast that the man who I thought wasn't a ten out of ten on the looks scale but seemed to have some level of handsomeness and charm actually looks like a garden gnome, is about the same height as one but has a worse beard.

'I'm good, very good. I knew it was you. You look just like your photos. Stunning,' he says, eyes glaring at me.

Jane's eyes leave her chips to focus on me. She twists her face, which has smears of tomato sauce painted across.

I manage an awkward laugh, offering Duncan a chip to try and fill the awkward silence whilst I engage my head in a pleasant response, as opposed to what I'm actually thinking. What I want to tell him is that the feeling isn't mutual, and I almost do, given I've been guzzling prosecco all night and I know no amount of beer goggles will make this little garden hopper appealing to me. So, I say the only thing I can think of.

'Thanks.'

'So, maybe we can arrange that date, then?' says *Snow White*'s sidekick, still looking at me with excited anticipation.

Jane gives an insulting 'pfftt' as she focuses on getting the corner blob of tomato sauce spread across the remainder of her chips.

'Erm, we have to go, Dosey, I mean, Duncan. Uber waiting. Have a great night.' I drag Jane from her seat and make sure I keep my chips upright. I don't look back once we get outside.

'Who the hell was that?' Jane asks, eyes and hands still on her chips. 'You need to raise your game, hun. He can't even take a joke.'

She's still sniggering about the encounter thirty minutes later when she gets dropped off at her front door after telling the Uber driver about a law-shagging fairy tale character.

***

I wake up to a tongue that feels the size and hardness of a brick. I grapple for the bottle of water next to my bed and drink almost all of it in one go. Making an exaggerated sigh, I put the bottle back and flop my head back down onto the comfort of my teddy bear fleece pillowcase.

'Happy New Year,' I say sarcastically, feeling a little sorry for myself. Picking up my mobile, there are multiple messages from friends and family wishing me all the best for the year ahead. 'Sod off,' I say to my phone, returning it to the bedside cabinet. I roll over and go back to sleep.

Two hours later, I wake again due to a very full bladder. I stagger to the toilet, sit, have the longest wee in history and realise I have two choices: to continue to pity myself and be ungrateful of all the other great things in my life or just get on with life and if a relationship happens, it bloody well happens. I could tolerate a little more of the 'you're *still* single?' bullshit and the pitiful 'when will you settle down?' I could even probably stomach some of the 'you aren't getting any younger, mind, Kitty, think of that biological clock ticking' insensitivity. Or I could just avoid being around idiots as much as possible.

I crawl back into bed and decide I will do what I do every year, perhaps with more thought, dedication and insight. I will write my goals for the year.

It takes over an hour and I have to go back to them four times to make sure they're right, but they are here, forever, in my i-notes.

New Year Goals
1. *Save money—goal £3,000.*

2. *Exercise three times a week minimum.*

3. *Read 20 books.*

4. *Buy less fast fashion and buy more second-hand clothes, but only when I actually need something!*

5. *Eat more veg.*

6. *Put up with no crap.*

7. *Fall in love.*

8. *Plan my lessons better and be more creative.*

9. *Spend more time with family, especially Narna once born.*

10. *Learn a new hobby.*

11. *Travel somewhere new, in or out of UK.*

12. *Batch cook more.*

13. *Believe in myself more.*

14. *Stop eating chocolate every day.*

15. *Pay random people more compliments (filter people. Do not wish to look like a creep or give a creep the wrong idea).*

16. *Get more sleep.*

17. *Prepare packed lunch night before work.*

18. *Get a rescue cat.*

19. *Decorate bedroom.*

20. *Wear sunscreen daily.*

I smile to myself as I put my phone on charge and get out of bed. Even writing the list made me feel a surge of motivation. I have a month left of Soul Mates, and I won't be renewing my subscription. If I haven't met anyone by then, it isn't for me and it wasn't meant to be. Satisfied with my efforts, I jump in the shower, desperate to wash the smell of stale alcohol and garlic mayonnaise out of my skin and hair.

Chapter 37

It's soon the beginning of term again and time to return to Richardson High. The kids are usually full of energy coming back and the teachers just full of beer, chocolate and Pringles, making us sluggish and fully embracing the January blues. I, on the other hand, have my goals to focus on, and it feels like a fresh start.

I've still been going on Soul Mates and have actually arranged a date for tomorrow with 'TIMidUntilI-KnowYou' (Tim), who isn't exactly timid but has secured a date with me after a very entertaining chat about late 1990's childhood TV programmes. Duncan sent me a message after our unplanned meet in the takeaway. He was very sweet, paying me compliments. I thanked him and diplomatically told him that I wasn't feeling any chemistry. I'm done with wasting my time, and I don't want to waste anyone else's.

Despite seeing Sadie a few days ago, she still instigates a scene like something out of *Long Lost Family* when she spots me across the car park. As she screeches my name in her sing-song voice, students and teachers are immediately alerted of my arrival. I'm certain if it weren't for the fact she's five foot nothing, she would pick me up and swing me round. Instead, she settles on a show-stopping entrance and greeting. Instead of scooping me up, she pulls me in for a famous booby cuddle.

'Hi, Sade,' I say, eventually pulling away.

'Well, hello, my little Kitty-kins. Here we are, back at the devil's arsehole for another term with the little non-conforming twats, and the students as well.' She winks.

'Absolutely, and you'll still get the best results in the region,' I reply as we link arms and start walking into the school.

It's a long day getting back into the swing of work. Being a teacher, school holidays are great, but I always get into my natural rhythm of relaxation and routine after two weeks off, which means the return to the work regime can be brutal at times. Saying that, I can't complain. I have friends who have never had more than two weeks off work in decades of employment. But I've felt this feeling so many times, and I know I'll ease into things in the coming days.

Tim and I have arranged to meet at a new bar in Tynemouth, which hopefully will be quiet enough to chat but not too quiet to make it obvious we're on a first date. It's a bitter cold January, and Tynemouth is at the coast, so it's always a few degrees colder.

I pick out skinny jeans, a mint green mohair jumper and black boots. I add jewellery and a sparkly belt for a bit of glamour, along with a jewelled clutch bag. I can't resist putting my new black teddy bear jacket on over the top. I grab a hot water bottle for the car until the heating in my, now classed as vintage, old car warms up, and I set off.

I still have those first-date flutters of nerves, but they're distinctly less than when I began dating. Maybe it's confidence in myself, or maybe it's something about my expectations dropping. I haven't exactly been very successful so far. I shake my head. It isn't in my nature to be pessimistic, and I remember my goals. I can achieve them, I just have to find out how, and tonight with Tim could be a chance.

I soon arrive and go into the new bar—Oscar's. It's an airy, stylish venue with plenty of seats. I take a seat and patiently wait for Tim whilst scrolling through social media.

'Kitty?'

I look up from my phone to Tim stood right in front of me. With sparkling blue eyes, he has length to his hair that gives a little wave to it and the odd spattering of grey mixed within the dark reddish brown. He has a little stubble that adds character to his face. I'm guessing he's probably a little older than the thirty-nine in his profile. I could be wrong though. I'll be annoyed if he has lied, but I'm still attracted to him irrelevant, nonetheless.

'Hi, sorry I'm a little late,' Tim says politely, offering me his hand to shake, then realising it's too formal, he leans over and kisses my cheek. 'What would you like to drink?'

'Erm, a tea, please,' I reply, smiling.

I'm happy and intrigued when Tim goes to the bar and comes back empty-handed, opting for a cappuccino himself, which is brought over later by a waiter with my tea. I wonder if he has a no drinking rule like me, wants to keep in tune with my drink of choice or he would have picked it anyway. As we get chatting, he asks about my job, my family and interests. He's attentive, engaged and complimentary.

'So, I've just been talking about myself. What about you?' I say, conscious I don't want our chat to be one way.

Tim talks about his job as a mechanic and that he has an eighteen-year-old son who's just started university in

Leeds. 'So now my boy is about a two-and-a-half-hour drive from me and my wife.'

'Eh, sorry, did you say wife?' I ask, almost spitting my tea across the table.

'Yeah...' Tim looks into the steam coming from his cappuccino and sighs. 'I guess I haven't been completely transparent, Kitty.'

You're not bloody kidding.

'You see, my wife, Carmel, and I... well, we're in a bit of a rut, shall we say.' Tim gives me his best sincere look, with focused eyes and slightly tilted head.

'What do you mean, in a rut? Are you separated?' I snap, hoping this is the answer. It better be the answer.

'No, no, Kit, we aren't separated. I very much love my wife.' Tim shuffles in his seat a little, turning his body to completely face me.

'Then, what the bloody hell are you doing here on a date with me, Tim?' I enquire, louder than I should have. Or maybe I should have enquired even louder. I've been talking to a married man who I met on a dating site. And now I'm on a date with said married man. No, I should have enquired louder.

A man at a nearby table glances up from his newspaper and beer.

'Please, Kit, let me explain. I want to be honest,' Tim says confidently.

'Okay, okay. I'll listen,' I say, shaking my head. I mean, yes, I will listen. But that's where it will end.

'I love my wife, Kit.'

'You've already said that,' I interrupt with increasing anger and disgust.

'Okay. Well, the thing is, we are stuck, bored, at a crossroads, you could say. We want to start experimenting.' He raises an eyebrow, eyes boring into me expectantly.

I look back at him with the type of disappointment you express from winning one pound eighty-eight on the EuroMillions.

'We want to inject passion and excitement into our relationship,' he continues, after it becomes apparent I don't know what to say. 'Try new things after two decades together. So, I joined the site, and Carmel and I looked together,' he explains nonchalantly, like he's explaining how to plug a laptop in.

'Eh? You've been messaging women as a pair, pretending to be just you? Pretending to be single?' My hand tightens around my mug, the heat pushing through, into my hand.

'Kind of, yes. We both think you're beautiful, Kit. We would love to get to know you,' he propositions, smirking confidently.

'I don't bloody think so, Tim. Surely there are other sites for that type of, well, that type of weird stuff.' I put my mug on the table, afraid of smashing it. I feel disappointed and used. Deflated.

'Please, Kitty, consider it. Our next date could be at my house. Carmel is a stunning woman,' Tim replies, trying to convince me like you would convince a child to eat all their dinner before pudding.

'I'm not into women, Tim, and I'm even less into weird threesomes with stale couples,' I announce, getting up from my seat and putting my coat on. 'I would suggest you maybe being honest from the start next time and change your profile name. There is bugger all TIMID about your intentions, Tim,' I state as I storm off.

Rushing to my car, I can't quite believe what just happened. What the hell is wrong with people? Is this the new wave of marriage counselling?

'Prick.' I get into my car and start the engine. The only good thing about tonight is that my hot water bottle that's been sitting on the passenger seat is still warm.

Chapter 38

I haven't been on Soul Mates for over two days, needing some respite from the madness and disappointment. One more 'Fancy hooking up?', 'Would love to get a hold of you!' or 'Hey, Sexy' is going to send me over the edge and put me off men permanently. I'm having a short break before one last attempt in the last ten or so days of my subscription to find anyone half decent, non-psychopathic or not a complete and utter pervert. Until then, it's the end of the first working week of term and time for food shopping. I've eaten my body weight in nuts, chocolate, crisps and cake all Christmas, so I'm determined to buy plenty of healthy food and start focusing on one of my goals: eat more vegetables. I've been thinking of new recipe ideas all week, along with old favourites, that I can batch cook from scratch and freeze. I have my shopping list ready as I pull up at the supermarket and gather my bags for life.

Going inside, I begin with my list, which is written in chronological order of where the items are in the aisles. I'm equally as impressed by my memory as I am in thinking I'm a bit of a loser. The first aisle is filled with fruit and vegetables, so I pile them into the trolley. It's really cold, so I don't fancy salad; instead, I pick up eight packs of tomatoes to make batches of tomato and basil soup in the soup maker I received from my aunt and uncle for Christmas. I'm really excited to use it.

Is this what being in your thirties is about?

'Hey, I think you dropped this?' says a voice behind me.

I turn around, snapped out of my thought-zone, to see the guy who I'm pretty sure commented on my Christmas jumper as he left the shop and I went in a few weeks ago. At least, I think it's him from the small glance I got. Standing closer to him, I realise he's also the guy whose calves I rammed my trolley into a few months ago. Jeez, he must think I'm some scatty clutz.

I smile and take my shopping list out of his hand. 'Ah, thanks.'

'Bit old-school, a list on paper, isn't it?' he says playfully.

I look down at the list, then back up to his eyeline, rubbing my lip as I feel my cheeks heating up. 'Well, yeah, I guess it is. But my iPhone couldn't register the face recognition last year and the year before due to wearing masks, so I had to keep putting my PIN code in every minute. I went back to the traditional way of making notes.'

'You know what, that makes perfect sense.' A warm smile spreads across his kind face. So, my list does make sense, not just to me.

'Well, enjoy getting all those items and'—he looks in my trolley at the mass of red—'erm, enjoy your tomatoes.' He walks off with a nod of the head.

'Thanks, and it's for soup,' I say after him, feeling the need to explain.

'Bet it'll be delicious,' I just about hear him say as he continues with his shop.

I stand for a second, next to the broccoli and cabbage, and panic that my hair may have looked like a frizzy, burst mattress from the winter air or that my mascara has smudged. Shopping List Man is cute, and I have a feeling he may have been flirting. It's nerve-wracking having my usual, very insular and personal experience of shopping delved into by a stranger. I'm a bit self-conscious, but there's also a little dance of energy in my stomach. No, he probably wasn't flirting; he was probably just being polite. I'm buying only for myself when he probably has a family he's buying for and eating with. I hang back a little, embarrassed in case I see him in the next aisle. Yet something in me wants to see that warm smile again.

Chapter 39

This morning, I caught up with Jane at the gym. I told her about Threesome Tim, and she updated me on her last date with Dominic and their date tonight. In fact, she's probably on it right now. She lit up as she talked about him, and it not only made my heart smile for my friend in that moment, but it's also given me hope. Jane has never rushed or panicked about love; instead, she's been patient and placed boundaries, and it's paid off. Love has come to her. I know everything will be okay, for Jane and for me.

And that's why I'm now logging back into Soul Mates. There are a variety of inbox messages including an apology but please reconsider from Tim.

'Unreal.' I delete and block him.

There's a string of the usual inappropriate and unappealing messages and a few that are worth replying to, including some attractive men. However, I've realised from harsh experience that probably only a third, if that, of folk on here actually look like their profile photo, and many of their photos are from ten years ago, with the extra fabrication of adding ten inches to their height. Well, maybe I'm exaggerating.

I have just over a week left of my subscription to Soul Mates. The messages of discount codes, new sign-up procedures and incentives have started to arrive. I have no intention of continuing—it's all too stressful. Although Sophie and many others have found perfect luck and love on internet dating, I'm not sure an extra three years will help me, never mind three months.

The weekend is soon over, and I'm preparing for the work week ahead. I place containers of batch-cooked tomato and basil soup and vegetable curry carefully in the freezer, along with some homemade pitta breads.

I've been messaging two men on Soul Mates over the last twenty-four hours. One guy, 'Fred-wardScissorHands', is a barber and lives in the next town. The other, 'Sean85Rugby', coaches the local rugby team. Both seem interesting and have good banter. Sean is less of my type, with his dirty-blonde hair and clean shave, but he's still very handsome, so I'm giving the communication a chance. Fred looks a bit of a hipster, with his bouffant of thick, dark hair and styled beard. I chat to them both for the rest of the night, on and off, before an early night ready for the Monday morning rush at Richardson High.

The week brings a mixture of work, exercise and tea at Sadie's, along with some Soul Mates messaging.

At the staff meeting Monday morning, Mr Dryden announced that the student teacher training placements will start two weeks before the February half term and will continue until Easter term. It means we'll have eight student teachers arriving in the next month. We haven't had placements for over eighteen months due to the pandemic, so it feels nice to support the university again. Student teacher placements can be the best thing ever or feel like you're constantly standing barefoot in dog shit, and nothing in between. Whilst I've only supervised four students before for sociology, Sadie's had almost double figure students. Half of hers have been super lazy, clueless and she's had to 'wipe their arses', as she so eloquently put it. Or they've assisted at a high standard, therefore making teaching for the actual teacher much easier. Mine have all been great, have brought fresh ideas and eased my workload.

Mr Dryden gave us a twenty-five-minute lecture on the students' arrival, what we need to do to prepare and the responsibility. What he and the Board of Governors will expect from us as well as the university's obligations and requirements. We all feel out of the game, so time to prepare is essential, and an action plan will be designed and delegated over the next week.

I'll worry about preparing for the arrival of the student teachers nearer the time. For now, I've got a date with Sean tonight to focus on. I'm thinking about what to wear this evening, during a Sadie-free lunch break. I click on the app and notice he's messaged.

Sean85Rugby: Hey Kitty, so sorry, will have to give tonight a miss. I've been asked to step in to train the under 12s as the coach is poorly. How about Saturday afternoon? 4pm? x

I sigh, but understand these things happen.

Hi, no bother, that's fine. Yeah, Saturday would be good. Same place? X

Sean85Rugby: Thanks gorgeous. Yes, and I may even treat you to a pizza in the place next door to the bar – it's awesome . Speak soon x

I decide not to message back, but the 'gorgeous' comment and thought of pizza melt away the slight disappointment I have from the cancelled date.

There's also a message from Fred telling me a joke someone shared at the barbers' this morning. I chuckle to myself as I reply.

Me: Brilliant! What you up to at the weekend? X

Fred-wardScissorHands: Maybe taking this pretty girl out if she's free. She's called Kitty. Do you know her? x

Me: Yeah, I think I do. She's amazing x

Fred-wardScissorHands: I already know that! Is she free Saturday, about 2pm? Maybe for a walk and hot chocolate down the coast? X

Even though it's going to be cold, it will be nice to do something other than go to a bar or café; however, I'll be cutting it fine to meet Sean.

Me: Can you make 1pm and we've got a deal? X

Fred-wardScissorHands: Yup! I finish work at 12, so should make it fine. Will look forward to meeting such an exceptional woman xx

Wow, I'm not sure I've ever been called exceptional.

I return to the classroom, full from my couscous and beetroot salad, and a little full of myself.

Chapter 40

It's Friday again and a busy day at work after Mr Dryden shared the action plan in preparation for the student teacher training placements. It includes all marking and lesson plans up to date, which they technically should be anyway, but we all know some colleagues are lazy and unorganised. Weekly health and safety checks will continue, but all staff have to familiarise themselves with the paperwork again. Mr Dryden will be sitting in on each subject lesson over the next few weeks for any guidance needed and to assess the interaction with students. A spot check on assignment marking and lesson plans will happen as well.

'It feels like we're expecting the bloody queen,' says Kim, one of our colleagues. 'Don't see why we should be made to feel like we're getting inspected. We've enough of that with Ofsted, for crying out loud.'

We nod. It does feel a little like we're doing something wrong.

The day passes with some teachers moaning and twisting about the student placement prep and feeling scrutinised.

'It'll make the lazy arses up their game,' Sadie says at lunchtime as we share some pick and mix sweets she's brought in.

'So, two dates tomorrow, then. Perhaps one of them will get lucky?' She raises her eyebrows.

'*Sadie*, pack it in. I'm certainly not going to be jumping into bed with anyone cos the subscription of Soul Mates is ending. I'm totally cool about it, and what will be will be.'

'Yeah, but you might fall madly in love with these two foxes tomorrow and have another dilemma of who to choose,' Sadie says, clapping her hands.

I roll my eyes. 'Doubtful, but I like your enthusiasm.'

The afternoon is soon over. The kids are bursting to be out of the door for the freedom of the weekend, as are us teachers.

'Have a nice weekend, love. Update me tomorrow on your dating conveyor belt,' Sadie says as we part in the car park.

'Will do. Say hi to Stu from me.'

I have a quiet night ahead of me and have decided to have a long bath with a book, glass of wine and face mask. But first, my food shopping. Parking up and grabbing my bags, I click a trolley out and go into the shop. There are different fruits and vegetables on offer each week. This week, there's pineapple amongst the offerings. I love pineapple, but it gives me blisters on my tongue, mainly as I eat the majority of the whole thing in one sitting. I put one in my trolley, telling myself I will learn the art of moderation this year. Maybe I'll add it to my list.

I'm soon at the middle aisle, looking at all the random items. Many are super useful—drain unblockers, bubble-gum-scented disinfectants, noticeboards. Then there are the slightly bespoke items—sewing patches, animal cooling towels, glue guns, ski goggles. Lastly, the utterly random—hotdog toasters, inflatable ottomans and dancing alarm clocks. I mooch in the stationery that's mixed up with children's jigsaws.

'Getting something for the kids?'

I look up. It's Shopping List Man from last week, also known as Trolley Calves Ram Victim Man. He looks smart, wearing a light blue shirt and dark tie. A similar outfit to last week. I wonder if he also comes shopping straight from work.

I clear my throat and try not to smile. 'Erm, no. I, I don't have children. I just like stationery for work and that,' I reply, trying to be blasé but conscious I probably sound like a complete idiot.

'I like a bit of stationery myself, although not with space hoppers and giraffes on.' He chuckles, searching through the pile of notepads and lever arch files. 'Ooh, there's a less obscure pattern here. Look, diagonal stripes. Although it's a bit too feminine for my liking.'

'Maybe you could get it for your wife or partner?'

For the love of God, what did I just say? Too many bloody cheesy chat-up conversations on Soul Mates. Now I sound like a nosey, desperate, sleazy barmaid.

'Nope, none of those either.' He looks in the next basket of randomness, soon pulling something out. 'Think I'll just settle on some drill bits.'

I do a nervous giggle, wondering if I'll have to find another supermarket to frequent after hitting on Shopping List Man. I grab a notebook with illuminous giraffes on, plonk it in my trolley, smile through cringey, gritted teeth and begin trying to attempt to gracefully slope away.

'Well, nice chatting. Erm, have a good shop.' I push my trolley away, hoping I'm not the colour of the many packets of tomatoes I yet again have in my trolley.

'Thanks. You have a good one too,' he replies.

Feeling more cringey than watching a hall full of middle-aged dads doing disco dancing, I continue my shopping quickly and take sanctuary in one of the checkout queues. After paying for my shopping—that no matter how much or little I get, always seems to come in just under forty pounds—I walk to the exit, passing the other checkouts. Shopping List Man is waiting to be served. He waves and smiles, and I wave back.

I burst out laughing to myself as I put my bags in the boot. Regardless of my education and profession, I can be so useless and awkward in so many situations, living up to my fuckwit nickname from Sadie. I sit in my car for five minutes, playing over what just happened. As I put my seatbelt on, ready to start the engine, Shopping List Man approaches a white Audi diagonal to me. He sees me again and smiles. I smile back. It feels awkward but exciting. There is something very endearing about him, and it's more than him being good-looking. A genuineness maybe. A silliness maybe. Whatever it is, it makes me smile.

Chapter 41

'Wow, I like your time management,' says Jane as we work out on the ellipticals. She's referring to my planned dates this afternoon—1 p.m. with 'Fred-wardScissorHands' Fred and 4 p.m. with 'Sean85Rugby' Sean.

'Well, I'm up against the Soul Mates dating clock,' I reply. 'Seriously though, I think these two will be my last, regardless of the outcome. Not sure I can tolerate any more offers of dick pics or any more of the mundane and unimaginative "Hi, baby, how's you?" messages.'

Jane starts to laugh. 'Well, it's been, erm, entertaining, if nothing else.'

I'm tempted to tell Jane about Shopping List Man, but it seems far too presumptuous. I'm not the best at reading whether people are being friendly or flirty, and even though he said he doesn't have a wife or partner, he may be dating, gay or celibate. Or even not fancy me in the slightest and was just being a nice, friendly member of the community.

'How's things going with Dominic, then?' I enquire as I take a drink from my water bottle.

'Ah, Kit, he's great. He's so funny and, you know, just a thoroughly nice guy. Which is rare.'

I wipe my forehead with my flannel and let out a sigh. 'Yup, that's definitely rare. Although, to be fair, we women can be awful as well,' I jest.

'Speak for yourself. Honest, Kit, he's lovely. I really like him. But I'm just playing it cool; what will be will be, you know?' Jane shrugs, moving the incline on her machine down.

'Absolutely. Well, he's a lucky guy, and he definitely gets the friend's seal of approval. So far.'

We finish our workout and say our goodbyes. I head home to shower and eat before getting ready for my two dates. It will be puffer coat, hat and glove weather down the coast with Fred, but for my date with Sean, at a bar on a trendy street just outside of Newcastle, I'll take a change of coat and some dry shampoo to volumize my hair, which will no doubt be flattened by my hat. I choose skinny jeans and an animal print top, and I'll top up my makeup for a more evening look before meeting Sean.

I try not to feel hopeful as I get ready, but both Fred and Sean seem such nice guys. I've been here before though and attempt not to be naive, but I also don't want to be one of those women who think all men are arseholes, untrustworthy and out to get me. It feels like drinking a poison and expecting others to die. Even the terrible way Gary behaved, although it hurt at the time, I'm almost over it. I hardly think about him, and I know I'm a decent person and nice girlfriend. In reality, it's his loss. I just wish people could be honest.

I'm parked up, ready to meet Fred outside of a little café on Tynemouth Front Street. We're going to get a takeaway drink and walk along the beautiful coastline. It's stunning at any time of year, and today is no exception despite the bitterly cold mid-January chill.

I start walking to the café and spot him waiting outside. My stomach immediately does a flip at his attractiveness. Potentially better in person. Fred kisses me on the cheek as we greet, and he opens the café door for me. He's so polite to the server as he orders our drinks. It's clear he works with people, and his pleasant disposition is appealing. We take our drinks from the counter once he's paid and they're made, and we begin to walk.

We head in the direction to view the coastline and pass a few more shops.

'How's your morning been?' I ask, knowing he's been at work.

'Great, yeah, thanks. We are always so busy; it's non-stop. It's not great money and it's long shifts, but I love barbering. What about yours?' he asks, looking at me with his beautiful, chocolate-brown eyes.

I inhale, smelling the North Sea air as I update him on my morning, telling him about the gym with Jane, where we talk as much as we work out. He laughs, and I notice his perfect teeth.

We stop for a minute on the footpath, stand side by side, and look out to the coast. It's only ever beach warm for a few weeks of the year, but with the miles of beautiful caramel sand and the endless view of waves that crawl gently onto the shore, it is a sight I love to look at any day of the year. There's something about the coast that calms the soul, and Fred and I both take a deep breath as we silently absorb the beauty of nature.

Fred looks at me, and we smile at each other, then the coast, before continuing our walk. Fred has a more mixed-heritage complexion, and he tells me his late grandparents were Serbian and moved to America in the late 1960s. They had two children, his mother and uncle. Fred's mother moved to the UK in the early 1980s and met his father. His uncle still lives in America, in Brooklyn. He talks to me about traditional Serbian foods. I love the sound of gibanica—a pie of egg and cheese.

'It's making me hungry.'

'You never get hungry in Serbia; they don't let you.' Fred laughs. 'Food is the ultimate hospitality and love,' he says, touching his chest.

We walk for four miles, soaking in the stunning view, chatting non-stop about life, interests, work, past relationships. Fred tells me he's only had one serious relationship, which lasted about eighteen months. He had another long-distance relationship with a girl at uni in London when he was younger, but it fizzled out.

'How do you feel about long-distance relationships?' he asks, tilting his head.

'Erm, I've only really had one, when I was younger. My first boyfriend, Ryan, who was studying down south whilst I was doing my A-Levels. It worked for a while, but we were both young. I guess lots of students do it.'

'Yeah, what about as adults?' Fred persists.

I shrug. 'I suppose partners work away and stuff. I'm not sure it would be for me. I'm a home bird and like my routines. I think at my age, I want more of a settled life, you know?'

'Yeah, totally, although you are still only a bairn, as you Geordies would say.' Fred winks as we continue to walk along the coast.

Fred is interesting and funny, engaging me as we head back along the route we came. The cold North Sea air caresses my face, but the company and conversation keeps me warm inside.

Fred walks me to my car. 'Kitty, it's been a pleasure. I would really like to see you again.' I find his boldness attractive and a pleasant surprise, as I wasn't sure he fancied me.

'Yeah, that would be lovely. Just send me a message, and we can sort something out,' I say quickly, smiling as I press my hands together.

'Brilliant. May I kiss you?' he asks gently, eyebrows raised as he slightly tilts his head.

I immediately feel a little awkward and unsure about kissing on a busy high street in the middle of the day, but I do fancy him, and I'm happy he asked rather than just pouncing.

'Why not, eh?'

Fred leans in and gives me the most tender kiss. Our lips connect with such ease. Kissing him feels like silk, and he tastes of sweet hot chocolate. Pulling away, he looks at me, smiling. Not a smile like the sort where he's got what he wanted, more the sort where he's genuinely happy in this moment.

'Thanks for a wonderful date. Enjoy the rest of your day, pretty Kitty.'

I feel a flutter at 'pretty Kitty'.

'And you, Fred. Thanks.'

I get into my car as Fred walks to his. I sit for a second, biting my lip, feeling a 'wow' moment. The date was great. Fred is handsome, interesting, articulate, polite and kind. And he wants to see me again.

It's 2:45 p.m. I have time to go home and change properly for my date with Sean rather than getting ready in the car. I check the Soul Mates app to see if he's messaged. He has.

Sean85Rugby: So sorry Kit, I'm gonna have to postpone. Speak soon x

So, no excuse or reason for the postponement. I'm a bit annoyed at the short notice from Sean and the fact it's the second time. At the same time, I had such a nice date with Fred that it more than makes up for it. I'm not going to reply to Sean; he can chase me.

For now, I'm happy to go home, get my cosy loungewear on, put the heating on and have a big cup of tea and some biscuits.

Chapter 42

As like most Sundays, I go to see my parents, with the bonus of a feeding. Henry is there, but Sarah is at work. She'll be going on maternity leave within two months and has managed pregnancy well so far. Only the smell of fabric conditioner makes her sick, and that's fading as the pregnancy progresses. Henry's talking about the nursery and plans they have. They're not sure on names, but have a few short-listed, and just like me and Henry, the baby will have no middle name.

'You mean her middle name isn't going to be Narna?' I ask, looking seriously at my brother.

'Bugger off.' He laughs.

My parents are delighted with the prospect of becoming grandparents, as are Sarah's parents. My mam has bought so much already—practical items and cute little babygrows. Our new arrival will be cherished like the precious gift she is.

Fred has been messaging throughout the day. It's his day off work, and he and his housemate have been to the gym. Like Jane and I, they talk as much as work out. We message back and forth. It's nice to have some possible dating potential, given the string of disasters and let-downs Soul Mates has provided me. I was tempted to ask for a refund until I met Fred.

I haven't heard from Sean, and I'm not going to make the first move. He's obviously someone who always prioritises everything above a relationship, and I've already been in that position, for way longer than I should have tolerated. It isn't a good start with him, and it feels like it just isn't meant to be.

I give Fred my mobile number, since my time is ending on the site and it's easier than logging in. I'm confident he isn't going to pester me or send gross photos of his genitals. We arrange a dinner date for Wednesday.

The day of the date soon comes round, and I'm famished as I drive to meet Fred. I like my food and eat quickly, so I need to make sure I behave at the dinner table and don't look like a piglet. I showed Sadie a picture of Fred on Monday. She thinks he's good-looking. She then told me she's planning a holiday in the May half-term with Stu. It will be good for them to get away, although I will miss her. Hopefully, soon, I'll have my own Stu to go away with.

Fred is waiting outside the restaurant and greets me with a hug and kiss. I quite like the fact he waited outside, excited to see me again. He holds the door open for me before stepping inside himself, and we're shown to our seats. We look over the menu, with a few 'oohs' and 'ahhs'. Fred decides on a chicken burger and I choose veggie enchiladas. After ordering our food, we talk about our week so far and favourite boxsets. Fred mentions *The Sopranos*, which he recently watched for 'about the tenth time'.

'There's some programmes that just never get old; they're timeless,' he says, turning his palms up, 'and when you watch them again and again, there's always something new you interpret, something new you spot.'

I smile at him, nodding. 'I feel like that about *Desperate Housewives*. I watched it when it first came out, and I guess I forgot some of it. But when I watched it recently again, it was bloody marvellous,' I say, my eyes widening. 'The storyline, the characters. I was an emotional wreck.' I giggle, leaning forward.

'*Desperate Housewives* is brilliant, and Teri Hatcher is *hot*,' Fred says in a silly voice as he raises his eyebrows.

The food soon comes out of the kitchen, and it's delicious. I take my time savouring my food rather than wolfing it down. Fred is also a foodie, which is an attractive quality to me. It means we'd be able to explore different places to eat together, try out new meals and expand our palates. We talk about cooking and our signature dishes.

'I'll have to cook for you sometime,' Fred clasps his hands on the table.

'That would be lovely.' A little butterfly is fluttering its wings in my stomach.

'Kitty, I do need to tell you something though,' Fred comments, looking at me intensely.

A rumble of dread circulates inside me, scaring the butterfly away.

'Oh yeah, you married or something?' I say jokingly, although I'm not joking at all. Nothing shocks me anymore. And he wouldn't exactly be the first.

'God, no.' He laughs.

If that's his reaction to being married, it can't be worse than that, right?

'I'm leaving Newcastle at Easter for a few years.'

My mouth hangs open for a few seconds. 'Oh, I see,' is all I eventually offer, quietly and looking at my half-empty plate. There's still some hope, right? He didn't say where to. Maybe it's to Durham or Sunderland or...

'It's for a place at the Sassoon Academy in New York.'

Or New York...

'My uncle helped sort it. You see, there's too much competition here, and I can't ever make much money doing barbering.' He pauses, swallows and continues, 'So, the academy will teach me hairdressing as well, and I can get an intern at one of the big hairdressing chains hopefully. It's an opportunity I've wanted for a few years, and I can stay with my uncle in Brooklyn.'

I nod, my brain pretty much scrambled. 'Well, that sounds great, Fred. You'll be brilliant.'

'That's why I was asking about long-distance relationships when we met. I didn't want to assume anything would happen. I want a relationship, but you know sites like Soul Mates.' He rubs his forehead. 'I didn't expect anything serious. This chance of work came up when we were talking, and I guess I wanted to keep talking because I think we could be something special,' Fred explains, clearly anxious about my interpretation.

I take a deep breath and swallow my disappointment. 'Fred, this is amazing. It could be the making of you. These things happen, and you have to snatch opportunities. Don't worry about anything here.'

'So, you don't think you could have a long-distance relationship still?' Fred asks, staring at me with his melted chocolate eyes. Or is it me who melts when I look into them?

I know I'll probably regret what I'm about to say for a while, but I have to be true to myself and what I want. Life is short, and I want to be with someone who's there on my crappiest days and my best days. Plus, I got over Liam and Gary, so I can definitely cope with another broken heart, as much as I don't want to.

'No, I don't think so, Fred. Sorry, it's just not for me,' I say reluctantly.

We leave the restaurant soon after, and Fred walks me to my car again.

'Thanks, Kitty, for being honest and for the two dates. I've had a great time. You're a beautiful woman and a beautiful person, and whoever ends up with you is beyond lucky.' He looks at the ground before looking back at me with a sad smile.

We stand in silence, facing each other. I feel a pang of guilt, wondering if Fred is worth taking a chance on. I swallow and purse my lips. I need someone here with me, and if that means losing a potential good thing with Fred, it's a risk I have to take.

'Good luck, Kitty,' Fred says as he takes my hands.

'And to you, Fred. I hope you meet your Teri Hatcher.'

He sighs, kisses my hands and moves in the opposite direction, holding on to my fingers until they slip out of his grip. He walks backwards a few steps and blows me a kiss, the promise in his eyes now turned off.

I get in the car and watch Fred continue to walk away slowly with his hands in his pockets and head down. My tears begin to fall. I just want to be loved and to love someone. Why is it so hard? Why does everything that seems to have potential soon get flushed down the damn toilet? But the worst question of all... have I made a mistake? I finally have someone who hasn't ghosted, hasn't given me any red flags and would be willing to make things work irrelevant of distance.

Chapter 43

I slept poorly last night, dreaming about being a lonely old woman, eating nothing but biscuits and tinned soup. The feeling of isolation is still haunting me today at work. I closed my account on Soul Mates and deleted the app when I got in from my date with Fred. I also blocked his number. It felt harsh, but it was self-protection. I'm feeling massively vulnerable, and I can't have messages back and forth to draw me in even further. I already have worries that I could have said no to potentially the perfect guy. I can't have him making me regret or question my decision any further.

'Miss Cook,' Sadie bellows down the corridor as the students turn and look. Her crystal jewellery has her sparking.

I smile, but as she gets closer, she sees right through it.

She holds my shoulders and studies my face. 'What the hell is up, my love?'

'Well, it's over with Fred before it even began, Sade.' I sniff back my tears, knowing this is neither the time nor the place.

'Oh, come here, love.' She pulls me in for a cuddle. 'What happened?'

I explain our delicious meal and then the pudding of disappointment I was served as Fred told me his future plans in New York.

'You've done the right thing. You may not see it now, but I'm telling you, you have. You really think your loneliness will go by dating someone overseas who you'll hardly see for a few years? It will do nothing to fill that pit in your heart.' She puts her hand over my heart, and I hold her arm gently. I know her opinion is valid.

'Come for tea this week, love. Stu will make kiddy cakes for you, like chocolate cornflake cakes, and I'll make you my mash.'

I nod slowly, knowing her soul food will help. 'I'm pleased I tried internet dating, even just to know what I don't want,' I say, trying to be upbeat as we walk to our first classes.

'Me too, Kit, and I'm so pleased you know your worth,' she replies, rubbing my arm as we part ways in the corridor.

As the week goes on, I start to feel in a better fettle. Dinner at Sadie's on Thursday helps, as does a Tupperware box of Stu's homemade cornflake cakes to take away. Jane listened to me moan the night before at the gym. She's been a great tonic, and I'm comforted by my decision to just let love come to me rather than searching the internet for it.

My lunch at work today is a banana and three of Stu's cornflake cakes. Sadie has been roped into something for the teacher training students' arrival the week after next, so I'm taking the chance to read some of the latest book by a local author, R. A. Hutchins.

The working day soon ends. I say goodbye to Sadie, who tells me to pop over for a cuppa at the weekend if I'm at a loose end.

I head straight to the supermarket. It isn't until I get my trolley that I think about Shopping List Man. It's been such a strange and emotional week that I haven't even thought about the cringefest from last week. I roll my eyes, hoping he isn't going to be here, but at the same time, kind of hoping he will. List in hand, I get to work.

I soon reach the alcohol aisle and search for a new gin. There's so much choice, and the coloured bottles sparkle like gemstones. My go-to is anything citrus, but I'm going to live a little and try a different flavour. I lean in to read the labels.

'We have to stop meeting like this.'

I bite my lip and turn around slowly. I know that voice.

'I'm good at advising on gin, even if I'm no help when purchasing stationery,' he says, glancing at the shelves and winking.

I give a little laugh, and Shopping List Man's smile beams back at me.

'For the fine lady, I recommend the blackcurrant and raspberry.' He points to one of the many gins on the shelves.

I grip my trolley, feeling ridiculously nervous with him standing so close. 'Hmm, yeah, that does sound nice.' I pick up a bottle and put it in my trolley. Why not? Not like I could decide on a flavour anyway.

His eyes follow to my trolley, then back to me. 'I'm Rob, by the way. You can call me Supermarket Rob, if you want.' He shrugs.

'Hi, Supermarket Rob. I'm Middle-Aisle Kitty.' I decide not to mention that I already refer to him as Shopping List Man.

'Brilliant. Pleasure to meet you officially, Kitty.' Rob chuckles, and his grey-blue eyes smile with his mouth. I notice his laughter lines. He has full lips surrounded by a beard with sprinklings of grey in it. I guess him to be in his mid-thirties.

'You do come here often, I know that, so I can't ask it. But I guess you live local?' he says, raising an eyebrow as he rubs the back of his neck.

'Erm, yeah, just on the Bewick East estate,' I reply, smoothing down my hair.

He nods. 'Ah, I'm just off the main road before that estate, Lawson Road.'

'Oh yeah, I know it, near the pub.'

'Yup, The Windmill, my local,' says Rob, tapping his thigh.

There's a brief, awkward silence, and I start to feel a little self-conscious. I don't want to begin talking rubbish, desperate to retain some level of appeal. I look down the aisle, back to him, and I decide to continue with my shopping in the hope we may bump into each other in another aisle when I've had time to think what to ask.

'Well, it's nice to meet you properly, Rob, and thanks for the gin recommendation.'

'Yeah, nice to meet you too, Kitty. Maybe I'll see you in The Windmill at some point and not just in here.' He turns his palms up, then places his hands on his trolley. 'Have a great night.'

'You too,' I reply, walking off, trying to work out what just happened on the gin aisle.

Chapter 44

After a quiet weekend, it's Monday again and a week until the student teachers are arriving for placement, giving Mr Dryden another week to panic.

'Sod this, I'm bringing my whoopie cushion in next Monday to strategically place for each student across the week,' announces Sadie during the morning briefing, to laughs and looks of disgust in equal measures.

'Meet at lunchtime?' I ask her as the meeting ends and we all rush off to teach first lessons. She nods and blows me a kiss.

I spent much of the weekend thinking about Shopping List Man, who I now know as Rob. Each time I drove out of my estate and past the area he lives, I wondered what house was his and searched for the white Audi he got into at the supermarket a few weeks ago. Then I would give my head a bit of a wobble for overthinking, telling myself he's probably just being friendly. Yet something in me keeps returning to that friendly, handsome face.

I tell Sadie all about it at lunchtime.

'Oh, Kit, I love him already. He sounds lovely and a good giggle. He totally has the hots for you.'

'Whoa, I don't know about that, Sade, maybe he's just a nice guy.' Sadie's right, Rob does seem lovely and he's definitely made me laugh. But for all the dating and internet chatting and flirting, I still don't feel sure I can distinguish where the boundaries lie for friendship, desire and deviance, given my disasters so far. 'I'm scared, Sadie. It's been a rough few months with dating, and I'm not sure I even want to think that way after the disappointment of Gary and then Fred.' Despite my words, I'm thinking about Rob already and planning my outfit for the weekly food shop.

'So, take control, Kit,' she says sternly. 'If he's there Friday, which he will be, ask him for a cuppa. If you've got the wrong idea, which you absolutely haven't by the sounds of it, you can just say you were being friendly and neighbourly, then move on and perhaps shop somewhere else.' She laughs before prodding me. 'Only joking, hun, I can tell he likes you. Who wouldn't?'

I give her a grateful smile. 'I don't know what would be worse, rejection or having to learn the layout of a new supermarket,' I half joke.

Sadie grabs my hand and leans in. 'Love, you've had a hard time the last six months. But you're a strong, tough girl, and you must be brave and take this chance. Else I will be coming to that damn supermarket with you and making a scene.'

'Right, off you fuck, love. Get to your lesson. Mr Dryden will be hovering at the back like bird shit on the window,' she says, jumping up, the bangles around her wrist jangling.

I have no idea how Sadie knew he'd be in my class, but she was right. It goes well though, and afterwards, I reward myself with a Wham bar from my desk drawer. As it battles with my fillings, I think about what I could say to Rob if he's at the supermarket on Friday. Sadie's right, as per usual, about just a casual cuppa, maybe even at the café across the road from the supermarket. Not straight after shopping—I wouldn't want our freezer stuff to defrost—but maybe the Friday after, before the shop? Or would that be creepy then doing our separate food shop after sitting and having a cuppa together? Yeah, it probably would. Although he mightn't even want to go for a cuppa. Crap, he might be one of those weird adults who doesn't drink tea or coffee, or any hot drink. He may just drink pop.

'For crying out loud,' I say to the empty classroom, realising how stupid my snowball of thoughts are. Finishing my Wham bar, I take a deep breath and get my act together for the next lesson.

Rob hasn't been far from my mind the last few days, which feels stupid but somehow right. I'm on my way to the dreaded but exciting food shop, and I'm wearing my new skirt, thick black tights and a black roll-neck jumper. I've decided I'm going to ask if he fancies going for a cuppa, seize the moment and all that, so I have my cute, vintage leopard print coat at the ready in the back of my car.

The last few months have been exhausting, constant logging onto Soul Mates, chatting with men, making an effort and spending time getting ready only to meet some weirdo, perv or liar on most occasions. I'm kind of done with men for a while—it's feeling like a lot of effort for very little.

But Rob seems different. He can't take his face off and reveal a face perfect for the back end of a pantomime horse. He won't turn out to be someone completely different, visually at least. He clearly is single-ish, else he's some kind of weird supermarket-frequenting, trolley-for-one creep. I don't get the woman-hating vibes radiating from him. Rob seems as normal as anyone is, handsome, chatty, funny and, dare I say, interested?

If he agrees to a cuppa with me, maybe we can compare shopping lists? Actually, no, not compare shopping lists, that would make *me* the creep.

If this all goes wrong, there's a supermarket two miles in the opposite direction of my house. I will lay low there for a while and return on a different day of the week to my usual supermarket, hopefully dodging any future encounters.

Today at work was the final day before the teacher training students arrive on Monday. Mr Dryden has stopped flapping, as all is in hand. Everyone can now breathe, eat and sleep the preparation. This also means I've not had time to overthink what I'm going to do once I bump into Rob.

The drive feels much quicker today, whether from excitement or panic, I'm not sure. After re-applying my lipstick in the car, grabbing my bags and getting a trolley, I smooth down my hair and try to act casual as I walk into the supermarket. Given my almost photographic memory created due to familiarity of all the produce, I can have a quick look around for Rob but still get all I need. He was right about the blackcurrant and raspberry gin being delicious. I'll tell him once I find him.

I still haven't spotted Rob by the time I reach the middle aisle, with all my biggest distractions. I can't see him over by the checkouts either. My heart begins to sink a little.

I approach the last aisle of the supermarket, still with hope. I take a deep breath and round the corner, pushing my trolley into the aisle. I can immediately see one guy kneeling to look at something on the bottom shelf. My breath catches in my throat. It's not Rob.

I make my way to the checkouts, shoulders slumped. I pile my items onto the checkout and wait my turn, glancing round as I chew on my thumbnail. If I weren't a regular, I'm certain I would have looked like a shoplifter, given my eyes were going like the clappers to each direction of a compass.

After getting served and paying, I sigh and push my trolley out of the shop, pushing my hope of happiness further away with it.

Chapter 45

I spent much of my time alone over the weekend. I needed time off from the world and from talking about the same rubbish from my head. I drank a few gins, ate pizza and crisps, wore my pjs and watched boxsets. By Sunday night, after visiting my parents for Sunday dinner and some homemade flapjacks, I felt recharged and less pitiful and ready for Monday.

Today sees the arrival of the teacher training students. We sit in assembly, in those uncomfortable plastic chairs, at the side of the room, waiting for Mr Dryden to introduce the newbies to the school and explain to the kids how they'll be part of the school for the next eight weeks. The school hall is constantly freezing. It's like a train station in that it could be the hottest day of the year but it will still chill you to your bones. Sadie's sitting next to me, listening to me complain I'm cold for the tenth time. I tap my feet, trying to stop them getting colder as we wait for the assembly to get going.

Mr Dryden proudly stands on the stage, greeting the school and generally talking bollocks for a few minutes before announcing the students. Sixteen feet come traipsing onto the stage. Each student takes a seat, and I, and everyone else, has a look at the fresh teaching meat. Then, my heart sinks. I strain my eyes and look again, look away and back in case it's some optical illusion. Sadly, it isn't.

'Sade,' I whisper, nudging her.

'Yes, love?' she says back, still facing the stage.

'Sade, it's Gary; he's up there.'

'Ghosty Gary?' she says, eyes finally leaving the stage to look straight at me.

'Yeah,' I say, almost feeling the colour drain from my face, becoming ghosty too but in a different way.

'Well, that little prick can get straight back down and bugger off out of our school,' Sadie grumbles, loud enough for colleagues on the row to hear.

'Shh.' My eyes flit to the left and right, not wanting to draw attention to us. 'Oh crap, I can't believe it. What am I going to do?'

'You're doing nothing, Kit, cos you've done nothing wrong, unlike that pillock.' Sadie crosses her legs and her arms, glaring harshly at Gary.

I try to listen to the rest of the assembly whilst my heart beats in my eardrums. Mr Dryden introduces the students, and Gary smiles at his audience, clearly not spotting the woman he ghosted after so much promise. By the time we leave the hall, my eyes have rolled more times than a slot machine on the Las Vegas strip. Some of us are to greet the students, whilst others have classes. Luckily, I'm going straight to teach. Unluckily for Gary, Sadie is on meet and greet. There's nothing quite as scary as a protective Sadie.

'The Cockwomble won't get away with it, love,' she announces through gritted teeth and flaring nostrils.

I slope off, just wanting to bury the past where it belongs. Bury it deep, with the array of emotions I felt at the time and the current nervousness gnawing at my stomach.

I've managed to avoid Gary for two full days, and now we're on day three. As I'm no longer on Soul Mates and have blocked his mobile number, he has no way to contact me, and I know he wouldn't dream of emailing my work email. I'm certain he knows I'm here though. Sadie hasn't let on that she's my friend, but each student gets a prospectus of the school, which includes the latest Ofsted report, student newsletter and a 'Meet the Team' section with photos and information about each teacher. We also have our mugshots in the staffroom, displayed on the noticeboard for all to see.

'He's up himself, Kit. I can tell,' Sadie says, perched on the edge of one of the tables in my classroom. 'Has that sleazy confidence, like *James Bond*. Womaniser.'

I start laughing. 'Well, he didn't get very far with me, and then *Mission Impossible* became just that, as he aborted the operation.' I walk around the classroom, putting today's lesson plan on each table, ready for the students.

'I'm pleased you can laugh about it, love, but it's not funny. He's a disrespectful swine, and I hope he explains himself.'

'You know, Sade, I don't really care.' I finish up and stand facing her, my hand on my hip. 'I just would rather not bump into him. I know it's him in the wrong, but it's just all something I would rather not have to deal with.'

'About that...' She bites her lip.

'What now?' I sigh.

'You're about to be observed. By two students. One of them being—'

'Gary,' I finish.

Sadie nods. 'Remember, just do your job and ignore him. He doesn't deserve any more attention than what you need to give. If anything, you may get some closure.'

Sadie slides off the table. 'Good luck,' she says, massaging my shoulder gently as she leaves.

Within minutes, there's a knock on my classroom door, and I close my eyes, wanting to be anywhere but here. Gary and his fellow student come in. Gary gives me a quick nod before glancing to the floor as he jingles some change in his pocket. He doesn't look shocked though, just awkward, so it's clear he knew he was walking straight into my classroom.

'Afternoon,' his colleague says with a smile, none the wiser.

I stand up, trying to feel stronger. 'Hello.' I hope I'm coming off as assertively as I'm trying to be and my voice doesn't sound how I feel.

I grab two seats and drag them to the side of the classroom, gesturing for them to sit. They both comply. Gary looks at his feet before engaging in a brief conversation with his colleague and opening his notebook.

Turning away from them, I place my hand on my desk, trying to steady myself. I don't know if it's nerves or anger, but I want the next hour to be over. Luckily, the kids soon pile in, and I go into autopilot, doing what I do best. I wobble a little in voice and posture, but I don't think it's noticeable, and I try to avoid glancing in Gary's direction. When I do, he's making notes, or probably scribbling lies to add to his very own bullshit manual.

At the end of the lesson, the kids get up and leave. Gary's colleague thanks me and exits the room. I wait for Gary to leave with him, not caring about a thank you, just wanting him gone. He stands from his seat, but he remains stood, making no attempt towards the door.

'Kitty, I'm so, so sorry,' Gary says, still struggling to make eye contact.

'Okay,' I reply quickly, not wanting to interact as I start packing away. Hopefully the fact I've acknowledged his apology, even if I've made no attempt to accept it, is enough for him.

'Please, I'm really sorry.' He moves closer to where I'm collecting printouts and pens.

'I said okay, Gary. What more do you want?' I snap, shaking my head. I'm disappointed, hurt, angry and just want him to crawl away like the snake he is.

'To explain? To be friends?' he pleads.

I snort. 'No, not interested in either, thanks.' I stare at him coldly. 'And you're only saying that cos you're here and probably crapping yourself. Just stay out of my way and get on with your placement,' I say calmly and without emotion, leaving the classroom, trying to stand tall as my whole body stiffens. Gary watches me walk away, making no attempt to stop me or come after me. As much as I want to scream and even cry, he isn't going to get anything else from me.

I manage to avoid Gary for the rest of the week. I've asked Sadie not to mention that I know Gary to anyone, as I don't want people knowing my business or making things more awkward. A packet of Maltesers was placed in my pigeonhole in the staffroom Thursday lunchtime and today. It wasn't Sadie, so I know it was Gary, and I remember the conversation we had about favourite chocolate. I ate them; it's not in my nature to be wasteful. But whilst the chocolate melted in my mouth, my cold heart for Gary certainly didn't warm up in the slightest.

Leaving school, I'm relieved it's Friday and I don't have to worry about bumping into Gary for at least a weekend. For the first time today, I think about Rob. At least I can thank Ghosty Gary for the distraction in my current lack-of-love life, ironically. After not seeing Rob last week, my hopes aren't as high as usual today.

I drive to the supermarket and quickly rush inside and out of the winter-chilled air. I glance around to no sign of Rob, so I get on with my shopping. My heart hasn't dropped as much this time. I think I'm getting used to disappointment. Pears are on offer this week. They always remind me of my late grandmother. I pick them up and put them in the trolley, knowing there's probably an eight-hour window through the week to eat them, when they aren't hard and yet to turn to mush. Strolling on, I pick up some veg. I've been making soup and want to try making a chunkier broth with root veg and pulses. I search for a small turnip, already knowing it will be a workout trying to cut it but thinking it will be delicious in my soup.

'Nothing better than turnip on a roast dinner with loads of gravy and mint sauce, is there?'

I grin to myself before turning around. Rob is standing there, smiling.

'Yeah, I agree, although this is for homemade soup.'

'Ah, now you're talking. You'll have to share the recipe.'

'I kinda just make it up as I go along, adding in whatever. But maybe I can keep you a portion,' I reply, shocked by my boldness.

'Sounds an offer I can't refuse. I could've done with it last week. I had the man flu.'

Maybe that's why I didn't see him shopping last week.

'Oh, it would have been perfect medicine. Glad to see you're better now.' I'm struggling not to stare into his eyes, which are cool but have such warmth and depth I can almost see the kind soul I'm certain is inside him.

'Erm, that gin was nice, thanks for the recommendation,' I say, feeling a little flustered.

'My pleasure. I can also recommend some great bake-at-home bread rolls that go lovely with homemade soup.' He winks.

I feel myself blushing. 'Well, perhaps we could have a cuppa at The Windmill sometime, and if you aren't a psycho, I'll treat you to some of my amazing soup after,' I say with as much confidence as I can muster. I'm not even sure how I managed to get the words out of my mouth. Every second he takes to reply, my heart speeds up.

Rob laughs. 'I like your style, and I'm intrigued to know about your psycho benchmark assessments. A cuppa sounds lovely. I might even fancy a shandy.'

I giggle, looking at his handsome face and the light lines that are painted on it when he smiles. I really want to kiss him. Although I've been bold so far today, that would be a boldness beyond my capabilities.

'How about Sunday afternoon?' Rob asks.

I swallow to catch my breath. So, he wasn't just agreeing to it to prevent awkwardness, he's actually planning a meet. 'Yeah, that sounds lovely. Erm, do you want to take my number?'

'I thought you'd never ask.' He keeps his eyes on mine for just those few seconds longer.

I feel myself blush again as I put my number in his phone. He rings me immediately so I have his. Another action to show he's not just all words.

'Okay, well I better get my shopping done, then,' I say, really wanting to hang around and talk with Rob all night, but feeling like a bit of a tool hanging around the turnips and carrots as people try to get in for their veg.

'Yeah, of course, me too. Have a good shop, and I'll look forward to seeing you outside of this place, Kitty.'

He brushes my outer arm gently with his hand as he walks past, and I swear I feel electric. I want to jump up and down on the spot with excitement, but I'm desperate to play it cool. Instead, I give him a head start as I save his number in my phone and send a text to Jane and Sadie telling them I have a date with Rob. Putting my phone back into my coat pocket, I let myself absorb the feeling that maybe, just maybe, this is the start of my romance luck changing.

Chapter 46

'O-M-G, he's so into you. He sounds perfect, Kit,' Jane says after I talk through my meeting with Rob. I'm beaming.

'I hope so. He's so nice, Jane. You know when you just get the vibes from someone?' I say as we move from the exercise bikes over to the ellipticals. 'He seems super genuine and warm, and he's absolutely gorgeous. Tall and strong-looking, with such a handsome, friendly face and a really sexy salt and pepper beard,' I gush before taking a gulp of water and putting my bottle in the machine's drink holder.

'Sounds just your type, hun. I'm keeping everything crossed that your date goes well and we can soon have double dates.' She speeds up on the elliptical, the excitement pushing her on.

Things are going great for Jane and Dominic. It's fantastic seeing her radiate with happiness. Jane's never needed a man to complete her, but Dominic's made her soul shine, and the bounce in her step is adorable.

I've arranged to meet Rob at 3:30 p.m. tomorrow afternoon. We were texting last night for a little, but I want to play it cool. By the time I get back home from the gym, he's sent a photo of a cat who befriended him on his morning jog. It's a cute gesture, especially after

I told him last night about my love of cats. I also really like that he's into his fitness. He said that although he likes a night out with the lads he went to school with, at almost thirty-five years old, he's kind of over going out on drinking binges every weekend. Instead, he enjoys a weekend of exercise, visiting places, seeing family and chilling out. He hasn't asked loads of personal questions about my relationship past, which I find refreshing and endearing after the scrutiny I sometimes faced on Soul Mates and with dates I met.

By the time Sunday afternoon comes, I'm more nervous than I've felt in a long time. I've been to the toilet three times and my stomach is still performing an orchestra. It's less than a ten-minute walk to the pub, so I see no point in driving. I wear small-heeled boots, my leopard print, long coat over skinny jeans and a vintage Guns N' Roses T-shirt from the 1990s. I wrap my black pashmina across my neck, tucking it into my coat to keep extra warm, and put my gloves on. I hope I don't have to dart off to the toilets as soon as I get to the pub. I've put a bit of smoky eye makeup on and lip gloss with a pale pink tinge, which I immediately regret, as my hair blows into my mouth the second I leave the house. My legs feel wobbly as I walk to the pub, and I panic I'll get my kitten heel caught in the pavement, which, of course, has never actually happened to me, but there's always a first.

I arrive at the pub with ten minutes to spare, so I go to the toilets to reapply my lip gloss and calm down a little, which feels silly, since I've seen Rob several times in the supermarket. He's seen the sanitary towels I buy and the kiddie waffles and spaghetti hoops, yet I'm standing by the sink in the ladies toilets of The Windmill, thinking my guts may explode for the fourth time in less than a few hours.

The truth is, I'm scared. Scared to be hurt, frightened I'm not enough, worried of disappointment and petrified of never finding true happiness. I know Sadie would say something along the lines of 'Put your big girl pants on, my little fuckwit, and let him see the real Kitty Cook. If he doesn't like it, he's not for you, but don't you ever change or compromise.'

Sadie must have read my mind, as a message comes through from her.

Love you, my Kit, be your beautiful self.

There's also one from Jane. *Enjoy, hun, have a blast. Love you lots.*

I have the greatest friends, and if nothing happens with Rob, I'll still have the greatest friends and the greatest family.

Rob walks into the pub as I walk out of the toilets. He waves and walks towards me.

'Hi,' he says, leaning in to kiss my cheek.

I fluster and touch my cheek when he pulls away, immediately realising I look like a right idiot. I let out an awkward giggle.

He seems nervous as well, which I find both massively comforting and endearing. He smells of a forest in my dreams—woody, crisp and fresh. I inhale his scent subtly before he stands back.

'You look lovely, Kitty. Shall we get a seat?'

'Yeah, and thanks, so do you,' I reply, my eyes darting away from him.

Rob does look lovely, in dark jeans, a checked flannel shirt and a Levi's Sherpa coat. His style is exactly what I like, and it's strange seeing him in more normal clothes, as at the supermarket, he's always in a shirt and tie. He goes to the bar and orders us pots of tea. We've already established via text that we both love Yorkshire tea. It's already a big check on my list.

I find out that Rob works as a manager at the local council's planning department. He's lived in his house just off the estate for eight months after renting nearby for two years whilst his divorce went through and the former marital home sold. He speaks about his ex-wife with no disrespect.

'I spotted you ages ago in the supermarket, you know. Not that I was spying on you like some weirdo stalker, so don't put this in your psycho assessment,' he says jokingly as we pour our second cup of tea. 'But I saw you, and I saw the cute expressions on your face as you pottered around the shop, in your own little world.'

I definitely will not be putting that on my psycho assessment. If anything, it makes me feel better after the disappointment I was holding at the supermarket the other week when I didn't see Rob. As long as he wouldn't put me on his psycho assessment for that, I think it's fair to say we've equalled each other in that department.

'I saw you before Christmas as you were crossing the road. It was the week after you were looking in the middle aisle at the stationery. I tooted, but you looked into the car like you wanted to rip my insides out.' He chuckles.

'Oh my, I remember that.' I put my hand to my mouth, slightly cringing. 'I thought you were tooting at me for crossing the road and telling me off. I couldn't see you properly in the dark, but I did think you were familiar.'

We both laugh.

'How long you been single, Kitty?'

Although I know I found it appealing that he hadn't asked about my dating history, I knew that the subject would be approached at some point. And after Rob revealing all about his divorce, it's only fair for me to disclose my past. So, I give him the overview of Liam, without going into detail, then the highlights, or should that be the lowlights, of Soul Mates.

'Wow, sounds like a bad film. What a nightmare. I'm sorry on behalf of men everywhere that you met so many maniacs and pervs and that you had to listen to so many lewd suggestions. If it's any consolation, when my ex and I split up, I went on, and I had a load of middle-aged women wanting to, shall we say, soothe more than my broken heart.'

I grimace and my eyes widen, yet I kind of want to know more. I wonder how different my Soul Mates journey would have been if he'd been on there when I was. Maybe we would have discovered each other without the need for any of the other failed dates.

Rob and I get lost in conversation, and we've soon been chatting non-stop for hours. I'm starving, and I'm debating whether to invite Rob back for some homemade soup. I don't want him getting the wrong idea. Homemade soup most definitely isn't code for Sunday night sex. Technically, Rob is still pretty much a stranger, but I can't deny the connection, chemistry and comfort I feel in his company.

'Let me walk you home?' he asks as we get our coats on to leave.

I bite my lip and clear my throat. Rob almost reads my mind.

'Or even just to the end of your street, just to make sure you're safe.'

'Thank you,' I reply, and we walk out of the pub.

As we cross the road and begin the walk to my housing estate, we're side by side. Rob rubs his gloveless hands together and puts them in his coat pockets. I slide my arm into his, linking him. He smiles, and I'm pleased it's a little dark as I blush.

We soon reach the start of my cul-de-sac. I start to panic, not ready for someone to come to my house due to the nerves of unknown expectation. It's been almost six months since I split up with Liam, but no other man has been in my house, except for Dad and Henry, of course. I'm not ready to let anyone know where exactly my sanctuary is. I've been let down by Gary. I've been let down by others. It feels different with Rob, but I want to be sure.

'This is your street?' Rob asks, possibly sensing my nerves.

'Yup, this is me,' I say, unlinking my arm from his. 'Thanks, Rob, for this afternoon. It's been lovely. Maybe I can make soup for you sometime soon?'

'That would be lovely. Whenever you're ready. I'm in no rush, and the tinned stuff is fine for me until then.' He smiles, moving from foot to foot on the spot to keep warm.

He understands, and his response is perfect. I know he's different. I'm almost certain of it.

'Will you be okay walking back?' I check.

'Of course. I will text when I get in.'

Rob leans in and kisses me on the cheek. It's warm and tender, and the forest of dreams still clings to him, just as potent as earlier. He embraces me, his cuddle soothing, his body strong and protective. I never want him to let go.

'Thank you,' I whisper.

'No, thank you, lovely Kitty.' Rob pulls away, but it feels reluctant. 'Now, get yourself home and fed. Speak soon.'

He turns around and heads back towards The Windmill and his home as I walk the hundred metres or so to my front door. I take my coat and shoes off once I step inside, and go straight upstairs. I quickly get my pjs on, scoop my hair into a bun and then go downstairs and pop some soup in the microwave as I try to process the thoughts bouncing around in my head about Rob, wondering if it's all too good to be true.

Chapter 47

I can hardly keep the smile from my face at work as I update Sadie on my date with Rob. Our knees face each other as we drink a cup of tea in the staffroom. Sadie leans forward, her eyes focused on me as she absorbs everything I say about the date.

'Sade, he's just so lovely. There's a real genuineness from him. A warmth.' I beam. 'And he's really funny and asks loads of questions. Wanting to get to know me, but not in a creepy way.'

'He sounds marvellous, Kit, he really does. When will you see him again, outside of you both being supermarket stalkers?'

'Hopefully this week. He asked me to check when I'm free. I just don't want to get carried away; I'm still scared of getting hurt, and you know what happened last time.' I look down at my hands.

Sadie puts her cup on the table in front of us and edges a little closer along the sofa to where I'm sitting. She grabs one of my hands and touches my chin, tilting my head back up. 'Now, come on, you can't keep punishing yourself or any potential bloke because of a crappy experience.'

As if on cue, Gary walks into the staffroom. He looks over and smiles as I look away.

'Talking of crappy experiences. Prick,' Sadie sneers quietly. 'I get you're frightened, love, I really do. But don't let other people's dick-ish behaviour and inadequacies'—she looks over at Gary—'be projected onto others.' She turns back to me, her serious face checking I'm listening and absorbing her message.

I nod. 'I know, you're right. I need to get out of that mindset. I need to stop thinking all will go wrong. Being pessimistic will just drain my enjoyment and sabotage my possible happiness. I'm gonna try and be relaxed about it and not go psycho if he doesn't message back straight away. At least he's not on a damn internet dating site, and I don't know his surname yet, so haven't Facebook-stalked him.' I laugh.

I get up to wash my cup in the sink at the other side of the staffroom. Gary is shuffling about, so I look in the opposite direction. Another student teacher is at the sink, so we have a quick chat before I return to where Sadie is still sitting, applying her lipstick after lunch.

'Cockwomble has just put some chocolate in your pigeonhole,' she announces casually.

I look over and see the familiar red packaging of my favourite chocolate treats. I roll my eyes as I turn back to Sadie, who's shaking her head. I wish he would just leave me alone. I could do without the awkwardness, and my waistline could do without the chocolate, but I hate waste. I grab the Maltesers on my way out to teach, blowing Sadie a kiss after making sure Gary isn't behind her to think it's directed at him.

I update Jane on my weekend, and she updates me on hers as she keeps glancing across the gym to a smiling Dominic, who's lifting weights. He and Jane are a great match, and the more she talks about him, the more I'm certain my friend has met someone special. I'm buzzing for her.

'When we having a double date, then?' she asks.

'Well, let me get to five dates or so outside of the supermarket first, eh?' I laugh.

Despite feeling Rob has potential to reach five dates and beyond, I still want to find out his surname to double check his relationship status on Facebook. I don't think he's lied, but internet dating has proved you can never be too careful. I know a ton of other things about him though, like his favourite food is an all-day breakfast, minus mushrooms, which he's been unable to stomach after finding them growing in his garden last summer. He loves photography and has won an award for photos of the local coastline. I know he has a younger brother and nieces and nephews. He's travelled the world, from the slums of Mumbai to San Francisco. Rob fascinates me with his stories and stimulates me with his conversation, but he also asks about me and is genuinely interested. It felt like so many people I met and chatted to on Soul Mates and so many people in real life want to talk about themselves or direct everything back to them, but Rob *wants* to know about me.

I have to stop trying to burst my own bubble and learn to enjoy the happiness, so once back from the gym, I tell Rob when I'm free this week and ask him if he fancies coming round for some of my famous soup.

Rob: Wednesday sounds brilliant—the soup and the company . I will bring the bread and pudding. Soup is never enough to fill me. Xxx

We continue to text, and Rob sends a silly meme that makes me giggle. I decide now is as good a time as any to do my check and hopefully settle my head.

Me: By the way, are you on Facebook? Xxx

Rob: Yeah, I'm under Robert Albom. xxx
Me: Okay, I will add you, if that's okay? Xxx
Rob: Absolutely. It means I can have a look at your beautiful face whenever I want xxx

I bite my lip as I feel a rush of excitement. Beautiful. I can't believe he thinks I'm beautiful. Please work out, please work out. I open the Facebook app on my phone and search for Rob. His profile pic is his lovely, smiling face, and he looks to be on a boat. He's wearing a shocking Hawaiian shirt, but I can forgive that, as he looks so happy, healthy and handsome. I quickly send a friend request, hoping he'll respond soon so I can spend some time scrolling through his photos and wall posts.

A notification flashes—Rob has accepted my friend request. There are loads of cringey photos on my Facebook page, but all in fun, and I've deleted albums full of photos of Liam. There are no dodgy wall posts, and the people on my Facebook are friends, not strangers.

Notifications keep popping up as Rob likes and comments on my photos. I'm doing the same on his, as he has some fun photos of nights out and travel and some adorable ones with his family and his dog who passed away last year. He also has some of his photography up, and I can see how it won him awards. There are no comments anywhere that feel like red flags, not from Rob or his friends. He seems just as nice and genuine on his social media as he comes across in real life.

'Better than spaghetti hoops or a bowl full of kid's crisps,' Sadie jokes as I tell her that Rob's coming over for dinner today and I'll be making soup.

Every morning, Rob texts, wishing me a great day, then sometimes sends a photo of lunch or a meme early afternoon and then in the evening. He's consistent and engaging—two qualities I admire.

I start laughing with her as Gary walks past.

'Can we talk, please, Kitty?' he asks quietly as he rubs his hands together.

Sadie shoots him a look, then looks at me.

'Please?'

'Erm, okay, I have a free period at two, how about then?' I say as Sadie raises an eyebrow of disbelief.

'Yeah, great, in your classroom?' Gary asks, clearing his throat.

'Yeah.'

'Thanks, see you then.' He turns and hurries away.

'What the frig did you do that for?' Sadie asks, shaking her head.

'He's not going to go away any time soon, Sade.' I shrug. 'And as much as I enjoy Maltesers, I don't want them every day. I just need to tell him to forget it, be the bigger person so we can both try to at least not seem so awkward whilst he's here.'

'Well, I think you should just tell the cockwomble to bugger off.'

I know she's defending and protecting me, but I can't keep avoiding Gary. I'll tell him all is fine, even if deep down I don't forgive him.

Getting to know Rob has been refreshing, and I feel less angry and disappointed with the male part of the world now. He's helped me forget Fred and realise any emotions with Gary were pointless. It's the past, and it all happened, along with the other disastrous dates, to possibly get me to where I am now. I just have to remember that when Gary comes out with whatever bull he's preparing.

And I'm still prepared for that potential bull at 2:05 p.m. when there's a knock on my classroom door.

'Come in,' I shout.

Gary walks in with a bunch of flowers. I can't help but smile despite not wanting to at the beautiful yellow roses.

'For you. An apology, a grovel, a "I'm the biggest idiot on the planet", whatever you want to call it, they are for you,' he mutters, placing the flowers on my desk and leaning against the desk opposite. His nerves seem to have faded slightly at my smile, and I could almost kick myself for dropping the emotionless face so easily.

'Erm, thanks, they're beautiful,' I say, picking them up and looking at their pretty heads.

'I remember you said yellow roses remind you of your gran,' he says, smiling.

I nod, trying to regain some composure and control over my face. 'Yeah, they do, they were one of her favourites. Thanks.'

'Listen, Kitty, I know I screwed up, massively,' he says, moving from foot to foot. 'I know I made mistakes. I was stupid, scared, unsure, of myself, not you.' Gary looks at the floor and runs a hand through his hair. Looking back up at me, he exhales and continues talking, 'Anyway, I screwed up, and I did what us stupid men do—I ran away. I'm sorry. I really regret it.'

I take a deep breath, trying to stay strong. 'So, if you hadn't had your placement here at Richardson High, you would never have bothered apologising?'

'I couldn't get through to your phone, so I assumed you blocked me, and I couldn't find you on Soul Mates.'

It's like a hammer is hitting my head and my heart at the same time. He actually tried to contact me to apologise? How long ago was this? I'm not sure how I feel about this revelation.

'I didn't renew my membership. Funnily enough, I kept meeting disappointments.' There's anger and irritation in my voice.

Gary picks at his thumb. 'Listen, Kit, I was messaging a few girls. I wasn't sure if I just wanted to be single. I... I didn't know. Everything felt a bit fast. But then I kept thinking about you and didn't know how to tell you cos I couldn't get in touch and didn't know where you live.' He's talking really fast and animating with his hands, his eyes now piercing into me instead of the floor.

I can't deny that Gary has a point. And now I can't work out how I feel. I can't work out if I should have not been so hasty with the block button to see what could have happened between me and Gary or if I'm glad I used it so quickly because things seem to be going well with Rob.

'I wanted to get in touch, apologise, ask for another chance. Then, I came here and saw you and vaguely remembered you mentioning Richardson High. Then, well... it felt like fate. Like we were meant to be. I'll beg if I have to. Kitty, please give me another chance? I think... I think I could be falling for you.' Gary keeps his eyes locked on me. Eyes filled with hope and expectation.

If there were a world record for the amount of time spent lost for words, this moment would have smashed it right now. Gary can surely see the pure shock on my face. With the amount of it I feel, I must be showing it. I certainly wasn't expecting a declaration of him falling in love with me. I assumed it would be more around him wanting his student placement to be as least awkward as possible and for us to be amicable.

I look at Gary, his gorgeous face and deep brown eyes, and I smile against all of my will.

'I've missed that beautiful smile. Let me take you for dinner one night this week so we can talk and clear the air. Tomorrow?' he asks, eyes wide with anticipation as he leans forward.

Before I can think about it, I've said yes, and we quickly arrange a time and place before he rushes off to a class. As he shuts the door, I watch him wave through the classroom window, and as I wave back and he walks away, I realise what I've just done.

Time seems to move slowly until the end of the day as I grapple with my mind. I rush out of the classroom the first chance I get at the end of the teaching day to meet Sadie and tell her everything.

'*He's manipulating you,*' Sadie snaps as she grimaces at the flowers in my hand.

Something inside me knows she's right, but something also lingers in the fact perhaps Gary is being honest.

'He couldn't have contacted me though, Sade; I blocked him,' I persist.

'Kit, come on, you're making excuses for him. He blanked you and said his gran was poorly. Have you asked him about that?' She shakes her head at me.

My mouth remains shut for a while, the issue of his gran not having entered my brain. I know Sadie is looking out for me. I blow my cheeks out as she stares intently at me.

'Maybe I just need to chat with him and clear the air if nothing else. I mean, we have to work together for the next month and possibly longer if Dryden takes on any of them as trainees. I don't want an atmosphere, Sadie, it's too stressful.' Of course part of me is finding any reason for Gary to be right, and of course part of me wants to see if he's being honest and we could really make a go of it.

'I'm not having him worm his way back in, Kit. You should be stringing that cockwomble up.' She crosses her arms tightly. 'Be careful, or I will kill him and make him into fat balls for the birds. Seriously, Kit, don't lose something possible with Rob for the sake of someone who may mess you around again. Trust your gut.'

What is my gut telling me?

We head off home for the day, but as I drive, a wave of sickness comes over me. Rob's meant to be coming for dinner tonight. There's no way I can concentrate on getting to know him more and catering for him, despite it only being soup, after what Gary's declared.

'*Shit.*'

I know I need to get things finalised with Gary, to clear the air or whatever else it may be. At this point, I can't process possibilities. I don't want to ruin things with Rob, but I have to tie this up.

I click my indicator on and pull over to the side of the road. I quickly send Rob a text.

Hi, you, so sorry, can we postpone tonight? Had an awful day at work and my head's stotting. I need an early night. Xxx

I put my phone back in my handbag and pull off. The sinking feeling of doubt is in my stomach all the way home. Rob has already text back by the time I step into my house, so understanding, which makes me feel even worse.

Hi beautiful, no worries at all. I hope you're okay. If you need anything, let me know. Take care and hopefully catch up soon xxx

I feel awful for lying, for possibly messing him around and for the emotional tug of war going on in my head. I turn my phone off. I need some peace and quiet to clear my mind, to think about this logically, think about what I want and think about my responses to Gary's possible disclosures and excuses tomorrow night. In the meantime, not communicating with Rob feels the kindest thing to do. It will only be for twenty-four hours or so.

I spend the next few hours going over things in my head and making a list of pros and cons about Gary and Rob.

Gary	Rob
Pros	**Pros**
Gorgeous	Gorgeous
Fun	Romantic (so far)
Great chemistry/amazing kisser	Great banter
Common career	Attentive
Open with feelings	Lives local
Cons	**Cons**
Possible liar	May not have chemistry (not yet kissed)
Could ghost me again	May not be a good thing living local

I look over my list. Gary and Rob are really different in many ways. Whilst Rob appears more mature and attentive, Gary was super attentive those first few weeks. I haven't kissed Rob properly yet and don't know if we're compatible in that area. What if it all goes wrong and I keep bumping into him in the local area? But there's also that with Gary at Richardson High right now, possibly further on if he gets a job there. What if Gary is still on Soul Mates? What if he's just full of bull to make his placement easy, then he'll ghost me again?

I glance over at the yellow roses from him, which I've placed in a vase that used to belong to my late grandmother. I smile. There's a charm about Gary, a natural energy and charisma. And it could potentially get me into trouble.

I put my list on the shelf on my coffee table, pour myself a glass of wine and run a bath. I'll try and relax and ring Jane in the morning for some advice. I'm going to go for dinner with Gary, there's no harm in that, and right now, Rob and I haven't discussed what this is between us, let alone if we're even dating.

So, why do I feel so bad?

Chapter 48

Ever the diplomat, Jane told me this morning to 'listen to your gut instinct'. Right now, my gut's telling me I'm likely to be running to the toilet most of the day.

I hear the familiar 'Kitty-kins' shouted across the car park as I get out of my car. Sadie's frantically flapping like she's waving me off on the *Titanic*.

'Morning, love,' I say, greeting her.

'Still going out with cockwomble tonight?' she asks, raising an eyebrow.

'I have to, Sade.' I frown. 'I need to get this sorted in my head. It's not fair on anyone if not.' I run my hands through my hair.

Sadie nods. 'Well, I think he doesn't deserve it, but I understand, and I'll always have your back.' She pulls me in for a side hug, which automatically makes me feel better.

The day drags, and I struggle to concentrate. I've already ignored the morning message from Rob, who thoughtfully asked how I am and if my headache has gone. At lunchtime, I ignore the meme of a cat doing the moonwalk to Michael Jackson music, even though it makes me laugh and I want to tell him that. I can't engage in a conversation; it just feels too much to compute. Gary's left the daily bag of Maltesers with a white label stuck to the front. *I can't wait to see you later xxx.* I smile, then tell myself off for smiling.

After what seems like the longest day in time, I leave work after ironically not seeing Gary all day around campus. Driving home, the niggles of doubt resurface, and my stomach gurgles. As I rush to get ready, I check my phone. No more texts from Rob, which feels both good and disappointing.

For God's sake, Kitty, they can't win with you. I hold my hands to my head. What the hell am I doing, and what the hell am I going to do? Things are complicated, and I'm worried they're going to get a lot more complicated.

I finally finish getting ready and drive to Tynemouth. I park and walk to the tapas restaurant where Gary and I arranged to meet. He's waiting in the foyer and moves in to kiss me. I instinctively back off a little, to his shock, frowning. Does he think me agreeing to meet means he can put the lips on me immediately?

'I'm sorry, Kit, I didn't think.' He steps back from me.

A member of waiting staff comes over and saves the awkwardness. 'Table for two?' he asks in a jolly fashion.

I nod as Gary thanks him, and we follow him to a cosy corner booth.

Gary orders us soft drinks, and I wish I'd left the car so I could have had at least one or two for courage. Then again, I can't afford any lapse in control against Gary's charms.

'You look beautiful, Kitty. You always do. I struggle to keep my eyes off you when I see you at work.' Gary rubs his hands together nervously.

I push straight to the point, not caring for any more conversation about my appearance. 'Why did you have to ruin it all, Gary? We were getting on great. *You*'—I jab the table with my index finger—'well, frankly, *you* screwed it all up, and it hurt.' I try to control my emotions. Damn, I'm definitely glad now that I haven't ordered anything alcoholic.

'I know, Kit, I absolutely know, and I've regretted it every single day since. Then when I started placement and kept seeing you...' He shakes his head. 'Well, shit, it just made me see even more. You're everything. You're beautiful, clever, everyone loves you. I...' He puts his hand to his mouth and glances at the table before raising his head and staring at me. 'I think I'm in love with you, Kitty. I've made a mistake, and I've regretted it every day since. Please, let me have another chance.' Gary reaches over the table for my hand.

'Lemonade?' A chirpy voice interrupts.

Gary nods.

'And yours must be the blackcurrant and soda?' he says, smiling at me and placing our drinks down.

'Thanks,' I say as I exhale slowly. My mouth is dry, and I take a big gulp of my drink.

'Ready to order?' he asks enthusiastically.

'Erm, not yet. Five more minutes, please, mate?' Gary replies, tapping the table.

'Not a problem,' says Chirpy, turning around and almost skipping away.

'I need the toilet. Can you please just order me the veggie special?' I say quietly, desperate for some space.

I get up and head to the toilets. I enter a cubicle and lean my hot head against the white wall. There's a decent-sized window in here that I'm pretty sure I could fit through and escape out of. Gary has confessed his love to me, for the second time, and I feel sick. Sick that my feelings are battling in my head and heart, sick with fear of missing an opportunity but also of making a wrong move, sick of how there's a third person to consider here.

I shake my head and sigh. I've spent ages trying to find someone, and now I'm at a man crossroad, not knowing which path to take.

I leave the bathroom and return to the booth where Gary's sat, looking gorgeous, which isn't helping the situation.

'Your mate at work threatened me today,' he says flatly.

I laugh and look at him, my laughter soon drifting off at the sight of his unamused face.

'Sadie? What did she say?' I try to sound concerned, knowing it will be something scary but bound to tickle me.

'She told me that if I so much as hurt a hair on your head, she will find my address, kidnap me, pull all my fingernails and toenails off, chop me up and feed me to the seagulls.'

I try to hold back a snort.

'Kitty, it's not funny. She's totally warped.'

'She's not warped, Gary. She was the one who soothed me and looked out for me when you ghosted me. You were a dick, and she picked up the pieces. So, actually, her threat of torture is more than warranted,' I say assertively.

Gary says nothing and looks down at the table. Our order arrives, and although I have little appetite, I start eating.

'The way I see it, Kitty, you have two options. You can forgive me for the mistakes I know I made and I'm massively sorry for or you don't and we ignore each other for the rest of my placement. And you break my heart.' He looks up from his plate, his eyes burning into me.

I frown. 'Hang on a minute, Gary. I'm not having the emotional blackmail of breaking your heart. You didn't give a damn when you stopped answering my texts and said your gran was poorly. I mean, was she even really poorly, or was that a distraction whilst you "decided what you want"?' I ask, unable to keep the rage from my voice. I briskly put my fork down, realising a good portion of my food now has stab wounds in.

'Yes, she was poorly actually,' Gary says sulkily as he tucks into some patatas bravas.

'Listen, Kitty, I'm trying to be honest with you. I know I wasn't, but I want to be now. I wasn't sure what I wanted, it was overwhelming and we hadn't talked about being exclusive.'

I give him a 'don't you dare' look.

'I wasn't sleeping with other women, I was just dating them, and I wasn't sure if I even wanted that,' Gary says, shrugging as he turns his palms up. 'It's a bit mad, all that internet dating stuff. I'm sure you were talking to a few men at a time.' He wrinkles his nose and momentarily looks the other way.

I make a 'hmmphhh' noise. 'Gary, talking to and dating multiple people is different. We weren't exclusive, no. But maybe you should have thought about your approach and your emotional investment.' I stop for a second and swallow the emotion in my throat, unsure if it tastes more like anger or upset. 'The attention you were giving me, and God knows how many women, see how that could be interpreted as someone interested. You indicated we had a future, then poof, you were gone like a fart in the bloody wind.'

Saying sorry and understanding his behaviour seem two separate things to Gary. He stirs his food around his plate, not making eye contact with me.

'It seems to me you develop emotions quickly. You're professing your love for me now, but you probably say that as often as you say hello. Tell me, Gary, is all this just to make your placement easier?'

He looks up, then back down at his food. No words come from his mouth, and he's clearly wounded. I don't want to hurt him, despite him hurting me, but I'm determined to say what's on my mind and for him to realise the impact his crappy behaviour had on me.

'You can't do that to people, Gary. It's disrespectful, and you'll always come off worse for hurting people. It's karma.' I pick my fork back up and continue eating. Getting everything I needed to say out seems to have drained most of my anger away. That doesn't mean it can't come back though.

'Well, I know that now, don't I? That's why I'm here, *trying* to explain. But it sounds like you're having none of it.' His eyes plead with me. I melt a little and look away, not wanting to show I care.

'You're a dick, Gary,' I say, half-smiling.

He laughs. 'Your mate thinks so as well.'

We eat in silence for a minute. Not awkward, more reflective. He moves his hand across the table and touches mine.

'I mean what I said. I want to try again, Kitty. Properly, officially, exclusively. Whatever and however you want. I want to try. Please think about it.'

For all the uncertainty I felt when he stopped replying to my text messages, something about his voice and face makes me believe that he absolutely means it. With everything needed to be said out of the way, we manage to talk about work as well as our past as we finish our meal. It feels more relaxed with Gary now, and I let a little of my guard down.

After leaving the restaurant, Gary walks me to my car.

'Do you think I could at least have a cuddle?'

I give a half-hearted embrace, nervous in case my heart tries to dominate my head. He touches my face, trying to gauge whether it's a green light to kiss me. I pull away and see the disappointment in his eyes.

'I have a lot to think about, Gary.' I put my hands in my pockets, stepping closer to my car. 'I've moved on, in lots of ways. I need time.'

'Is there someone else?' He puts his hands in his pockets too, mirroring my body language. 'I don't want to ask, but I feel like I have to.'

'Perhaps.'

'I'll fight for you, Kitty. I won't just give up.'

'No "my balls are bigger than your balls" rubbish, Gary. We aren't in high school, even if we do teach at one.' I open my car door and get inside, pulling my seatbelt on and starting my engine, then rolling the window down. 'Goodnight, Gary,' I say as I start to drive away.

'Goodnight, Kitty. I'll look forward to seeing you tomorrow.'

Chapter 49

I'm exhausted from a terrible night's sleep after my evening with Gary. It's 5:30 a.m., and I can't get back to sleep despite my eyes struggling to stay open. I need to text Rob, especially considering I'll probably see him at the supermarket later today. It will look dodgy if I don't go. The situation is already way too complicated.

Hi, Rob, so sorry for crap communication. I still felt poorly yesterday but better now. How are you? Good week? Xxx

He texts back just after 6:30 a.m.

Rob: Morning, pretty lady, I thought I must have been given the boot . Pleased to hear I haven't and that you're feeling better. I'm good thanks and yeah, a canny week. You got much planned for the weekend? xxx

Me: No, no booting here . Going to the theatre with my friend Jane tomorrow and then family Sunday, nothing much else, well, except for the food shopping haha! What about you? Xxx

Rob: Sounds great, especially the food shopping. Highlight of the week! I hope to see you there maybe we can go around together . Doing Park Run in the morning, then catching up with the lads. Let me know when you're up for a meet up, would be lovely to see you in and outside the supermarket xxx

I sigh. I don't want to look off, and I still feel the same about Rob. I really fancy him and want to get to know him better. I don't want to risk sabotaging anything even though my head is scrambled. I feel like I have to see him again and then make my decision.

Me: How about tonight, after you put your shopping away? Xxx

Rob: Sounds perfect xxx

I get out of bed and have a long shower. I'll need to apply more makeup than a clown this morning to not look like I was on a bender all night. How come my face is getting old and I'm still dealing with college romance dilemmas?

I've already decided I'll avoid Gary at work. Luckily, Friday is one of my busiest teaching days, and I'll go to Sadie's classroom for lunch to avoid the staffroom, although it will mean I'll miss my Malteser collection.

I'll see Rob tonight and then I'll make a decision on what to do. I know Rob is the safe, trustworthy, reliable bet, but something about Gary keeps niggling at me. I don't agree with Gary's actions over Christmas and I'm not sure I can forget them either, but something feels unresolved, and something about his declaration of feelings towards me lingers with a host of what-ifs.

'You should just have one of those flasher macs and a plastic nose on,' Sadie mocks after I tell her I want to avoid Gary.

'Like a deviant *Inspector Gadget*?' I laugh, picking at my sandwich in Sadie's seat as she leans against her desk.

'Just tell him to shite off, love. Get rid.' She's clearly not deviating from 'Team Rob'.

I puff my cheeks with stress and confusion.

'Ah, love, sorry. I know your brain is feeling used and abused. I just can't see you being hurt. What about Rob?

I feel invested in him.' Sadie tilts her head and gives me a gooey eyed look, like she has seen a homeless puppy.

'I'm seeing him tonight, then I'll know. I'll know what I want and what I need to do, and I'll have to make a choice before my brain gets further molested.'

'Oooooh, Matron, molest my brain,' she squeals, leaning over to where I'm sitting and rubbing her hands all over my hair as her bangles play a tune.

I burst out laughing as she turns my hair into a tatty cow pat with her tiny hands.

'I'm going to do a wee right here, right now if I continue,' she says, crossing her legs. 'Seriously, Kit, your plan sounds like a good idea. I'm always here for you, you know that. And I'll always support you, whatever you decide. You're my little fuckwit, and I just want you to be happy.' She rubs my forearm and squeezes my hand before taking a crisp from the bag that lies open next to my sandwich.

I feel emotional, partly because I've only had four hours of sleep and partly as I just want things to be easy. It will be okay though in the long run; at least, I hope so anyway. I just have to get adulting, decide and get on with.

I drive to the supermarket, my nerves on edge. I managed to dodge Gary all day. At one point, I heard him shouting my name from one end of the corridor, so I discreetly scooted off and went into the ladies toilets for fifteen minutes. The coast was clear when I eventually left. I still have Gary blocked on my mobile. I'm not going to unblock him until I make a decision and only if my decision is him.

The weekly shop now feels so different knowing Rob likes me. I constantly worry I have a spot or fuzzy hair or that I look like Mrs Twit under the harsh supermarket lighting. On top of nerves about having to make a decision, I also have to acknowledge, of course, that Rob may not want to see me again after another date or a kiss. Having two men after me is making my ego overinflated, and it's way more than I can handle.

Rob is coming down the second aisle by the time I enter the supermarket. His smile immediately makes my temperature rise. His beard is slightly longer than last time I saw him, with a little more grey peppered amongst the very dark brown. He's so handsome in a rugged way.

'Well, hello there,' he says, the words almost a melody.

'Hi.' I smile awkwardly.

He comes round the corner, back into the first aisle, and leans in to kiss my cheek. I blush but enjoy the warmth of his lips against my skin. We stand for a second, just looking at each other. It feels, for a moment, like it's just us in the busy supermarket. Our moment, surrounded by fruit and veg, no other human in the place as our eyes and smiles connect. There really is something special about Rob, a depth that I'm yet to reach, but something in his eyes that feels like a comforting, secure blanket.

'Well, I need to get my shopping in for a handsome date coming round. I'm afraid the famous soup has long gone, so I'm hoping pizza and wine will suffice?'

'Perfect, pizza is my second favourite food after—'

'All-day breakfast,' I interrupt, smiling more naturally now. 'Seven okay for you? The house number is sixty-eight, by the way.' Just giving the number of my house out feels so surreal as it leaves my lips. There's a level of trust with Rob that I haven't found easily since Liam.

'Perfect. Well, I'll let you get on, but don't worry if you see me checking out your bum as you're doing your shopping.' Rob gives me a cheeky wink.

I giggle like a thirteen-year-old, the words somehow not feeling seedy coming from Rob.

I say goodbye and get on with my shopping, my head spinning again. It's a quick shop, as I want to get home and pour myself some wine and get showered and changed before Rob comes over.

At seven on the dot, Rob's on my doorstep, a bottle of wine and a cheesecake in hand. He comes in and takes his shoes—without me asking—and coat off. He's wearing jeans and a striped Ralph Lauren T-shirt. He looks great in a T-shirt, with muscular arms and broad shoulders. He kisses my cheek and waits in the hallway for me to tell him where to go. His aftershave is the same fresh and woody scent from the pub.

'Come through, make yourself at home,' I say, nervously gesturing him into the lounge. Instead of going straight in, he follows me into the kitchen. He's holding his bottle of wine and cheesecake for dear life, and it's obvious Rob is as nervous as me. Despite my many recent dates, I'm self-conscious and desperate to impress. Maybe it's because Rob is here, in my home, my sanctuary. Maybe it's because of Gary. Maybe it's because I like Rob. I don't know, but I do know what will help: wine.

'Thanks for these,' I say, taking his shield of wine and cheesecake from him.

'My pleasure. Thanks for the invite.'

I pour us both a glass of wine, deeply concentrating on not spilling it, and we go into the living room, where I have music playing via Alexa.

Sitting at opposite ends of my sofa, the nerves are erupting inside me despite the head start on the wine. We begin to talk about our day at work. As he talks, I nod and study his attractive face. The nerves aren't calming, so I take a large gulp of my wine.

'Thirsty?' Rob asks playfully. 'You look beautiful, by the way,' he adds as his body position mirrors mine.

'Erm, thanks, and you too. I guess more handsome than beautiful. Although men can be beautiful, can't they? Don't you think? I can't think of an example of a famous beautiful man, but I will.' I stop for breath, and Rob lets out a strange, bewildered laugh.

Oh, shut up, Kitty.

'I'll just check on the food,' I say, getting up before I say something else silly.

'I'll help,' Rob says, standing from the sofa.

'Honestly, there's no—'

Rob's lips are on mine before I can finish the sentence, his hand holding mine, pulling me close, against him. His kisses are gentle, and I'm struggling to keep myself up on weak knees. His lips are full and taste of wine and mint. It's a kiss of gentle longing, and my lips dance with his in a beautiful waltz. It's a kiss like no other I've experienced before, as if we're made for one another. I always thought I had chemistry with Liam, I thought I had chemistry with Gary, but neither of those sent sparks through me like this kiss right now. I absolutely know who I want to be with.

I reluctantly pull away, not wanting the pizzas to burn. Rob follows me to the kitchen, despite the start of a protest before the kiss, and fills our wines up before helping me with plates and cutlery. It's attractive that he wants to help. Pizzas cut and served, we return to the lounge and eat as we chat. The conversation is as engaging as it was at The Windmill. I can't stop thinking about kissing him again, and I wolf my pizza down so I can go and brush my teeth, ready for snog number two, three, four...

'I'm just popping to the toilet,' I say, putting my empty plate on the coffee table.

I head upstairs, phone out, already texting Sadie. I want to brush the herbs and pizza out of my teeth for an amuse-bouche of kissing.

It's him, Rob, I've made my decision! Xxxx

I send the same text to Jane. They both reply whilst I'm brushing my teeth, with congratulations, heart emojis and words of encouragement.

I reapply my lipstick, hoping it will soon be smudged all over, and giggle to myself, confident things are going to work out. I'll worry about what to say to Gary on Monday later, but there's no going back, and it's all absolutely concrete in my mind.

I rush back downstairs to Rob and freeze on the bottom step, hand clenching the banister. 'Erm, what's up? Where you going?' I slowly take the last step, brows creased.

'Look, Kitty, I really like you, but I don't know what's going on.' Rob's face is expressionless as he pulls his coat over his shoulders. His shoes are already on.

'What do you...'

He steps to one side silently, the list of pros and cons about Rob and Gary on view on the living room table. 'I found this when I was grabbing a tissue from under your table.'

I squeeze my eyes shut, foaming at myself for being so careless. I wonder if this whole situation will go away if I squeeze them shut tight enough or keep them shut long enough. But Rob is still looking at me sadly when I open them, although the list is now in his hand.

'I know we haven't known each other long, and I don't know who Gary is, but I hoped I was more than just your shopping list. So, I'm gonna go, and you can have a think about what you want.' He bites his lip, his gaze dropping from my face. 'I probably need to have a think about what I want as well.'

My heart drops, as if a weight has been tied to it, and I wonder if it will ever resurface. How could I have been so stupid to even pit him against Gary? Ghosty Gary versus Sweet Supermarket Guy, who's never ghosted me, never caused me heartache, never made me doubt myself, never made me feel not good enough. 'Rob, please. I... let me explain.' I place my hand on his shoulder, willing him to look at me again. 'It's complicated.'

'But that's it, Kitty... I don't want complicated.' He holds my wrist gently, removing my hand from his shoulder. 'I want honest and easy, fair and normal. I want to fall in love, to love with my whole heart and be loved back. Not to be hurt and messed around. So, I need to go, and we can talk later. We need space. Thank you for dinner.' He looks back at the list, and my heart sinks. I feel awful. 'You've kissed him already. Were you seriously trying to work out who the better kisser is to use it as a pro?' He shakes his head.

He opens the door and shuts it quietly before I have time to say anything else. Even in a situation like this, he's gentle and kind. I sit at the bottom of the stairs and sob. What the hell have I done? I've risked losing probably the nicest man I've ever met for a quick line from someone who disappeared on me and didn't give a damn. Someone who was seeing other women and doing God knows what with them whilst stringing me along.

I stand up, my head in my hands. '*Fuuucccckkkk*,' I scream as I kick the bottom stair, then scream at the impact on my slipperless foot.

I absolutely know Rob's the one I want to be with. The one who makes me smile in a safe but excited way. The kind, handsome, mature and interesting one. The one I trust to not break my heart.

I've ruined it all, burnt it like overdone toast, and as I collapse against the wall, sobbing into my hands, I'm almost certain there's no going back and that I won't see Rob again.

Chapter 50

I'm pleased it's the weekend as I wake up Saturday morning after another lousy sleep. I've written and deleted a text message to Rob at least ten times. I keep remembering a concept from the book *Men Are from Mars, Women Are from Venus* by John Gray—men like to retreat into their cave after an argument or disagreement and women like to deal with things immediately. I want to deal with things immediately, desperate to text Rob and try to explain, apologise, grovel, whatever it takes. But I know it will make it worse, and I need to give him some space. I just hope and pray the space he needs won't be forever.

Despite feeling less than up to it, I meet Jane at the gym. I have waning energy but a need to chat.

'Oh shit,' she says when I update her on last night.

My legs wobble on the elliptical, the little energy I have depleting. When Jane has nothing to say but 'oh shit', you know it isn't good.

'What should I do?' I ask as I clutch my warm cheek and frown.

'Give him space, like you have been, Kit. Perhaps text him later on, but something without a question maybe. Was he super miffed?'

'He seemed more disappointed. He wasn't angry, just upset, I guess. I felt so awful, Jane. I still do. I feel like I've lied to him.' I put my hand to my mouth, feeling myself getting emotional.

'Kit, you didn't lie, you just didn't tell him where you were at emotionally.' She stops exercising and looks at me. 'Really, after one date, I personally don't think you owed it to him to pour your heart out and possibly put him off anyway.'

I stare at her for reassurance, my legs having given up a while ago without me realising it.

'It's not ideal, but this happened to you as well as Rob. Gary turning up, changing his tune and stirring the pot, well... that's what's caused it in reality, isn't it?'

I nod. Bloody Gary. I'm so annoyed with him. He's messed things up again. Sadie's right— he's manipulative. And now it might have cost me Rob. I just needed that time and that kiss with him to be sure. I was confused, gullible, stupid and weak, but it's Rob I want to try with. And Gary, well, Gary can bugger off.

Wanting to change the subject, I bring up Dominic and our trip to the theatre this evening to see *Calendar Girls*. We're looking forward to the performance, and I'm desperate for the distraction.

We leave the gym forty-five minutes later, and we arrange for me to pick Jane up this evening and park in town for the theatre show. I have all afternoon to nap and think about what to text Rob.

Back home, showered and fed, I lie on the sofa with my fleece blanket over me and pick up my phone. After drafting and deleting a few times, I settle on a text and send it to him.

Hi, Rob, I'm so sorry. Someone I dated came back on the scene. I was confused and needed to close that chapter properly. I didn't want to mention it as, well, it felt a bit intense, since we had only had one date. But then last night, with you, I just realised how much I like your company and you, I really like you! I'm sorry you had to see the list, but I know I don't want anything to do with Gary, even if you don't want to see me again (which I hope isn't the case). Sorry xxx

I put my phone down and close my eyes, hoping for a power nap.

It's a cold, late January night in Newcastle, so I wrap up, with an extra pashmina to put over me in the theatre in case it's chilly. I certainly won't be indulging in half-time ice cream, but I have two bags of sweets for Jane and me to share.

Rob still hasn't replied, but I take a small slice of comfort in the fact that I've said how I feel, and although sad anxiety dances around my being, I'm satisfied I've been honest and approached my explanation the right way. Worst case scenario, he tells me to do one and I change my shopping night and hopefully never bump into him on the estate. It would be awkward, but there would be nothing I could do about it, and it wouldn't be the end of the world. Well, not completely. I just have to keep reminding myself of it as sprinklings of sadness keep landing on me throughout the evening.

Jane and the theatre are good distractions, and we laugh, yet feel moved by the play. We cuddle outside her house as I drop her home before arranging to go to the gym again next week. Driving back home, I immediately start thinking of Rob. He still hasn't text. I'm glad Gary is blocked, as feeling rejected and wanting some reassurance can lead to seeking it, even if it's from the wrong person.

Damn relationships, I think to myself, angry that I'm in this situation. Angry with myself for being so easy to manipulate and so quick to be flattered by Gary's charm. Angry with Gary for ghosting me, then crawling back, professing his love. It's now been seven hours since I text Rob, and there's no reply. I wonder whether I should text him again. I re-read the message I sent earlier. It's honest, open and explains the situation. I was apologetic and indicated I like him. Did I miss anything out? Should I have begged? Shit. I don't know what's for the best, and I'm beginning to feel desperate now I'm alone in my house with too much space and thinking time.

I put the kettle on, make myself a cup of tea and get changed into my pjs. I take the cuppa to bed and look at my phone, willing it to ping or make a decision for me. My skin almost feels itchy with impatience and feelings of uncertainty. I hate feeling out of control. I have to text him. I draft, then send a text. I couldn't even leave it an hour and go back to it, like I've advised friends so many times over the years. 'Draft and go back, see if you still feel like that in an hour', I've said on multiple occasions. Stupid cow. I throw my phone down on the bed next to me in frustration.

Rob, I understand if you don't want to see me again or speak to me, but please will you just tell me to leave you alone if that's what you want? I'm truly sorry, but if you don't want to hear from me and it's over before anything really began, it would be kind for you to tell me. Maybe I don't deserve kindness, but it will get me off your back and I'll leave you alone. Xxx

Exhausted from lack of sleep and emotional drain, I roll over and pull the quilt high, feeling like I may cry. I snuggle into the pillows that have been beside me since I asked Liam to leave all those months ago. The void has been here every night since, and it's not got much easier. A few tears dampen my cheeks as I start to drift off, feeling helpless and painfully lonely.

Chapter 51

It's a little after 8 a.m. when I wake up. Rare for me, as my body clock likes me awake, if not always alert, by 7:15 a.m. at the latest, even on weekends and holidays. I reach for my phone, willing it to have a message from Rob. Nothing.

'Argghh,' I shout.

I haven't told Sadie about what happened, telling her we'll catch up Monday and not to worry, but there's a text from her saying she'll call me at 10 a.m. She clearly knows something's up. There's another from Jane, thanking me for a great night and hoping I'm okay.

I get up and think about breakfast and plans for the day. As I strip the bed, ready to put the bedding in the wash, self-pity begins to grow around me. Whilst living with Liam wasn't exactly like having a home help, there were the odd tasks he would do. Even someone making me a cuppa feels like winning the lottery these days. I'm tired of doing everything myself, all the washing, making the bed alone, constantly cleaning and cooking and rolling round the house like a penny in a train station, echoing and in solitude. I know I could connect more with friends and visit my family, but something about being single makes me feel like for all I crave company, I can't stand to be around people at times. I don't want to wear the mask and nod, smiling when inside I'm feeling low, craving love and stability. I take the pillowcases off and throw them on the floor, exhaling a quiet welp.

They can all do one, the lot of them. Every single last man. They can all bugger right off. I fling the last pillowcase on the floor with frustration. Well, all except Dad and Henry and Sadie's Stu. Oh, and Dominic and Sophie's Chris. The rest though, they can go and jump.

After shoving my bedding in the washing machine, I make a cup of tea and pour a bowl of cereal before sitting down with the TV on. I pick up my phone and stumble to unlock the screen as fast as possible when I notice there's a text from Rob.

Hi Kitty, sorry for the late reply, I needed to think. I still need to think. I don't want to be hurt again and I want to trust you. I need some space to think about what I want. And I want you to have space to be sure of what you want as well. I'll be in touch, just give me time please. Take care xxx

I read the message. Then I read it again and again, trying to deconstruct it, analyse it and comprehend any hidden messages. It isn't a 'no, I don't want to see you again', but it also isn't a 'all is forgiven' message either. Surely it's progress though. After being blanked for thirty-six hours, it feels like a result, even if only a small one.

When Sadie rings, I talk through it all with her.

'He's hurt, Kit, naturally. You would be too.'

I nod even though she can't see me as I flop onto the sofa and let out a monumental sigh.

'But Rob seems such a decent guy, I think he'll be fair, and I think his decision will be final. I just hope it's what you want, love,' Sadie says, gentle support in her voice. 'What about Gary? What you going to do about him, Kit?'

I restlessly get up from the sofa and begin to pace my lounge. 'I'm going to tell him it's over. I don't trust him, not fully, he just swept me out to sea with his charm, words and his good looks. But he'll leave me without a life jacket again, I'm almost certain of that. I made a mistake listening to him.' I rub my shoulder, feeling the tension of the recent stress.

'No, Kit, you didn't. You were you; you were understanding. You gave him the benefit of the doubt and wanted him to be sorry. You craved seeing the best in him. That's why you're you and why you're such a wonderful soul. Don't ever change who you are, love, but never let anyone exploit your kindness,' Sadie says firmly.

I feel the tears start to come.

'Sending you a cwtch down the phone, love.'

'Thanks, Sadie, I can almost feel that cuddle.' I wrap one arm around myself, as if holding Sadie's cwtch to me.

'Now, pull those big girl knickers up and try to enjoy your day. It's not a negative from Rob, so that's one thing. Go and see your folks and get fed, and I will bring you extra treats into work tomorrow.'

I laugh. Sadie knows the way to my heart; I'm as happy with food treats as a toddler or dog.

'Thanks, Sadie, have a good day. Love you, send love to your Stu.'

'Love you too, little one. See you tomorrow.'

And with that, I put my big girl knickers on, do some housework and go round to my parents' for a feed and a few hours of distraction.

My plan works, kind of, and I spend Sunday trying to focus on other things than Rob and Gary. I do, however, know that I have to have a conversation with Gary tomorrow. Even if Rob tells me to bugger off and that he doesn't want to see or hear from me again, I know a future with Gary doesn't exist. Trust has been broken, and no amount of yellow roses, Maltesers and smiles from his attractive face could change that. I was caught up in the moment with his charm and words, but I have to trust my gut instinct. It's Rob or neither, and I'd rather have none than the insidious torture of mistrust and uncertainty. I'll seek out Gary tomorrow or, undoubtably, he'll find me, and I'll have an honest conversation with him, in an adult fashion. I'll regain control and make it amicable.

The future with Rob, however, feels less under my control, and something that will hang over me until he decides our fate.

Chapter 52

'You're making a massive mistake, Kitty. You know you are,' Gary pleads at my desk in my classroom at lunchtime.

He isn't taking it well, and part of me wonders if it's because I'm rejecting him and, being so good-looking, he clearly thinks he can get any woman he wants.

He puts his hands to his head, staring at me. 'I'm falling in love with you. You can't do this to me... to us.' He walks back and forth across the classroom, making me dizzy.

'Gary, *you* did this to us. The us that was new and exciting and had potential, that you sacked off for titillation and attention from other women.' I shake my head in disbelief as I rise from my seat. 'I clearly wasn't good enough for you then, and I never will be. You would've known if I was. I can't go back from that, and I... I just don't want to,' I say defiantly, crossing my arms.

He stops pacing and stares at me, wounded and clearly disgruntled that he's being rejected. 'You'll regret it, Kitty. We could've been the best. We *would* have been the best, and I can guarantee I would have been the best lover you'll now never get.'

I hiss through gritted teeth, 'Gary, I'm almost thirty-one. I'm not interested in sexathons... I want a meaningful, loving relationship. Perhaps if you'd thought about that rather than your dick in the first instance, we wouldn't be having this conversation. Unbelievable.'

I glance out the window, away from his annoying face, before I return to deliver my final say. 'Look, I want to be civil while you're here and professional, so please just accept it and leave. I have a class in fifteen minutes to prepare for.'

I start searching in my drawers for something I know isn't there, in the hope that when I look back up, Gary will be gone. I hear the door slam, and although I feel a bit of a cow, I know it's the right thing, especially considering what Gary did to me in the recent past. I breathe out all the tension that's been weighing on my body, then text Sadie.

Mission complete! Xxxx

By Friday morning, I still haven't heard from Rob. I've been checking my phone 578 times a day to see if he's text. Each time, I've been greeted with a blank screen and my heart sinking a little more into the ocean of 'forever going to be alone'. Even the Maltesers in my pigeonhole have ceased, so I don't have the comfort of chocolate. Sadie has increased the gingerbread treats though, which are hungrily and gratefully received. Hey, if I'm going to be single, at least I can enjoy my grub.

I've been debating whether to go elsewhere for my weekly shop or go the next morning. Part of me dreads the uncomfortable tension of bumping into someone I've hurt and I'm clearly being rejected by, but part of me is absolutely desperate to see him and hopefully not look like a dog left in a rehoming shelter.

'Go there, and if you see him, speak to him. Don't change your routines for him, Kit; you can't hide away, love,' Sadie advises as we sit and eat lunch together.

She's right, I just don't want either of us to feel awkward, but my life has changed a lot over the last six months, and I've learnt so much about myself. I've learnt even more about the strange phenomenon that is men and dating, and I don't want anything or anyone to make me feel uncomfortable in my own skin, in my home or in my community. My routines are important to me, and I don't want to have to change them, nor should I have to. After all, it's Rob who wants space and isn't communicating with me. So, I figure if anyone will change their shopping day in order to avoid, it surely will be him. Maybe he's shopped already.

'You're right, Sadie. I might just put on extra makeup to try to look irresistible though, just in case I see him,' I say back, trying to sound confident but shattering like glass inside.

'Kitty, you'd be beautiful in a potato sack with your hair tied back and not a scrap of makeup on, my girl. The right man will always see that in you. Your beauty radiates from your heart and soul.'

She takes my hands, and I smile at her. Sadie always knows what to say. She makes the darkest of rain clouds dissipate to let the sunbeams through. She's such a cheerleader, as are Jane, Sophie and my family. For all I may not have the partner I want or I may have sabotaged any possibility of getting closer to the man who's living rent free in my head, I have more love in my life than many could even imagine. I'm wealthy in love and care and, for that, I will always be grateful.

My stomach is gurgling, doing its usual fretting obstacle course inside my body as I drive. I feel like I'm going for an interview, on stage, in front of an arena of strangers. Yes, I really am that nervous, but I'm also determined. I have nothing to lose, and hiding away isn't going to help. Rob has been in his *Men Are from Mars, Women Are from Venus* cave for almost a week. I have to get on with life, with or without him.

I'm not feeling as assertive when I push the trolley into the supermarket with trepidation. I'm chewing my lip and mentally telling myself to stop. I want the lip gloss to stay on, the supermarket lights harsh enough to make me look like *The Scream* painting by Edvard Munch. With my list in my hand, I walk slowly into the first aisle, knowing I'll struggle to concentrate on what I need as I look around for Rob. I can't see him, and I don't know if it's disappointment or relief that I'm feeling.

I put my list in my trolley for a minute, pick up two mangoes and juggle them, trying to decide between them.

'I find the ones with around fifty percent red to them the best.'

I tense at the breathy whisper of the voice behind me on my neck, my fingers pressing against the peel of the mangoes, leaving fingertip depressions.

'Well, they were when I spent two months working on a mango farm in New Zealand. Can't stomach them myself now after literally eating, breathing, working and stinking of mango for eight full weeks.' He laughs quietly at the end of his statement and moves to stand next to me, his gaze going straight to the mangoes. 'Although, looks like you'll have to buy both of them now.'

There he stands, Rob, in his beautiful glory, even under the harsh lighting. He looks even more handsome than I remember, with his perfect beard, full lips and slightly tired eyes smiling.

'Thanks for the tip,' I say, sounding more nervous than I planned to. 'I've missed you,' I add without thinking. I look at my feet, worried about further rejection.

'Me too. I mean, I've missed you, not missed myself.' A grin flashes on his face.

My gaze moves from my feet to his eyes. 'I'm sorry, Rob, I really am.'

He nods, moving closer to me, trying to not get in everyone's way as they rush by impatiently or stroll by on their phones, distracted by life.

'It's a big deal for me to let someone in again, Kitty. I know women talk about getting hurt, how men have done this, that and the other. How they've had their heart broken, ripped out, stamped on. But so have men... we just don't talk about it.' The smile always reaching his eyes dulls away. 'I don't want to feel like that again, and I want an easy life. I want consistency, I want boring with pockets of reliable excitement. I want loyalty, I want to know I'm someone's first option, their choice, even from the beginning.' He pauses, but I can see he isn't finished. 'Things don't always work out, I get that. But I want a head start on it having a damn good chance.'

'I understand if you don't want to see me again. I'm sorry. I wish I hadn't been confused and wrote that stupid list. But I also didn't want to be hurt, and I had to work things out in my head.'

'And have you? Worked things out in your head?' Rob asks.

'Yeah. Yeah, I have.' I swallow, knowing that this is my one and only chance to convince him. Rob is exactly what I want, exactly who I want. I've just been stupid or scared, or both. I inhale and continue, hoping he sees I'm being genuine. 'I knew what I wanted before you found that dumb list. I knew it was you, and I've dealt with Gary.

I told him we have no future even if I've ruined things with you.'

A woman leans between us to pick out some mangoes, smiling awkwardly at each of us, knowing she's right in the middle of something. She shuffles away but stays near, clearly desperate to hear the outcome of this week's episode of *Confessions in the Shopping Aisle.*

'What did he say?' Rob asks.

'Does it matter?'

'Yeah, it matters to me.' He leans against his trolley, making it obvious he isn't going anywhere until he gets an answer.

I sigh. I don't want to have a full-on relationship counselling session in the fruit and veg aisle of the supermarket, but I have little choice, and I want this to end permanently or start again, whatever it's going to be.

'Well, he was upset and said I was making a mistake. That he was falling for me and that.'

'And do you think you've made a mistake telling him you don't want to be with him?' He taps his fingers against the metal mesh of the trolley.

I wait a few seconds as a man and child walk by us. 'No, I don't. It was unexpected from him. I was flattered and we had unresolved issues that needed sorting. They're sorted now,' I say, emphasising the last few words as I stare at Rob. 'No, I don't think I've made a mistake, and if it still meant not being given a chance from you, I would have still told Gary there's no future with us. I'm not interested in him.' I frown. 'But I was, I *am* interested in you,' I add quietly. I'm desperate for Rob to just hug me and say everything is going to be okay. I wouldn't even care about the onlooking shoppers. I feel like crying, screaming, running away and staying all at once.

I keep my head tilted down but sense Gary stepping closer to me. He touches the side of my head, pressing my hair gently against my cheek. His tender energy and warmth feel like home. He cups my face in his hands, tilting it back up, leans in and kisses me, full-on, in front of the mangoes. His soft beard grazes my chin. It's just us in the supermarket Friday teatime... just us kissing. We could have been in Paris, by the Seine River, the Eiffel Tower in the background. Just us.

A light noise pulls me from my imagination. I open my eyes and look to the floor, to the two mangoes I was holding in my hands for the last five minutes bouncing along the white tiles. They land at a woman's feet.

Rob puts his arm around my waist and chuckles as the woman picks the mangoes up. 'I really have missed you.'

Chapter 53

We walk to the local country park, with an essential flask of tea and a packet of chocolate biscuits. The trees and landscapes look so beautiful, as if adorned with glitter as the sun slowly dissolves the frost against the winter morning. We venture about a mile before cosying up on a bench and having our cuppa and snack.

As much as I wanted to see him last night after the supermarket, I wanted us both to absorb what the other had said over the mangoes. After telling Rob that Gary declared his love to me, I had to make sure Rob was okay, given Gary's working with me, albeit probably only for a few more weeks.

As Rob leans in close to me, I feel the excitement of new adventure and a new relationship, along with the comfort of positivity. Rob feels like a cosy pair of slippers... a very sexy, endearing pair of cosy slippers.

'Fancy going back to mine for lunch?' Rob asks. 'I've seen your house now, so it's only fair you visit mine. Plus, I make some mean cheese on toast.'

Going to Rob's house would be another step in our dating, and I feel a little giddy with anticipation. I let out a giggle of nerves. 'Sure. How could I say no to cheese on toast?'

After walking some more, we go to Rob's. Although I slowed down past his road a few times, I never worked out which house exactly is his.

'Here we are,' Rob says, pointing to his home. It's a well-kept semi, with a neat garden. Walking up the path, I notice a red Acer with its pretty, cherry leaves and pots either side of his front door, housing Buxus plants.

He opens his door, and I peer inside before stepping onto the grey runner on the wooden floor of his hallway. I go to take my shoes off, more out of habit, and Rob raises an eyebrow at me.

'You're fine leaving them on if you want. In fact, if you have smelly feet, definitely leave them on.' He nudges me playfully, and I open my mouth animatedly, pretending to be offended by his comment.

'Come on through.' Rob gestures along the hallway and takes us into the lounge before showing me around the rest of his home—it's immaculate, stylish and homely.

'I see you've got good taste in interior design as well as women.' I wink.

He leaves me to continue nebbing around his home whilst he makes the cheese on toast. There are photos of his family, smiles adorned on all their faces, love radiating from the memories captured in time and hung on the walls. Rob just seems so real, so transparent and with such integrity. He seems the type who always tells his mother he loves her at the end of a call, who never forgets a birthday, who doesn't mind being the taxi on nights out.

I let out a breath of contentment as I walk into the kitchen, where he's muttering away under his breath as he flaps a tea towel towards the grill.

He pulls out the tray, revealing our burnt lunch. I laugh as he puts the hot tray of blackened crusts and bubbling, burnt cheese on the kitchen bench.

'Shit, sorry,' he says, glancing at the tray, then me. 'I think I might have oversold my cheese on toast.'

I grin and walk over to him, slipping my arms around his waist from behind. 'I'm pleased that's happened, as I was beginning to think you're too perfect, in some sort of creepy robot way.' I giggle. 'You've finally exposed your weakness.'

He turns to face me and kisses my forehead. 'Yeah, I'm absolutely rubbish at cooking. I just have no imagination. That's why I was so excited about the soup that I never got.' He elbows me light-heartedly. 'I just eat bread and convenience food.'

'Well, that's fine, as I love to cook, and I'm really fussy about some things I like to eat, so I guess it'll be me who does the cooking in our relation—' I bite my lip to stop the rest of the word coming out, my face taking on a hot glow.

'Is that what you want, Kitty? To be in a relationship?' Rob asks, expectation in his eyes. I wait for him to frown, to back away, to maybe even tell me to leave, but he doesn't.

'Yeah, I do.' I bite the inside of my cheek nervously. 'I know this is technically only date two, but we've been supermarket dating for a few months, and I just feel like I've known you for ages, Rob. It feels so right... *you* feel so right.'

Rob nods expressionlessly and doesn't say anything for a few seconds, although it feels like forever. I brace myself for rejection.

He puts his hand to my face and tilts my head up to his. 'Kitty Cook, will you be my girlfriend?'

Time almost freezes in my head as I try to absorb the words Rob just spoke. I feel a massive grin spreading across my face as I look into Rob's eyes. Eyes of such warmth and depth. Eyes that make me smile. Eyes that have never made me feel anything less than enough when I've looked into them.

'Y-y-yes,' I stammer. 'I would love to.'

Rob kisses me and holds me close, his strong arms enveloping me. When he lets go, tenderness and kindness are etched on his handsome face.

'Brilliant, you've made me the happiest man on the estate,' he jokes. 'Now, what do you fancy for lunch?' The sorry state of the previous burnt offerings are still sat on the kitchen bench behind him, now cold as well as blackened.

'Have you got any spaghetti hoops?'

I stay at Rob's for the rest of the day and night. He drives me back home briefly to shut the blinds and leave the timer light on. I grab some pyjamas that actually match and don't resemble nightwear worn frequently in a retirement village. I place some makeup, toiletries and matching underwear into a bag, along with my slipper socks and my Velcro slippers—I won't compromise on those.

Back at Rob's, we cosy up on the sofa with pizzas he's managed to not burn—I told him when to take them out of the oven—and some gins. We talk until midnight, with intermittent kissing. I'm giddy with excitement and elated that I have a boyfriend after months of catastrophic dating and uncertainty. To think someone as wonderful as Rob was on my doorstep all along, like a twenty pound note blowing in the wind around the street.

'You know that first time we met in the supermarket?' Rob asks. 'Well, actually, we didn't exactly meet, you rammed the trolley into my calves.'

I chuckle. 'Eeeh, honest, I'm in a world of my own at times. Sadie always wonders how I've managed to get through life. I bet that really hurt though.'

'Yeah, it did actually; I had a graze and a bruise for a week after.'

I can't help but rub his leg even though I know for a fact it's well and truly healed.

'Well, Fridays were never my shopping day, it was always a Wednesday. Fridays were mainly a few pints after work with my team or meeting the lads at The Windmill or in the village. But then I got assaulted by you and, well, I thought you were brilliant, Kitty—so beautiful, magnetic and I liked that you were a bit scatty.' He smirks, balancing his nearly empty gin glass on the arm of the sofa. 'So, I changed my shopping day the week after, hoping to bump into you again. Just hopefully not as literally.'

My eyes widen as I let out a breathy, nervous giggle. I hardly noticed him at first, too absorbed in Soul Mates. And once I did notice him, I spent so long panicking that he hadn't noticed me in the same way. Yet, this whole time...

'You didn't have a basket, evidently by my attacked calves, so I kinda thought Fridays must be like a weekly shopping day for you.' He chews on his bottom lip, as if wondering if his next admittance should stay as purely a thought. 'Friday became my regular day, and most of the time I got to see you, even if you didn't always see me.'

He leans back on the sofa, the sofa sighing in a way that I'm sure he wants to right now. 'That last bit sounds a bit creepy... it wasn't meant to. It was meant to basically explain that I adored you from afar, more Shakespearian than *Silence of the Lambs*.'

I touch his face, the soft bristles of his beard brushing the palm of my hand. 'That's really sweet, Rob, but I do wish you would've made yourself a bit more visible and not hidden behind the beans with binoculars. It would have saved me many a disastrous date. Plus, you could've helped me put my shopping in the boot.' I grin, and he grins back, all worried tension easing from his face.

'Come here.'

I squeal as Rob pulls me gently into his arms and places his lips on mine, kissing me passionately.

'You're gorgeous, Kitty, I could kiss you forever,' he says between kisses.

I tug his bottom lip gently as I pull away. 'Well, how about we go and kiss upstairs so I can take these nanna slippers off?' I lift one of my legs up, wiggling my toes inside the comfy monstrosity on my foot.

Rob laughs, standing up, and takes my hand to lead me upstairs. We fall back on his king-size bed and continue kissing. I can smell his fresh bedding and his aftershave as he kisses my neck. His caress is gentle, as if his hands were made for my skin. I tremble with his touch, the anticipation and the joy of his tenderness on my body.

'Are you okay?' he whispers in my ear as his hands explore me.

'Yeah, everything's perfect,' I reply, kissing his shoulder.

We undress and make love, our souls connecting as well as our bodies. It's been so long since I've experienced this sort of passion and affection, but it all comes naturally, the need for Rob overriding any worries.

The moment ends, and we lie in each other's arms until we fall asleep, our breathing in synchronicity as I dream about a future with the man I've waited a lifetime to meet.

Epilogue

Rob and I are lying on the sofa, snuggled up with a fleece blanket over us, our bodies breathing in sync as we fit together perfectly. I'm leaning into him, his arm around my shoulder. He kisses the top of my head, and I close my eyes, feeling utter contentment as I squeeze his hand. We've been together over three months, and it's been the best three months of my life. Rob makes me laugh, he's gorgeous and his heart matches the beauty of his shell. He's become my best friend and the love of my life all in one. I've not once felt anything less than safe, supported and loved. For the first time, I feel enough.

Jane, Sadie and Sophie were the first to find out when we made it official. They were all so happy and supportive, still are, and most likely relieved to hit the end of my dating dilemmas and emotional instability. I'm back to being the consistently supportive best friend, not the one always needing advice and to offload, although I know my friends are here for me, like I am them. Opening up has been a massive learning curve. I'm now able to receive advice and support as well as give. I tried to get Sadie to share her cheese and leek mash recipe with Rob, hoping it would help him on his learning to cook journey... she still hasn't agreed to part with her secret and absolutely addictive recipe. Rob hasn't met Sophie and Chris yet, but we've spent a lot of time with Sadie and Stu and managed to fit in some double dates with Jane and Dominic. Thankfully, Jane is still as happy as ever.

Luckily, there was no atmosphere with Gary at work before the end of his placement. I even saw him flirting with another member of staff on a few occasions—I definitely had a lucky escape there. He hurt me, and it was undoubtably awful at the time. He knocked my confidence, but, ultimately, I'm grateful for Gary, his sly ghosting and for all the others I dated from Soul Mates. All of those disasters, all of those conversations and decisions, some of which were out of my hands, led me to Rob. How could I ever not be grateful for that?

I wish Gary all the best in whatever he does. Maybe he's learnt some lessons from his short time with me, maybe he hasn't, but it's not my problem, and I have no hard feelings. He finished his placement with us at Richardson High, along with the other teacher training students, and I haven't seen him since. He's officially part of the past that brought me to my present and future: Rob.

I was nervous to meet Rob's family—his mam Patsy, his older brother Brian, and his nieces and nephews—but I had no reason to be. They've welcomed me into their home and lives with ease and warmth. Rob met my parents before meeting Henry and Sarah. My parents think he's great and took an instant shine to him. There was a level of communication and connecting immediately with Rob and my parents that I never truly felt or saw with Liam. Maybe it's a sixth sense they have as my parents, a protective unconsciousness or something they see in Rob that makes them believe he's just about good enough for their daughter.

Rob was more nervous to meet Henry—the older, protective brother—than my parents. The night we arranged to visit them for an hour was the night Sarah went into labour. Sixteen hours later, Eliza was born, and Rob ended up meeting my brother, Sarah and my niece all at once, which was an intense but lovely situation. Rob has a real paternal vibe, and he managed to soothe Eliza's cries better than me on that first visit. I think watching the way Rob is with Eliza has really helped Henry bond with him. Even on that first visit, I noticed Henry watching Rob interact with his daughter, and I saw his wall slowly start to crumble and the trust grow in his eyes, although I'm sure he won't admit it.

We're all going to my parents' today for Sunday dinner, so we'll need to start getting ready soon. Even though it's only been three months, it's always just presumed that Rob will be coming with me.

'Let's book a holiday later,' Rob says, iPad in hand. 'Where do you fancy going?'

'Erm, I don't know... I mean, anywhere.' I think about where I've always wanted to go, to see sights from all the movies and where romance seems to dance on the streets. I turn to Rob and clap my hands with excitement. 'What about New York?'

Rob grins and stands from the sofa. 'Yeah, let's go to New York.' He picks me up, and I wrap my legs around his waist as he spins me around.

I squeal and giggle. 'Are we actually going to do it?' I'm already thinking about what I want to buy there.

'Of course we are. Later. For as soon as possible.' Rob stops spinning, and I rest my head on his shoulder. 'You know, Kit, it will be amazing. Even a trip to the supermarket with you feels like an adventure.' He turns to me and places his hands gently on either side of my face. He kisses me tenderly, then gazes into my eyes. 'I love you.'

I can't imagine ever getting tired of those three words. Even now, he tells me he loves me countless times a day, and I still feel as giddy as the first time.

'I love you too.' I smile into the crook of his neck, the familiar fresh and woody scent surrounding me. 'And I can't wait for all our adventures to come.'

Acknowledgements

Thank you so much for reading The Life and Love (Attempts) of Kitty Cook. I hope you enjoyed her journey to find love. The inspiration for this book came from my own dating experiences, many of which, like Kitty's, were unsuccessful, laughable, and extremely odd! However, dating can also be character building and similar to Kitty, I learnt what I did and certainly did not like!

It may seem strange but I'm grateful for all the disastrous dates (and wow, there were many scoring top points in the bizarre and grotesque departments!). If I never had those rubbish, disappointing, borderline scary, and revolting dates, I wouldn't have found my true love. So, thank you to all of my own first dates, even second and third dates, that ultimately never progressed but led me to Paul.

Thank you to all the people who believe in my writing and support me constantly. Cassandra and the team at Cahill Davis Publishing. You are a joy to work with and I still pinch myself that you believed in my writing from day one. Thank you to my family, who encourage, support, and champion me. My mam, Sheila, for eternally being proud of her "baby." My dad, John, for asking every bookshop if it stocks my books. My auntie Carole and my auntie Eleanor for always asking, reading, and encouraging. Special thanks to my sister, Joanne for reading the draft of this book and being part of it. But thank you to all my family, you are all a wonderful support.

Further thanks to the friends who not only held me up during my single, lonely, and unpredictable dating era, but who continue to show love, support, and encouragement even now, without the "Will he text back?" dilemmas. Special thanks to Debbie and Sylvie, who inspired Sadie and Jane, and were always there for me. Thank you to Caroline, who inspired Sophie, and who always offers to read my draft manuscripts, and provide words of encouragement. Also, thanks to Lesley who used to listen to my dates with horror or smiles of reassurance over many a night in or out! Further thanks to Rachael, who heard about the manuscript and eagerly read it overnight.

Much thanks to my social media friends, who feel like a big, global hug. People who clicked into my life and now, I can't imagine not having them there.

Thank you, reader! I write to make even one person laugh, smile, feel seen and heard, or feel hopeful. I have had so many heart-warming messages of support and feedback that a character has been relatable and has made an impact. That's why I write and I will forever be grateful. If you've reached the end and would be kind enough to leave a review on whichever platform you're most comfortable, that would mean so much to me. And if you post about the book on social media, please use the hashtag #TLALAOKC so I can find your post!

If you would like to find out more about my writing, please visit www.helenaitchisonwrites.com and follow me on
Facebook: Helen Aitchison Writes
Instagram: @helen.aitchison_writes
Twitter: @aitchisonwrites

Also by Helen Aitchison:
The Dinner Club - available in paperback and ebook.